For two terrific women.
My daughters, Beverley and Maxine

Thanks to copy-editor, Sandy Draper, for sorting the
wheat from the chaff. Great job!

Brides of War

June Tate

Allison & Busby Limited
12 Fitzroy Mews
London W1T 6DW
allisonandbusby.com

First published in Great Britain by Allison & Busby in 2015.
This paperback edition published by Allison & Busby in 2015.

A CIP catalogue record for this book is available from
the British Library.

10 9 8 7 6 5 4 3 2 1

ISBN 978-0-7490-1847-4

Typeset in 10.55/15.55 pt Sabon by
Allison & Busby Ltd.

The paper used for this Allison & Busby publication
has been produced from trees that have been legally sourced
from well-managed and credibly certified forests.

Printed and bound by
CPI Group (UK) Ltd, Croydon, CR0 4YY

Chapter One

27th January 1946

Gracie Rider, née Brown, stood waiting at the rail of the SS *Argentina*, a grey-painted American ship sailing for New York, carrying the first GI brides to their new homeland. The weather was cold and wet. The drizzle did nothing to cheer those who searched for familiar faces standing huddled on the quayside. There were only about a hundred people as the families had been advised to stay away, but Gracie had seen her parents, standing, waving, her mother wiping tears and her father trying to look cheerful.

The small crowd were singing *Anchors Away* and *There'll Always Be an England*. Passengers shouted back, 'We won't forget you!' Gracie's own tears trickled slowly down her cheeks, as she waved furiously as the ship slowly pulled away from the dockside. She waited until there was nothing but water to be seen and walked slowly away.

It had been a very long day. Before dawn, buses had arrived at the barracks at Tidworth Camp to start loading their human cargo for the drive to the ship. Then on board there had been an allocation of cabins. Hers was to accommodate up to twelve people. The bunks were in two tiers and every other bunk was folded up, but there was little room between them to move.

The women chatted as they tried to sort themselves out. Some had got to know one another at Tidworth Camp, so there was a sort of camaraderie among them, which helped the situation along.

The first meal on board was a luxury with food not seen during the austere days of rationing, and this went some way to cheer the women who were facing such a dramatic change to their lives. Roast beef was devoured with great enthusiasm and the pudding with ice cream savoured slowly, but many found it was too much too soon and were unable to eat all that was put before them. Such rich food had been off their table for too long.

After dinner, Gracie and Valerie Johnson, another war bride whom Gracie had befriended in the camp, put on their coats and walked on the decks to get some fresh air. It was cold and dark with just the deck lights giving any illumination. The sea beyond looked black and the sky was devoid of a moon. It was an alien environment. Soon they found their way inside and to comfortable chairs in a public area. There they sat down, pleased to be in the warm. The smell of new paint lingered on the air.

Taking out a packet of Craven A, Gracie offered one to

Valerie. They puffed on the nicotine eagerly to help settle the nervous tension both were feeling.

'Well, we really are on our way!' Gracie eventually said. 'I can't believe it, can you?'

Her companion shook her head. 'No, it seems unreal to be honest, as if it's happening to someone else and I am a part of it whether I like it or not.'

'Is your husband meeting you in New York when we dock?' Gracie asked.

'Yes. He lives in New York, so we don't have a long journey. You?'

'Yes, Jeff said he'd be there. We have to go to Denver in Colorado, wherever that is. I've looked it up on the map, but America looks so vast against the map of Great Britain and I just can't visualise it at all. To be honest it scares me to death. We are staying with his family until we find a place of our own and I can't say I'm looking forward to that. What if they don't like me?'

'Or you don't like them!'

'Oh my God! I never thought of that!'

'Fortunately Ross has found us an apartment so I don't have that problem,' Valerie told her. 'But of course I'll still have to meet his family.'

'What's Ross's job in civilian life?'

'He works for his father who has a law practice.'

Gracie wasn't surprised. From the beginning she'd assumed by Valerie's demeanour that she was well educated and from a moneyed family, unlike her, but it hadn't stopped them from becoming friends.

'What does your husband do for a living?' Gracie was asked.

'He's a salesman, but I've no idea what he sells.'

She frowned and thought, *I don't really know much about the man I married at all!* During the heady days of their courtship it didn't seem to matter but now the future with him loomed and she was scared. She hadn't seen Jeff for six months and, although he'd written regularly, she was nervous about meeting him again. Would he seem a stranger? She rose to her feet, needing to be alone with her thoughts.

'I'll see you later,' she told her friend and walked through the door leading once again to the deck and solitude.

Jeff Rider had come to Gracie's rescue at a dance held by the Red Cross to introduce the American GIs to some of the local residents. One of the soldiers, somewhat the worse for drink, had been hassling her for a dance and was becoming a nuisance when she declined. He'd grabbed her by the arm, but Jeff had stepped in and pushed him away.

'Take off buddy, she's with me,' and he'd led her on to the dance floor.

Gracie thanked him profusely.

As he took her into his arms, he smiled and said, 'Well I couldn't see a damsel in distress and not come to her rescue could I?'

After that, they had spent the rest of the evening together.

The dance was well attended by the young women of the town who were intrigued by the soldiers who seemed far more exciting than the local boys. They were brash in comparison, full of confidence . . . exciting and generous. Chocolate and nylon stockings were on offer, but in many cases, the prize came with a price. Sex was not something a decent girl was prepared to pay for such a return, but there were those who were happy to accept. Jeff hadn't been like that. He'd bought her a drink and treated her with respect and so they'd started to meet regularly.

Gracie leant back against the bulkhead and closed her eyes, remembering how it felt to be in his arms and feel his mouth on hers. He'd been so much more experienced than the young men she'd dated before. He hadn't rushed her and took his time before his caresses became more intimate, making her aware, as never before, of her own sexuality. It had been a revelation – and eventually he'd had a weekend pass.

They had been to the cinema and as he walked her home, holding her hand, he stopped and drew her into a shop doorway, held her close, kissed her longingly, then spoke.

'Gracie honey, I've got a weekend pass,' he said softly.

'How lovely! How are you going to spend it?'

She could see his face in the light of the moon. He stared into her eyes and hesitated for just a moment. 'I would love to take you to Bournemouth, book into a hotel and spend the whole time with you.'

She was taken aback. 'You mean you want me to sleep with you?'

He smiled, amused by her shocked expression. 'Is that such a bad idea? You must know how I feel about you by now.'

But she didn't. He'd been attentive, loving, but that was all. Now this! She'd had several boyfriends and almost got engaged to one, but she'd never been intimate with any of them. But Jeff – Jeff had made her feel like a woman, not a girl. She was twenty years old and a virgin! She knew that a few of her friends had slept with their boyfriends but she had never allowed herself to be persuaded, although several had tried. She was now confused because she knew she wanted to go with him. Be with him, to know what it was like to be made love to.

He caressed her cheek. 'I've fallen in love with you, Gracie and I want to show you how much I love you. Please say you'll come with me. We can leave on Saturday morning and return early on Monday morning.'

She thought quickly. She could tell her parents she was going to stay with her friend Betty, another clerk who worked in the same office. It wasn't unusual. The two girls often stayed at each other's houses. She gazed into the eyes of her boyfriend and saw the longing mirrored in them. At the same time her body betrayed her with its message.

'Yes, all right, I'll come,' she said.

It had been so easy. Her parents didn't question her when she told them she'd be at Betty's for the weekend and would go straight to work from there. Jeff had promised they'd catch a train in time for her to get to her office on Monday morning.

'It'll give us an extra day together,' he told her, 'and I don't have to report back until noon.'

On Friday night, she'd packed a small overnight bag, with some trepidation. As she lay in bed alone that night, she tried to envisage how it would be when she was sharing a bed with Jeff. Although she was extremely nervous, she was also excited. However, she didn't know what was expected of her. Would he be disappointed with her lack of experience? How dreadful that would be! She now began to wish she'd said no!

Jeff was waiting outside the train station for her. He took her case, kissed her and ushered her inside where he bought two return tickets to Bournemouth. As the train drew in, they boarded and were able to find two seats together in a crowded carriage where they settled by the window.

After placing their cases on the overhead rack, Jeff sat down and put an arm around her shoulders. 'You OK, honey?'

She smiled and nodded, trying to ignore a few hostile glances from one or two of their travelling companions. Not everyone had welcomed the arrival of the American troops in the town. 'Overpaid, oversexed and over here!' was the well-known cry from many. In particular from the British troops, who were not as well paid as the Americans, whose uniforms were not made of such fine material and who resented the fact that the GIs were more popular with the females of the town. Elderly female citizens were appalled at the behaviour of some of the girls who were seen with them, many of who were prostitutes that had swarmed into Southampton where business was brisk.

When the train arrived at Bournemouth, they took a taxi to the hotel, left their cases at the reception, as their room wasn't ready, and went in search of coffee and breakfast.

Once settled in a nice café, they ordered a meal and poured the coffee when it was served. Jeff reached across the table and took Gracie's hand.

'I can hardly wait to get you alone,' he said quietly.

Gracie felt the colour flush her cheeks. 'Shh!' she exclaimed.

'Don't be embarrassed,' he said, 'you have no idea how much I've longed for this moment. To be able to hold you, love you.'

Gracie looked round quickly to see if anyone had heard him, but the other diners were far too busy to be interested.

'Please, Jeff, not here,' she pleaded.

He laughed at her discomfort. 'You look so guilty, darling. Don't be. We are going to have a great time.'

Fortunately the waitress served them, which stopped any further conversation.

After the meal, they walked around the shops, looking in the windows before making their way to the promenade, where they sat looking out over the sea.

'This couldn't be more different from my home in Denver, where I live. It's at the foot of the Rocky Mountains. There are lakes, of course, and beautiful scenery like you wouldn't believe. Everything seems so much smaller here in England. Quaint even. The folk are more conservative, but then they've really suffered during the Blitz. We in the States have been lucky, except for Pearl Harbour, of course.'

As he told her about his home and country, Gracie couldn't help but think it sounded like a different world altogether. Then they made their way to the hotel.

Jeff had signed the register on their arrival and so, after picking up the key to their room, he took her into the bar for a drink. As he passed her a gin and tonic, he smiled at her.

'For goodness' sake Gracie honey, relax! You're not going to the electric chair you know!'

She suddenly started laughing. 'Oh dear, does it show that much?'

'Yes it does. You don't have to do anything you don't want to you know. If you just want to lie in my arms, that's fine. I've never forced any woman against her wishes and I don't intend to start now.' He squeezed her hand. 'Besides I want you to enjoy yourself, understand?'

She felt as if a weight had been lifted from her shoulders. 'Yes, I do understand but you must realise this is new to me. Does that surprise you?'

'Not at all, darling, I know you're a good girl. Why do you think I love you so much?'

'Do you really?' She frowned waiting for an answer.

'Enough to take you home now, if that's what you want.'

'You'd do that?'

'Of course. Do you want to stay or go?'

Suddenly everything felt right. 'No I want to stay . . . very much.'

'Great, then drink up.'

They sat at the bar chatting and after her third drink, Gracie felt relaxed and a little tipsy. When they left the bar and took the lift to their room, any inhibition she'd had seemed to fade as Jeff took her into his arms, rained kisses on her and slowly undid the buttons on her dress. She was completely carried away with it all and when he too undressed and led her to the bed, she went willingly.

Jeff, knowing of her innocence, was gentle. He held her, kissed her and caressed her until she was filled with longing

15

for him, surprised by her own wanton behaviour.

His mouth took her nipple, gently raking his teeth on it, making her squirm with excitement and when his kisses covered her stomach, then her thighs, she thought she would die with longing and eagerly spread her legs for him arching her back as he slowly entered her. As she lost her virginity, she cried out in ecstasy, winding her legs around him, tossing her head on her pillow as he increased his pace. She had never known the feelings that were flooding through her body and she was carried away on waves of sexual pleasure.

Jeff lay on top of her completely exhausted. Gracie beneath him was silent; her eyes closed hardly believing what had taken place but having loved every moment.

'Oh, Jeff,' she sighed.

'You all right honey?' he murmured as he slid off her, holding her in his arms. 'I didn't hurt you did I?'

She didn't answer, just kissed him, her mouth lingering on his.

He chuckled softly. 'Mm, that good was it?'

'It was wonderful! I had no idea sex was anything like that.'

'Oh Gracie, you are quite a surprise,' he whispered and kissed her slowly and gently.

They lay in each other's arms. Jeff telling her how he longed for the war to be over so life could again be normal. Of the friends he'd lost, how futile war was. Talking about his home town and his family, she wondered if he would ask her to share his life, but he didn't. Not then, but three months later, after an evening meal in a restaurant, he took her hand.

'Do you think you could leave all this behind, your home, your family?' he asked.

She felt a moment of panic, as she looked across the table at him.

'What do you mean, leave it all behind?'

His eyes twinkled with amusement. 'I'm asking you to come with me to Denver as my wife. I love you Gracie. Will you marry me?'

She felt as if someone had knocked every breath from her body. He was asking her the question she'd been longing to hear, but suddenly the consequences of saying 'yes' were staring her in the face. It was a huge step to take: to move across the Atlantic, to leave her family and the world she knew – and suddenly she was scared.

At her hesitation he spoke. 'Do you love me, Gracie?'

'Yes I do. Of course I do.'

'Do you want us to have a future together, a place of our own, children?'

She looked into his eyes and knew she didn't want that with anyone else.

'Yes, I really do.'

He held her hand tightly. 'I know it's asking a great deal of you to come to the States. It won't be easy for you to say goodbye to your family here in the UK, but it's the only way we can be together. You know I'll always take care of you, love you and, in a few years, we'll save enough to come back for a vacation.' He paused. 'What do you say honey?'

She felt the smile spread across her features. 'I say yes, darling. I will marry you.'

* * *

As she walked slowly around the deck of the ship, she relived the excitement of what had passed, the never-ending questions from the American military authorities before they eventually gave their permission. The wedding, her pale green utility suit bought with borrowed clothing coupons, the buffet in the local hall, with everyone making contributions to the food. The weekend honeymoon back at the hotel in Bournemouth and now . . . she was en route to her new life, filled with trepidation. She left the deck and made her way to her cabin.

Chapter Two

Valerie Johnson climbed into her bunk and started to read, shutting her ears to the buzz of conversation from the other brides who were in the cabin getting ready for bed. She found reading emptied her mind of all the concerns she had about moving to America and starting a new life. Being at sea didn't bother her; as a child she'd spent her childhood in Singapore with her family, as her father worked for the government and had been posted there. They had returned when war seemed imminent. She didn't suffer with sea-sickness as some of her travelling companions did.

For her, the change of country was exciting and she had the comfort of knowing her father had opened a bank account in New York in her name, giving her enough money to come home if she wanted to. She remembered his words. *Life is full of uncertainties, Valerie. Ross is a good man but when you live together with a person it's a different matter. Only then do you find out what they are really like. I just want to know that if you need to, you have the means to return. It's a kind of security.*

She had thanked him profusely. Not that she had any doubts about Ross. He had been a captain in the US Army and, when they started to see each other, it was a joy to find they had similar outlooks on life and shared interests. He was well educated, had attended Harvard, trained as a lawyer and would be able to keep her in the lifestyle she was used to. They both liked the theatre, opera and played bridge. But she was concerned about meeting his parents, not knowing how they felt about having a British daughter-in-law.

At that moment, Gracie returned. They chatted briefly as Gracie undressed for bed and settled down for the night.

The voyage was beset by bad weather and when the ship eventually docked in New York, it was later than expected. The women were packed, ready and waiting to be collected by their husbands with mixed emotions. Would their late arrival make a difference? Would their men be there? If they were, would they still feel the same when they saw them? The air was charged with uncertainty.

Gracie was called forward. Standing waiting was a man in a suit. It took a moment for her to recognise Jeff. She had foolishly expected to see him in uniform. He stepped forward, grinning broadly.

'Gracie, honey, it's me!' He took her into his arms. She burst into tears!

'Hey, steady now. Everything's going to be fine.' He held her tight, giving her time to recover.

Wiping her eyes, she looked at him and smiled shyly. 'You look so different in civvies,' she stuttered. 'I wasn't expecting that.'

He chortled. 'I've been out of the army for some months now, honey.' He picked up her bag. 'Come on, we'll get a cab. I've booked us in at the Taft Hotel for the night, before we make our way home to Denver.'

She followed him down the gangway, gripping hold of his hand as they walked through the dock to a cabstand. Then, sitting in the back, still holding his hand, she looked at the tenements as they drove past, thinking how shabby they all looked and her heart sank. However, as they began to enter the centre of the city, she felt relieved. The shops were brightly lit, the traffic was heavy and there was a buzz about the place that filled her with excitement. At one set of traffic lights, she saw a couple of American police officers and was surprised to see they were armed. The guns in their holsters, worn on their hips, were a strange sight to her, as was the fact that the traffic drove on the other side of the road.

They reached their destination and, after Jeff paid the driver, they checked in at reception and left Gracie's bag to be taken to their room before making their way to the café where Jeff ordered some coffee.

He gazed across at her and smiled. 'You look great honey. I began to wonder just when I'd see you again. It seems such a long time.'

'To me too,' she confessed. She looked around. 'I still can't believe we're here together.'

'I thought a night in New York would be a good start for you. It's a great place, very different from Denver but you'll love the shops. I'm going to take you to Macy's. You won't need clothing coupons here, darling. Then tomorrow we'll go home. You'll get to meet my folks.'

Gracie felt her blood chill at the thought. 'What do they think about us getting married?'

He hesitated for a moment. 'Well, they were surprised of course. Mother felt a bit cheated not being at the wedding, if I'm honest, but Dad was fine.'

'How long do we have to stay with them?' she asked with some trepidation.

'A couple of months maybe, until I've saved enough to furnish an apartment.'

'Can't we get one already furnished?'

'We could, but they're more expensive and I thought with our own stuff it will be a start for when we buy our own place.'

'I see,' she said, but hoped it wouldn't take that long. She didn't want to start married life living with anyone, especially Jeff's parents.

'Come on,' he said, 'let's go shopping. We can catch a bus outside.'

Macy's was a revelation to Gracie. It was huge and she could well believe it was the largest store in the world. As they entered the front doors, the smell of perfume filled her nostrils, then she saw the many counters displaying exotically shaped bottles and the women standing testing various brands. There was a whole floor selling lingerie, filled with the most glamorous negligees, bras, petticoats and panties in a vast array of colours, trimmed with lace.

Jeff bought her two nightdresses and two sets of underwear. The sizing was different here but the assistant came to her rescue and explained it to her for future reference. Gracie was delighted with her purchases. Two hours later, they emerged from the store with several bags filled with new clothes.

They stopped in at the Brass Rail for coffee and a snack and to rest their sore feet, and as Gracie sat down she started laughing.

'What's so funny?' Jeff asked.

'My father would die before he'd walk into a shop selling woman's underwear!'

'British men are more conservative, I'm American – we do things differently.'

'Oh Jeff, that was so much fun. Thank you for my presents.'

'Nothing's too good for my wife,' he said and, leaning forward, he kissed her. 'We'll go back to the hotel, have a rest and this evening we'll go out for a few drinks and look around. You must see Times Square at night.'

They caught a cab back to the hotel and checked into their room. Gracie kicked off her shoes and flopped onto the bed exhausted – the excitement of the day catching up with her. Jeff removed his coat and jacket, and went to the bathroom. When he returned Gracie was fast asleep. He looked at his bride and smiled, then lay beside her, covering them both with a blanket before taking her into his arms, and he too slept.

* * *

23

Gracie woke with a start. The bedroom curtains were open and the lights from the street below lit up the room. She felt the arms of her husband around her.

Jeff too stirred. He looked at her. 'Hello Mrs Rider,' he said and he kissed her.

Their lovemaking was long and languid, neither of them wanting to rush this moment for which they had both waited so long. For Gracie it was like coming home, and any doubts she had about coming to America were washed away as she lay in his arms. Tomorrow she'd have to face his parents, but tonight was hers to be enjoyed with the man she loved.

Enjoy it, she did. Well wrapped up against the cold, she and Jeff caught a bus to Times Square. The lights were something to believe. Times Square was bright and brash. The huge face on a billboard puffed smoke rings as it advertised a cigarette brand. The latest news flashed in a long strip around a building and the shops were still open.

They went into a nearby hotel bar and listened to a pianist playing, bought hot dogs from a barrow on a street corner and soaked up the spirit that was New York. Gracie had never experienced anything like it in her life before. Nothing could be more different from the quiet of Southampton. It was like walking through an American musical.

They walked along Broadway arm in arm, stopping to look in the shop windows, full of enticing things to buy. For Gracie it was such a thrill to see such displays after the shortages she'd suffered during the war. America was thought to be the land of plenty, and so it seemed to her that night as she soaked up the strangeness of this amazing city. If Denver were the same just how thrilling would that be! She couldn't wait to write home to her family and tell them all about it. She'd do that once she was settled with her in-laws.

The following morning, they checked out of the hotel and took a cab to Grand Central Station, which seemed absolutely huge to Gracie. There were shops here too, and she wondered just how much money did the Americans have to spend.

Jeff bought their tickets and they climbed aboard the train and settled in their seats. It would be a long journey until they reached their destination and then she'd meet Jeff's parents. She secretly sent up a prayer asking that the meeting would go well. She looked briefly at her husband, wondering if she disagreed with his mother over something, which side would he take? She knew that some of her friends had said their mother-in-laws were possessive of their sons. She hoped this wouldn't be the case with the other Mrs Rider.

As the train started to move, she decided to put such thoughts to the back of her mind and enjoy the journey. After all, it would only be for a short time, then they'd move out to their own place and she'd have Jeff all to herself.

Chapter Three

Valerie Johnson wasn't surprised to see her husband in a smart business suit, as he'd sent her several photographs after he'd left the army. She'd thought he looked very much the well-dressed businessman and had been pleased to see how stylish he was. When she was called for him to collect her, she ran straight into his arms.

'Hello darling,' he said as he kissed her warmly. 'God it's been an age and you look just as beautiful as I remember!'

They took a cab to a prestigious-looking block of apartments in New York's classy Upper East Side, with a uniformed doorman on duty who greeted her warmly.

'Welcome to America, Mrs Johnson! I hope you'll be happy in your new country.'

She was delighted. 'Why thank you, I'm sure I will.'

He looked at Ross. 'I could stand and listen to the

British accent all day long,' he said as he opened the main door for them.

Inside was a small reception desk with a uniformed guard sitting behind it. Ross walked over and introduced his bride.

'Hank, this is my wife. Anything she needs you see to it if I'm not around. OK?'

'Yes, sir.' He smiled at Valerie. 'Nice to meet you, ma'am.'

They took the elevator to the second floor and Ross took her along the corridor to the apartment that was theirs.

It was roomy inside and open plan, as opposed to her home with its separate rooms, and she liked it. It was light and bright, and the central heating was on, so it was warm and welcoming. He showed her the bathroom, which had both a bath and shower, and the two double bedrooms, beautifully furnished as was the living room. The kitchen was roomy and along one wall was a waist-high counter separating it from the living room so whoever was cooking could still be part of any conversation with her husband or guests who might be sitting relaxing, watching the television, which she saw immediately.

'Oh my, the television!' she remarked, 'and so big!' Not every home had a television back in Britain and those that did had a small cabinet housing a very small screen.

She ran into his arms. 'Oh, Ross, this is just lovely.'

'I'm so happy you like it darling. I'll make some coffee and we can catch up with each other, then we'll have a shower to freshen up and I'll take you out to dinner, just the two of us, to celebrate. Tomorrow Mother is having a dinner party for you to introduce you to our friends.'

'How very kind of her,' Valerie said without too much enthusiasm.

'Now you're not to worry,' said Ross sensing her reluctance. 'After all, everyone is dying to meet the woman who stole my heart. My English rose as they call you.'

She forced a smile. 'I just hope they like me,' she said.

He drew her closer. 'You are my wife and in time they'll love you as I do. They just have to get to know you, that's all.'

They sat and drank their coffee, exchanging news about what they'd been doing in the months they'd been apart.

Ross was telling her about returning to work. 'It took a while I have to admit. Some things have changed since the war, of course, and after being in command in the army I had to learn to step back a little, which wasn't easy at first.'

'And now?' she asked.

'Now, I have my own clients again so I guess I am in charge of those.'

'What about working for your father? Does it seem strange now?'

He paused. 'We don't always see eye to eye over how to run the business, I must admit. I've moved on, learnt a lot in the army, whereas he's still stuck in the same rut. It makes for some heated discussions sometimes.'

Valerie sensed there was a tension in the office, but

made no comment. She was used to mixing with people on all levels in her private life through her father's connections, but beneath her ladylike appearance was a rod of steel. She would bide her time and see how things were. She was a good judge of character and felt she would be an asset to her husband in more ways than perhaps he ever imagined. And if things didn't work out, she had the financial means to leave. This she kept to herself.

By the time they'd finished talking, it was well into the evening and they quickly showered and changed to be at the Four Seasons in time for their booking. Valerie loved the look of the restaurant with its wall frescos, depicting spring, summer, autumn and winter. The meal was lovely and the champagne cooled. They both relaxed and, by the end of the evening, they were tired. A cab took them back to the apartment where they stood at the window overlooking the city, drinking a nightcap, arms around one another.

'I can't tell you how great it is to have you here by my side,' Ross whispered against her ear. 'I've dreamt of this moment for what has seemed like an eternity.'

'I know,' she replied. 'Me too.'

They emptied their glasses and made their way to the bedroom and undressed. As Valerie picked up her nightdress, Ross caught hold of her arm.

'What's the point of putting that on sweetheart, I'll only take it off again!'

Valerie laughed quietly, threw it on a bedside chair and climbed into bed.

Ross drew her into his arms. 'God, Valerie, you have no idea how I've missed you.'

'I know. After you left for the States, it seemed to me as though meeting you and getting married had all been a dream, and as the months passed the reality of being your wife seemed unreal.'

'Well we can soon put that right darling,' he said, slowly caressing her breasts and kissing her.

She returned his kisses, the hunger that was within her was overwhelming and their lovemaking was not slow and gentle, but full of passion that had been denied for so long until they lay, breathless and exhausted.

'Now do you feel like a married woman?' he asked.

She let out a deep sigh of contentment. 'Oh yes! You have no idea how much I needed that.'

He laughed softly. 'Indeed I do! I have been celibate for far too long.'

'I should hope so!'

The following morning, they took a cab to Central Park and walked through the snow, wrapped up against the cold wind, stopping for coffee and a brandy to warm them. They took another cab back to Saks, Fifth Avenue, where Valerie enjoyed looking at the clothes and household goods before buying a dress to wear that night at her in-laws. She also purchased nylon stockings, which had been in short supply back at home. To her it was like Christmas with all its goodies. After such austerity at home, it seemed almost indecent, but she, being a woman, loved it!

Ross took her out to lunch and then showed her the sights. They went to the top of the Empire State Building so she could look out over the city that was to be her new home. She'd decided to buy a map of New York and, when Ross was working, would familiarise herself with the place, walking it block by block. It wouldn't be difficult. The city was laid out in a grid system: streets running one way, avenues the other. She supposed in time, she'd get used to the skyscrapers, the hustle and bustle – the pushing and shoving of folk who always seemed to be in a great hurry. It would be interesting she felt sure and a necessity if she were living there.

They returned to the apartment and, whilst Ross read the paper, she unpacked the rest of her clothes, pressing her new black dress and choosing her jewellery for the dinner that evening.

Valerie was tall, slim and elegant, with blonde hair and pale skin; a typical English rose, with fine features and wide blue eyes. Her classic good looks came from the genes of her mother and father, a handsome couple, and, as she applied her make-up and dressed, she turned and looked at herself in the mirror and thought, *yes, you'll do*. She had no idea what her in-laws were like, but she'd be herself. She was used to formal dinners, having attended many through her father's government connections, and decided to treat tonight as one of those. Be charming, be natural.

They took a cab to Riverside Drive, overlooking the Hudson River, where the Johnsons had a penthouse.

As Ross explained, 'It's easier to travel by cab in the city than to drive.'

It was obvious that this was an expensive block from the entrance and the doorman, who greeted Ross warmly.

'Good evening, sir, your folks are waiting for you, they told me you were coming.' He tipped his hat to Valerie. 'Good evening ma'am.'

They took the elevator to the top floor. There was only one door here and Ross, taking her arm, walked towards it and rang the bell.

As it opened, Valerie held her breath. A maid stood there, smiling. 'Evening, Mr Ross, come in.' Behind her was a buzz of conversation, which stopped as they walked through the hallway into the sumptuous living room.

An elegant woman stepped forwards and Valerie caught a waft of expensive perfume. Gloria Johnson smiled at Valerie. 'Welcome to New York!' But Valerie saw her smile didn't reach her eyes.

'Thank you, how nice to meet you.'

Ross's father stepped forward, a tall, well-dressed man with firm features and a stubborn jaw. He kissed her on the cheek. 'Hello, Valerie, my dear. I am Leo, your father-in-law, welcome.' His greeting was genuine. He took her arm and introduced her to the other guests. She sensed a certain tension as he reached the last one, Laura, a younger woman, glamorous in a hard way, thought Valerie, but she was surprised at the hostility she felt behind the handshake and greeting and wondered why.

Ross's brother introduced himself. 'Hello, Valerie, I'm your brother-in-law, Earl and this is my wife Bonny.'

Bonny was petite and full of fun, Valerie could see that from the brightness shining in her eyes and her laughter as she hugged her.

'Hi, Valerie! Am I glad to meet you. I'm longing to hear all about England and its quaint ways. I do hope we can be real friends.'

Valerie liked her instinctively. 'I'd really like that. You can help me get used to everything American.'

'Gee! I love the way you Brits speak! So ladylike.'

Cocktails were served with delicious canapés and the others approached Valerie, asking innumerable questions about Britain and the war until dinner was served.

The dining room was large and the table long enough to seat twelve people comfortably and set with great elegance. Valerie was seated with her father-in-law to her right and, on her left, one of his business associates who turned out to be charming.

She noticed that Ross was beside Laura and it was obvious to all that she was flirting with him, making him look uncomfortable and annoyed. Bonny caught her looking at them and winked at her. She obviously knew what was going on.

Gloria played the perfect hostess, bringing her guest into the conversation sometimes, but there was a definite coolness in her tone and Valerie knew instinctively that she would not be her friend.

At the end of the meal, Valerie asked to use the bathroom

and Bonny jumped to her feet. 'I'll take you, I need to powder my nose too,' she said and, taking Valerie's hand, led her away.

The bathroom was like a first-class hotel, with two washbasins, a huge bath and a separate toilet.

Bonny collapsed on an easy chair. 'Christ! I do so hate these family gatherings!'

Laughing at this sudden outburst, Valerie asked why.

'Well, Mrs Johnson, our mother-in-law thinks she's the first lady and as for that bitch Laura, I can't stand her!'

'Who is she exactly?'

Bonny sat bolt upright. 'You don't know?'

Shaking her head Valerie said, 'No. Should I?'

'Oh yes, you certainly should! It was expected that Laura and Ross would marry after the war. Oh my, when Ross wrote saying he was marrying an English girl, she went crazy! She's the daughter of a very rich father who dotes on her every wish, but this was something he couldn't fix.'

'I see,' said Valerie. 'Ross never mentioned her to me.'

'Well, of course not. Yes, they went out together but it was the two families who had planned their future, I'm not sure they ever told Ross and, if they did, he wasn't playing. You be careful of her Valerie, she's trouble!'

Taking out her powder compact, Valerie now understood everything. The girl, Mrs Johnson's coolness. She had ruined all their plans. 'What about Leo? Was he in on this too?'

'Probably not. Dad is a lovely guy. All he's interested in

is business and golf. He indulges his wife for a quiet life.'

Valerie started chuckling. 'Well, Bonny, now I know what I'm up against. I can't thank you enough.'

Bonny got up and stood behind Valerie and studied her reflection in the mirror. 'If I'm not mistaken, I'm sure you can cope with both of them.' And she laughed. 'Welcome to the family!'

It was almost midnight when Ross eventually booked a cab to take them home. They said their goodbyes and Valerie thanked her hosts for a lovely evening.

Bonny kissed her goodbye. 'I'll give you a call and we'll go shopping,' she said.

'I'd love that,' Valerie told her.

Once in the taxi, Ross let out a sigh of relief. 'There! I told you it would all be fine.'

'Yes, it was lovely. Your mother went to a lot of trouble.' She paused. 'You didn't tell me about Laura ever, why was that?'

He turned quickly and looked at her. She gazed back at him without blinking.

'There was nothing to tell, that's why. Sure we dated for some time, but that was all. I came to England a free man.'

'I don't think that's how your old girlfriend saw it,' she said softly.

'I never made Laura any promises. We never spoke about a future together.'

'What about your mother? Did she ever say you two would make a great couple?'

His jaw tightened. 'My mother doesn't and never has run my life.'

She smothered a laugh. 'I don't think she believes that for one moment, Ross darling, but she certainly will never run mine!'

Chapter Four

Gracie and Jeff Rider eventually arrived in Denver, after a long and tiring journey. Jeff had booked them into a hotel overnight to give them time to rest and freshen up for the morrow.

Although there had been a heavy snowfall, the streets had been cleared. After dinner they took a walk. Gracie was overwhelmed by the bustling city with its shops and restaurants. They stopped in a nearby bar for a drink and when she told Jeff how exciting she found the city, he surprised her by saying this was not where they would be living.

She looked at him puzzled. 'What do you mean? I thought you said you came from Denver.'

'Well, just an hour or so away, thankfully. The city is very tiring to live and work in, no we are in a smaller place, thank heavens.'

She was somewhat disappointed. 'How much smaller?' she asked.

'About the size of Southampton, I guess,' he said laughing. 'I don't mean the backwoods, Gracie honey.'

She wondered if there was anything else he hadn't told her?

They had breakfast in the hotel the following morning and made their way to the Greyhound bus station. As they settled in their seats and the bus moved out and through the town, Gracie felt a little depressed to be leaving such a vibrant place and hoped that wherever they were headed wasn't some dreary town. She'd seen enough American movies to know that there were many 'one-horse towns', as they were often referred to, and as they headed out into quieter surroundings, leaving the bustle of the city behind for a snow-covered countryside and fewer houses, her heart sank.

At last the bus pulled into its destination and they alighted. Gracie looked around. There were several shops, much smaller and duller by comparison, and the folk walking about were not so smartly dressed as the inhabitants she'd seen in Denver.

They climbed into a cab and Jeff gave the address to the driver.

Gracie took in every detail as they drove away from the station. Yes, there was a town as such. There were shops and chemists, or drugstores as she had been told to call them. The vehicles parked there were not smart, but slightly battered, and there were several small trucks. There was a grocery store, then they passed a school and drove into a small residential area. The houses stood back from the road, their gardens unfenced unlike British gardens, and Gracie wondered how that worked out. Did the residents know which part was theirs, she wondered. It all seemed a bit strange and more downmarket than she'd been expecting after seeing Denver itself.

The cab stopped in front of one of the houses where the path had been cleared. It looked cared for, but it was very ordinary. Somehow, like many others coming to America for the first time and only having American movies to judge by, the reality was a disappointment. This was no Hollywood type area. Not quite a one-horse town, either, for which she was grateful. The next thing was to meet the relations.

The front door opened and a woman came walking down the path, a shawl around her shoulders. Gracie could tell by the physical likeness that this was Jeff's mother. The woman looking at her all the time as she approached. Gracie wasn't too sure if the look was friendly or not.

'Mother, this is Gracie, my bride! Gracie, this is my mother.'

Velda Rider shook her by the hand. 'I hope you had a good journey?'

'A long one but we stayed overnight in Denver to rest up, last night.'

'You'd better come in out of the cold,' she said and walked away. Gracie followed.

There was a long porch outside the house, but once through the door you stepped into a large open living room. There was another room that Gracie assumed led to the kitchen and a stairway to the upstairs. It was clean, and while the furniture had seen better days, it was comfortable. She stood by the fire to warm her hands.

'I'll put the kettle on,' said Velda. 'I hope you don't mind coffee, I'm afraid we don't drink tea in this house.' It was more a declaration than an invitation.

'Coffee will be just fine, thank you,' Gracie answered.

'Sit down, make yourself comfortable, after all this will be your home from now on.'

There was no warmth in her voice as she made the statement and Gracie felt her hackles rise.

'It's very good of you to take us in at the moment. I'm sure it's not an ideal arrangement as far as you're concerned, but hopefully it won't be for very long, Mrs Rider.'

Being challenged surprised Velda. 'Jeff is my son and it is my duty to take care of him.'

'Of course, that's what mothers do, but now he has a wife, so I can take some of the weight of care off your shoulders. After all, it's time you had a break don't you think?' Gracie smiled at the woman as she spoke but stared straight at her as she did so.

Velda walked into the kitchen without replying and Gracie could hear her banging about as she filled the kettle.

Jeff frowned at her. 'Be careful honey, after all this is *her* home.'

'I'm very aware of that, Jeff, and I hope she'll have it to herself again very soon!' As she spoke, Gracie vowed that somehow she would make sure they moved very quickly. After all, no two women enjoy sharing a kitchen and, in this case, a man. Yes, Jeff was the other woman's son but he was now also her husband.

After they had drunk their coffee and eaten homemade cookies, Velda took Gracie upstairs to show her the bedroom.

'This one here is yours and Jeff's, next door is mine and opposite is the bathroom and along there,' she pointed to a room at the end, 'is Rick's room.'

'Rick?' Gracie looked puzzled. 'Who is Rick?'

'Why Jeff's younger brother, of course!'

'Oh yes, of course,' Gracie hurriedly answered. She hadn't known that Jeff had a brother. He'd never mentioned him, but no way would she let her new mother-in-law know that.

The room was adequate. Not particularly big, but enough to hold a double bed, chest of drawers and a wardrobe. It was clean and the bed was made up, ready for them.

'Thank you, it's really nice, Mrs Rider.'

'I'll get Jeff to bring up your cases so you can unpack and get settled in,' she said, and left Gracie alone.

When Jeff walked into the room minutes later, Gracie immediately questioned him, 'You didn't tell me you had a brother and that he was also living here.'

He just shrugged. 'I've been away in the army and to be truthful, he doesn't figure much in my life. Never has, if I'm honest. The only thing we have in common is our parents.'

She let this pass. No doubt she'd meet her brother-in-law soon enough and she started to unpack, but all the time she

41

was wondering how soon they could leave this house for a place of their own.

'When you've finished,' Jeff said, 'I'll borrow Dad's car and show you the town. You'll soon get used to it, the stores you'll need to shop in. After all, we'll be here a while.'

'Can't we look at some estate agents at the same time? Perhaps we'll be lucky and find something. After all, I'm sure your mother would be pleased to have her house to herself.'

'Another time, honey. Today we'll just take it easy and familiarise you with your new surroundings. First things first, we need to get you kitted-out with warmer clothes. I'll wait downstairs for you.' And he left the room before she could argue.

A little later they climbed into the car and drove into town. It was a little bigger than she'd thought, but certainly not as big as Southampton, as she'd been told. Neither was it as classy. It amused her to see many of the men wearing Stetsons, sheepskin coats and jeans to keep out the cold. She smiled to herself and wondered when John Wayne would show up.

Jeff took her to a store and bought her some jeans, cowboy boots and a warm thick jacket that came just below her hips. She turned down a Stetson for a warm woollen hat with earflaps, wondering what on earth would she look like in such strange apparel.

He then took her to the local grocery store, pointing to the aisles of food and shopping carts, explaining that you walked around, choosing your goods then paying for them at the checkout. She thought how very different this was to shopping in Liptons with a list and asking someone behind the counter for the goods and then paying for them.

The roads and pavements, or sidewalks as she must remember to call them, had been cleared of snow but there was a chilling wind, so she was glad when Jeff suggested they stop in a diner for a coffee.

They sat in a booth and ordered. The place was busy and the waitresses fast and efficient. 'Bacon and two eggs on a raft, sunny side up,' one called out to the chefs behind the counter. Gracie looked puzzled.

Laughing, Jeff explained. 'It means two fried eggs on toast, without the eggs being turned over . . . sunny side up.'

'An entirely new language!' she exclaimed. 'I have so much to learn. A pavement is a sidewalk, the chemist is a drugstore, a lift is an elevator.'

'A boot of a car is the trunk,' he added, 'and a vest is a waistcoat.'

'Enough, Jeff! It'll take time but I'll get there.'

The waitress served the coffee.

'Thank you very much,' said Gracie.

'Aw gee! You English are always so polite,' the waitress remarked before she was off to the next table.

Gracie had a few things she needed sorted and looking at her husband she said, 'I need to know just what to do, sharing your mother's house. What about meals? Do I cook for the two of us?'

'Hell no! Ma would take that as an insult! I'll give her

money each week for our keep and she'll cook for the family. You can ask her what she'd like you to do in the house to help her. You need to work it out between you.'

'When do you go back to work?'

'Monday morning.'

'Where do you work, you've never told me?'

'I work in one of the outlets for men selling all sorts of things. Work clothes, ordinary clothes, jeans, shoes, equipment. It's a kind of general store aimed at the males of the community. We cover a large range of goods.'

'Perhaps I could get a job too,' she suggested.

'It's not as easy as that, Gracie. You have to apply for a green card first. It's a permit which allows you to take a job, you can't work without it I'm afraid.'

All Gracie could think was that she'd be spending far too much time around the house with her mother-in-law and that didn't sit well with her. She had to try and get along with the woman for both their sakes. With this in mind, she bought some chocolates, or candies – as Jeff explained – to take to her, but when they arrived home and Gracie gave them to her, Mrs Rider wasn't enthusiastic.

'Don't hold much with sweet things,' she said, 'they rot your teeth!'

Gracie was furious at such rudeness. 'Oh well, in that case I'll eat them. It would be a pity to let them go to waste.' She opened the box, took one and offered the box to Jeff, who also took one, which earned him a glare from his mother.

Picking up some magazines she'd bought, Gracie asked Velda if there was anything she could do for her and was very smartly turned down, so she settled in a chair and read.

Around half past five, there was the sound of a vehicle outside and then the front door opened. A tall young man a few years younger than Jeff walked in. He stopped when he saw Gracie. With a broad grin he walked over to her and kissed her on the mouth.

'Well hello! I'm Rick. I didn't realise my brother had married such a looker! Welcome to the family.'

Gracie saw the thunderous expression on Jeff's face, but he remained silent.

'When did you arrive?' Rick asked.

'Earlier today. Once we'd unpacked, Jeff took me into town to look around.'

Her brother-in-law sat beside her. 'So, what did you think of your new surroundings?'

'It's far too soon to know, really. Everything is so different. It'll take a while to get used to.'

'Well I think you're very brave, Gracie, to leave your country behind and come out here. It can't have been easy for you.'

'No, but then, of course, I want to be with Jeff, so there was no choice really. So here I am, although I hope for not very long. Your mother is kind to put us up, but we need our own place.'

He rose from his seat. 'I'm off to have a shower, so I'll see you later but I hope you don't move out too soon. It's kinda nice to have a beautiful young woman around the house.' He grinned broadly at her and left the room.

She looked at Jeff. 'Don't you two talk to each other?' she asked sharply.

'When necessary,' he replied and continued to read the paper.

Shortly after, the door opened again and an older man entered. Jeff put down his paper.

'Dad, come and meet your daughter-in-law. This is my Gracie.'

Ben Rider was tall, broad and powerfully built, dressed in jeans and a heavy short coat. He removed the woollen hat from his head, walked over to Gracie and shook her hand. His grip was hard and firm.

'Well, howdy Gracie. Welcome to Barton. I hope you'll be very happy here. You've had a long journey, you must be weary.'

'We stopped over in Denver last night, so we did have a rest.'

'Very wise,' He turned to his son. 'You alright boy?'

'Yes thanks, Dad. I took Gracie around the town, I borrowed your car.'

'That's fine, use it whenever you like, I've got my truck, so I only use it at weekends sometime.'

'Where do you work, Mr Rider?' asked Gracie.

'I'm working on a construction site,' he told her. 'We're building new apartments on the other side of town. Now if you'll excuse me, I'll go see my wife.' He left them and wandered into the kitchen.

Gracie could hear voices as husband and wife talked. She couldn't distinguish the words, but Mrs Rider sounded angry. Then Ben returned with two cans of beer and passed one to Jeff.

The two men sat and chatted and Gracie listened. She was thankful that they seemed on good terms after seeing Jeff with his brother. She liked her father-in-law. He had seemed friendly enough.

At suppertime, they all sat round the table and Velda served the food. There was a large meat loaf, sweet potatoes, corn on the cob and green beans. It was delicious and Gracie said so.

'This is so tasty. I haven't had these kind of potatoes before, they're so different and I really like them.'

For once Velda seemed pleased. 'I take pride in my cooking,' she said, 'men need a good meal in their belly after a hard day's work.'

Rick looked up. 'You'll have to cook us an English meal one night, Gracie, so we can see what that's like.'

Gracie was about to say how much she'd like to do that until she saw the look of anger on Velda's face. 'We'll have to see what your mother thinks, after all it's her kitchen.'

Velda remained silent so no more was said.

Later that night, when they were in bed, Jeff reached for her but Gracie caught hold of his hand on her breast. 'Your parents are in the next room,' she said.

'They are going to be in the next room every night,' he said, 'what difference does that make?'

'Oh Jeff, I don't know but somehow I can't relax knowing there is only a thin wall between us.'

'Now listen, honey. We will be living here for a while and you'll have to get used to the idea. After all, we are married and married people have sex!'

She knew he was right, but somehow the thought of seeing Velda in the morning, and her knowing they had made love, was enough to make her tense.

She snuggled into her husband. 'You just have to give me a bit of time to get used to all this, that's all. Anyway I'm too tired tonight.'

He chuckled. 'Don't you start having headaches on me.'

'No I won't,' she promised, 'but just not tonight.'

'I guess I can hold out for twenty-four hours, but we have a lot of catching up to do Gracie. We've been apart for too long and I have ached to hold you in my arms.'

From the tone of his voice, she knew he wouldn't accept her reluctance again. She closed her eyes and tried to sleep, but her thoughts were jumbled. She was going to live in a house where she wasn't really welcome by Jeff's mother and Jeff and his brother were obviously at loggerheads. It didn't bode well for the immediate future. Eventually she fell asleep from exhaustion.

Chapter Five

Whilst Gracie Rider was trying to sort out her difficulties, Valerie Johnson was enjoying her new surroundings. Ross had arranged for a cleaner to come in twice a week, which left Valerie free from too many household duties and, as Ross had taken a few days off to be with her, she enjoyed being taken around New York. They went to Radio City to see a movie and watch the Rockettes, a group of dancers whose precision was a joy to watch when they performed in the interval. They had been out to dinner, skated on the outside ice rink at Rockefeller Center and been shopping at Saks, Fifth Avenue. It had been a whirlwind and she'd enjoyed it tremendously.

Near by the apartment were intriguing small shops. A delicatessen, which sold a vast selection of fresh food as well as pasta, cheeses, olives, nuts and many varieties of unusual ingredients, long gone from the shelves of British shops due to the shortages of the war. Alongside, a shop selling fruit and vegetables, a grocery store, a dry-cleaners and drugstore. Everything that she would need without having to travel far. She was delighted.

Eventually Ross returned to his desk and Valerie planned to explore, but a call from her sister-in-law, Bonny, with an invitation to go shopping and out to lunch, delayed her plans. She'd liked Bonny when they met at her welcome party and looked forward to seeing her again.

The two girls had a great time shopping in Bloomingdale's then went for lunch in an Italian restaurant that Bonny recommended. After they'd ordered and the wine had been poured, Bonny looked at Valerie and raised her glass.

'Here's to a new friendship,' she said.

'I'll drink to that,' Valerie replied and they clinked glasses. 'How long have you and Earl been married?' she asked.

'Three years, long enough to know how the land lies in his family.'

'Oh dear, what does that mean?'

'It means that Gloria thinks everyone should do her bidding. That whatever she says is right. She tries to rule everyone!' There was a flash of anger in the other woman's eyes.

'But she doesn't rule you, I imagine?'

'Damned right!' Bonny leant closer. 'Don't you let her rule you either.'

Valerie leant back in her seat. 'I've met her type many

times over the years and I am certainly not frightened by my new mother-in-law, I can assure you.'

Bonny laughed with delight. 'I just knew you were a strong woman when we first met, but I have to warn you that she and Laura are joined at the hip and they will do their damnedest to destroy your marriage. Trust me!'

'I'm not sure how much notice Ross takes of his mother but I got the impression he is very much his own man. I do hope I've not been wrong about him.'

'No, you haven't,' Bonny assured her. 'Ross has always stood on his own feet but, of course, he works in Leo's firm so, in many ways, he's kind of tied up with the family even more.'

Remembering her conversation with her husband and the changes he would like to make in the firm, Valerie wondered if Ross would tolerate the restrictions his father still insisted on. It was an interesting thought. If Ross branched out on his own, he could run the business the way he wanted and loosen the ties with the family. It was worth considering, she thought, but she kept it to herself.

That evening, as they sat down to dinner, Valerie told her husband about her day out with Bonny. 'We had a great time,' she said. 'I really like her, she's a bundle of fun.'

'Yes, she's good for Earl,' he told her. 'My brother was under my mother's thumb until Bonny came along. She made a man out of him.'

'What about you, darling? How much of a hold does Gloria have over you?'

Laughing he said, 'Not nearly as much as she'd like! My

mother loves to control people, but she doesn't control me and never has.'

'I'm happy to hear it. How did today go in the office?'

Ross frowned. 'Fine, I suppose. As far as my clients are concerned I work my own way but the business wants updating. Dad hasn't moved with the times. Don't get me wrong, he's a good lawyer but the firm could make much more money, if he would only listen to me.'

'Have you ever thought of moving out and opening your own firm?' Valerie asked casually.

He looked at her in surprise. 'As a matter of fact, I have, ever since I came out of the army. I feel stifled.'

'Then I think you should think seriously about it, Ross. There's nothing worse than being unhappy in the workplace. It's unhealthy for one thing!'

He gazed fondly at her. 'I do love you. You and I think so much alike and that is so comforting.'

Valerie, pleased at the compliment, smiled. 'We should start looking for office space. If you want to branch out on your own, it would be better sooner than later.'

During the weeks that followed, Valerie took herself off on a journey of discovery around the city. She loved the vibrancy of it, the eclectic feel to the place, but she knew that eventually she would have time on her hands and had no idea how she was going to fill her days.

She wandered into a small café, took off her scarf and gloves then ordered a coffee and sat looking at a guidebook of the city, marking out further places to visit. She decided to sample the cheesecake and ordered.

A young man sitting at the next table leant over. 'You are English if I'm not mistaken?'

She looked up. He was neatly dressed in a grey polo-neck jumper and trousers, with an interesting face and green eyes that twinkled at her. 'Yes I am. The accent gives me away every time.'

With a smile he said, 'Don't ever lose it. To hear English spoken well by an English person is delightful to listen to. We have a common language, which sadly we Americans crucify!'

She couldn't help but laugh. 'I have noticed, but we are different people in a different country.'

He looked at the guidebook. 'Are you just visiting?'

'No. I've just moved here to be with my husband. We met in England during the war.'

'So, you are a GI bride?'

She nodded. 'That's right, there are quite a few of us, I'm afraid. I'm just exploring the city, trying to familiarise myself with it.'

'What sort of things interest you?'

'Art galleries, museums, I love to read and discovering all that is different here in New York. Believe me, after the restrictions in my country due to the war, the shops are pure joy to a woman!'

'Have you been to the Metropolitan Museum of Art?' the stranger asked.

'Not yet, it's on my list though.'

'It's one of my favourite places,' he told her. 'Look, I'm free today. Let me take you there. It's the least I can do for a person who is learning about the city. What do you say?'

Valerie was surprised by his invitation, but he seemed a decent type and she was feeling alone in a strange place. 'Yes that would be really kind of you,' she replied.

'I hope you're wearing comfortable shoes, it's a big place.'

She laughed. 'Oh, believe me, I'm well prepared. Exploration and heels don't mix, that I know. In any case, I'm wearing boots.'

He leant forward with an outstretched hand. 'Max Brennen.'

She took his hand and shook it. 'Valerie Johnson.'

The museum was a large imposing building. Inside the entrance there was a huge hall with a grand staircase. Here was a plan of the interior and the rooms showing paintings from all over the world. Valerie was thrilled. They started on the European artists then went on to look at the Dutch painters. They sat on a bench looking at a painting by Rembrandt. She was surprised at how knowledgeable Max was but when she questioned him about it he just grinned.

'In my youth I went to art school. I wanted to be another Goya or Constable, but I wasn't really good enough, so now I work in advertising for my sins.'

'Oh that's so sad. Do you still paint?'

'Oh yes, painting is my life!'

Several hours later, they parted. Valerie thanked him profusely for his time and company. He took out a business card and gave it to her.

'Call me sometime when you're at a loose end in your

explorations and maybe I can show you something else. I've really enjoyed today. Seeing things through different eyes is always exhilarating.' He shook her hand again. 'I've really enjoyed your company Valerie, I hope we meet again,' and he walked away.

She watched his retreating figure. He was tall and held himself well as he strode down the street, winding a long scarf round his neck. She had so enjoyed the day but wondered if Ross would be angry that she'd gone off with a stranger, not the safest thing to do anywhere. She decided not to mention it and put the business card in her wallet, called a cab and went home to rest her aching feet.

Two weeks later, over breakfast, Ross told her that he'd booked a table for dinner that evening and after they'd be going to an exhibition of local artists.

'I know how much you enjoy art,' he said. 'These evenings are always interesting. I've been to several and I have been known to buy the odd picture sometimes.'

'Really? Where are they?' she asked knowing there were none in the apartment.

'I have them on the walls in my office,' he said.

'We could do with something in the living room,' she said. 'The walls look a bit bare. I've looked at prints in the stores but haven't seen anything I like.'

'Perhaps we'll see something tonight.' He kissed her and said, 'I'll be home just after five.'

The art gallery was in the Village, so they dined nearby in a French restaurant before making their way there. It was well lit with the walls covered with paintings and a label beneath each one, giving the title of the picture, the artist and the price.

They'd left their coats with a young girl when they entered who'd also handed them a glass of champagne, and now the two of them were studying the works before them, mingling with many others, doing the same. It was fascinating seeing the different styles, but the talent that was on the wall impressed Valerie. But it was one sizeable painting in particular that took her eye. It was of a small bridge in Central Park at dusk, with the skyscrapers in the background. What impressed her was the use of light in the painting. It was remarkable and she stared at it for a long time.

Ross, who had been looking at another, joined her.

'This painting is absolutely beautiful,' she said, 'just look at the light, look at the buildings, some have lights in their windows, others have not, but see here,' she pointed to the bridge and the greenery behind it. 'You know almost what time of day it is by the colour of the sky. I love it!'

'You have no idea how happy that makes me to hear you say that.' The voice behind them made them turn.

Valerie turned and looked into the eyes of Max Brennen. She was so surprised she was speechless.

It was Ross who spoke. 'Are you the artist?'

'I am.' He looked at Valerie and smiled but didn't say a word.

'My wife loves this picture,' Ross said, 'she's looking for something to hang in our living room and I'd like to buy it for her.'

'Oh Ross! Really? Oh thank you, darling, I'm really thrilled.' She looked at Max. 'This is remarkable, the way you've caught the light. It's so atmospheric.'

'I'm so glad you like it,' he said, 'but would you mind if we kept it in the gallery until the show closes in a week's time?'

'Of course not! Everyone should see it.'

'Where do I pay?' asked Ross.

Max pointed out a desk on the far side of the room and when he and Valerie were alone he said, 'How lovely to see you again.'

'Well, I can't tell you what a surprise it is to see you and your work. Max, this painting is exceptional! Why on earth are you working in advertising?'

'To pay the bills. I do display my work at events such as these, but it's not enough to live the way I like. Simple really.'

Ross returned at that moment, which stopped any further conversation. Max shook his hand.

'Thank you, sir, if you give me your address and phone number, when the gallery closes, I can arrange to deliver the painting to you.'

Ross handed him his business card. 'I'm at the office all day but Mrs Johnson will be at home. Perhaps you could hang it for us at the same time?'

'It would be my pleasure. Goodnight Mrs Johnson. I'll see you in about a week's time.' He didn't take his gaze from her whilst he spoke.

Valerie felt a sudden frisson as she looked back at him. 'I look forward to it. I can't wait to see your work hanging on my wall.'

Max left them to speak to other guests and, shortly after, they left the gallery.

'Nice man,' Ross remarked as they sat in the cab taking them home.

'Yes, and very talented,' she replied, but she couldn't help a feeling of guilt creeping into her thoughts. Why on earth hadn't she told Ross that she and Max had met before? After all, it wasn't as if they'd done anything wrong. Now she felt as if she'd just left her secret lover and nothing could be further from the truth – and if she told Ross now, it would seem very suspicious.

However, when they arrived home, she walked into the living room and stared at the large blank wall in front of her, thrilled that soon she would have Max's painting hanging there.

Chapter Six

Gracie was becoming more than irritated with her mother-in-law. Once Jeff had returned to work, Gracie had made a great effort to get along with Velda and had asked how she could be of help in the house. The other woman had her cleaning the bathroom and toilet, polishing the furniture and scrubbing the kitchen floor on her hands and knees. This Gracie hadn't minded until one morning, when she'd gone out to do the shopping, she returned to see Velda cleaning the kitchen floor with a mop and bucket. She was enraged.

'Oh I see! That's how *you* clean the kitchen floor, but when it comes to *me*, I have to get down and scrub it!'

Velda blushed and looked uncomfortable, not knowing what to say. But Gracie was not lost for words at all.

'I have tried my very best to please you since I arrived. I know you resent me, well I can't help that, but I will not be used as a skivvy just to satisfy your jealousy.'

'What's a skivvy and what makes you think I'm jealous?' Velda blustered.

'A skivvy is a term for a person who is given all the worst jobs without any respect being paid to them and you are jealous that your beloved son has another woman in his life that he cares for. *You* are no longer his first choice. Well get used to it!'

The other woman looked furious. 'How dare you talk to me like that, you are in *my* house and you should be more respectful!'

Gracie calmed down. 'Look Mrs Rider, we both love Jeff and I wish we could be friends and get along. God knows, it's difficult enough you having to put us up and us having no place of our own, but for heaven's sake, do we have to continue resenting each other?' But she saw by Velda's expression that she was wasting her time. She turned and walked out of the house.

Gracie walked into town and searched out the realty office, as estate agents were called in the States, and entered.

The girl behind the desk smiled at her. 'Good morning, what can I do for you?'

'I'm looking for an apartment to rent,' she declared. 'Do you have any on your books?'

That evening, when he returned home, Jeff was surprised to see his suitcase and one of Gracie's in the hallway. He walked into the kitchen and saw his mother at the sink.

'What's going on?' he asked.

With a face like thunder she looked at him. 'Best ask that wife of yours. She's upstairs.'

He took the stairs two at a time and rushed into their bedroom where Gracie was packing another suitcase.

'What the hell is going on?' he asked.

'We're moving out.'

'Out? Out where?'

'I've rented a small apartment nearer the town,' she told him.

'You what?' he couldn't believe what he was hearing.

Gracie stopped her packing. 'Look darling, we are in the way here. Your mother resents me and we'll never get along, so we are leaving.' She saw the anger in his eyes. 'Well at least, I am moving. You have a choice, Jeff. You come with me or stay with your mother! It's entirely up to you.' She sat on the edge of the bed and waited for his reply.

'You should have discussed this with me first, Gracie and how did you manage the down payment?'

'With some savings I have.' She stared at him. 'Look, Jeff, if we are to have a life together, we have to start on our own. The rent isn't high. The apartment could do with a lick of paint, well I can do that when you're working, besides I'm a good manager with money, trust me.'

'It seems the decision has been made for me and I really don't like it, but in future, Gracie, we talk these things over. Understand?'

She rose from the bed and put her arms around his neck.

'Absolutely.' Then she slyly added, 'Just imagine, without your parents on the other side of the wall, how our sex life will improve!'

Shaking his head, he laughed. 'You are a minx, Gracie Rider.'

She didn't answer but just grinned broadly at him. 'Can we take your father's car to move our stuff?'

'I guess so. Do we have a bed to sleep on at this place?'

'We certainly do, it's furnished. Not anything special but it's clean and comfortable. With a few bits and pieces, we'll soon have it cosy.'

'Well, I'd better go down and tell Ma what's happening.'

'You do that and take these cases with you. I'll strip the bed and join you downstairs.'

She breathed a sigh of relief as he left the room. Well that old bitch can scrub her own floors now, she thought as she removed the top sheet.

As she walked down the stairs a little later, Gracie could hear raised voices in the kitchen: that didn't surprise her. Velda wanted her gone but not her precious son. Well now she'd lost and wasn't at all happy.

Gracie had started moving the bags outside when Jeff walked out looking flushed and angry. He picked up the remaining cases and took them to the car, packing them in the trunk.

'Is that everything?' he asked sharply.

'Yes, so let's go,' Gracie answered and climbed into the passenger seat and gave him the address. As they pulled out, in the wing mirror, Gracie could see Velda, looking furious, standing in the porch watching.

When they arrived at their new abode, Jeff unpacked the trunk and helped Gracie carry their bags into the apartment.

Putting the cases down, he looked around. The living room was small but comfortable, the kitchen, minuscule in comparison to his mother's but clean and workable. There was a small box room used as an extra bedroom and the main bedroom had a double bed, wardrobe, chest of drawers and bedside tables. It was adequate, if not a little cramped.

'Well?' Gracie waited for his answer.

He pulled a face. 'I've seen foxholes on a battlefield not much smaller than this,' he said.

'Maybe, but there is no enemy hiding here!' she retorted. 'We left her behind!'

'That's a bit unkind,' he chided.

She softened towards him. 'I'm sorry darling, I know she's your mother and I tried my best to get along with her but you are her son and she wasn't ready to let go of the apron strings. It would never have worked out, and in the end it would have ruined our marriage. I wasn't going to let that happen!'

He pulled her into his arms. 'I know, you're right, but this move was so sudden it took me by surprise and I'm not one for surprises. I like to plan ahead. We would have moved eventually.'

She tried to make him understand. 'Yes I know what you're saying but by that time our marriage would have been in trouble.'

He kissed her quickly and said, 'I know, but let's not argue about it. Have we any food in the house?'

Shaking her head she said, 'Sorry I didn't have time to go to the grocery store, but I thought we could go to the diner down the road for a meal tonight. What do you say?'

'I say we shop then go to a restaurant for dinner, as a way of celebration.'

She hugged him. 'Oh Jeff that would be great!' then she kissed him. 'Later we can unpack and have an early night.'

He grinned broadly at her. 'After all, Mom and Dad are no longer on the other side of the wall, so I'm expecting a lot from you honey. I expect you to make this move worthwhile!'

She laughed heartily. 'You men. You're all the same.'

They shopped for all their goods, with Gracie trying to familiarise herself with American dollars at the cash desk, then they went for a meal. As Gracie ate, she felt as if a load had been lifted from her shoulders. She would like to be able to work but without her green card it wasn't possible. She'd start proceedings for that as soon as she could and, in the meantime, there was a lot of work to do to get the apartment as she wanted it and she'd start tomorrow.

On their return, they unpacked the shopping, then their cases, had a coffee and went to bed, both exhausted, but Jeff still reached for her beneath the sheets.

'Come here,' he murmured.

This time Gracie was able to relax. It was like being on honeymoon all over again, except this time they were not in a hotel but in their own place and she gave herself willingly.

The following morning, she prepared a cooked breakfast for herself and her husband and when Jeff had left for work, she went to a shop and chose some paint for the living room. She decide that cream would make the room bigger, but had forgotten to take any measurements so didn't know how much to purchase. When she explained to the man serving her he was more than helpful.

'We have plenty of that colour in stock, so don't you worry now. You come back if you need more.'

She thanked him, took two pots and paid the bill. He handed her the change.

'Thank you ma'am, have a nice day.'

She smiled at him. 'Thank you I will.'

As she opened the door of the shop to leave, she collided with Rick, her brother-in-law.

'Hey! Steady there,' he said as they crashed into each other. 'My, if it isn't Gracie. What the hell are you doing here?'

'Oh, hello Rick, I'm buying some paint.' She held up the two pots for him to see.

He raised his eyebrows in surprise. 'I heard that you'd moved out when I got home just now!'

'I'm sure I'm not your mother's favourite person at this moment,' she said wryly.

'You can say that again!' Then he chuckled. 'I don't blame you. Two women in the same house never works. Can I drop you off? I've got my truck outside. You can show me around.'

Gracie knew that Jeff would not approve, so she quickly refused. She'd already alienated herself with the mother and, knowing how Jeff felt about his brother, she figured it would be most unwise.

Rick looked disappointed. 'Another time, maybe. You and I should get to know each other better, Gracie.' He gazed into her eyes as he spoke and she saw the desire reflected in them and heard the invitation in his voice.

'I don't think Jeff would like that,' she said.

'But you might,' he persisted.

'No Rick, I wouldn't! Get one thing straight, I love your brother and I'm not interested in anyone else.'

'We'll see about that,' he said. 'You might change your mind sometime in the future.'

She watched him walk into the store and wondered just how much of his chat was teasing and how much was serious? But he had a certain charm she couldn't deny that.

Chapter Seven

A week had passed since Valerie and Ross had visited the art gallery, so she wasn't surprised to get a call one morning from Max, the artist, whose painting Ross had purchased.

'Hello, is that Mrs Johnson?' a voice enquired.

Recognising his voice, Valerie said, 'Hello Max! I wondered when you'd call.'

'Valerie, I'm so pleased to have caught you at home. I did wonder if you'd be out on one of your explorations of our glorious city.'

'Not today,' she replied. 'So, when am I to see my painting?'

'How about this morning? I'm free, I can be with you in half an hour, if that's suitable?'

She couldn't stem the feeling of excitement inside her. 'That would be lovely! I'll be here.'

'See you then.'

Valerie quickly went to her bedroom to freshen her make-up and hair. She smoothed down her dress, sprayed on some perfume, placed two cups ready and made a fresh pot of coffee. Filled with expectation, she waited.

Max arrived shortly after, and carried the painting into the living room. He admired the furnishings and agreed with the wall space Valerie had chosen for his picture.

'It'll be perfect there,' he said. 'The light from the window is just right to show the full potential of the scene.'

'Would you like a cup of coffee?' she asked.

He paused. 'Let's get the painting up first, then I'd love a coffee, thanks.'

She watched as Max took his measurements and drilled the necessary holes in the wall and eventually she helped him lift the picture in place. They both stood back and looked at it.

'I don't think I'll ever get tired of looking at it, Max. It's really quite moving in a strange way.'

He looked at her and said, 'Only someone with the soul of an artist can see that. Have you ever done any painting, Valerie?'

'I've lived abroad a lot,' she told him, 'and I had a lot of time alone as my parents were busy, due to Father's work – and yes, I used to sketch. Each country we lived in had its own kind of beauty and I wanted to capture it.'

'Did you use watercolours or oils?'

'Neither, just ink sketches really.'

'I'd like to see them sometime,' he said.

She looked at him with dismay. 'Oh my goodness,

no!' She gazed at his work, then at him. 'I would be too embarrassed to do that. My efforts would pale in comparison to your obvious talent.'

He looked kindly at her. 'That's silly. I'm not going to make any judgements; I'm interested that's all. Do you have any sketchbooks handy?'

She hesitated.

'You do, I can tell. How about that coffee and you can show me whilst we drink it. Go on, don't be afraid.'

She reluctantly agreed and, after pouring out the coffee, she went into her bedroom and took out two sketchbooks from a case beneath the bed and, with her heart beating a little faster, took them into the living room and handed them over.

Max slowly turned each page, giving each sketch his undivided attention.

Valerie waited, hardly able to breathe. Eventually he looked up at her.

'Why ever were you worried? These are really good! You have a natural eye and feel.'

She could hardly believe what she was hearing. 'Honestly? I only did it for my own amusement.'

'You should do these scenes in watercolour, you'd be surprised how much better they would be. It would really bring them alive.'

'I've never tried. I always had a pen and pencil and a pad with me, paints would have been difficult to carry round. I would just see something that caught my eye and I'd stop there and draw.'

'I could always show you how,' he suggested.

Valerie immediately backed off. 'Thanks, but I really don't have the time.'

'Of course you do! You know you do. What are you afraid of?'

She knew the answer but she couldn't possibly tell him. Although she loved Ross, this man fascinated her and she was very aware of the fact and knew she had to deal with it.

'I'm not afraid of anything,' she lied, 'but you know I plan to find my way round New York and that is my priority, but thanks for the offer.'

He prepared to leave. 'That's a pity. If you change your mind, you know where to find me. Meantime enjoy your painting and keep in touch.'

As she opened the door to let Max out, she was surprised to see her mother-in-law standing there.

'Gloria!'

Gloria looked at her then at Max. She raised her eyebrows waiting for an introduction.

'Max, this is my mother-in-law, Mrs Johnson. Ross bought one of Max's paintings and he kindly came along to hang it for me.'

'Good morning,' Max said then turning to Valerie he said, 'I hope you enjoy the picture,' then he left.

Gloria swanned into the room as if she owned it and looked at the wall.

'Is this his work?' she asked sharply. 'Can't say it's to my taste!'

'But it is ours,' Valerie retorted. 'To what do I owe the pleasure?'

'I was on my way to Saks, so I thought I'd drop in and

see the apartment.' She looked round but said nothing.

'Can I offer you some coffee, it's freshly made?'

'For your painter friend no doubt.' The accusation was in the tone.

'Yes, it was the polite thing to do after he took the trouble to hang it. It's what we do in England, we like to show our appreciation.'

Gloria made no effort to hide her dislike as she said, 'I want to talk to you about Ross!'

This took Valerie by surprise. 'Really?' She poured the coffee into a fresh cup.

'Ever since he returned from the army, he's been unsettled in the office. He keeps wanting to change things. Well, it just won't do! Leo has run this business for years and knows what's best for the company.'

'And you've come to me because . . . ?'

'You must have a word with him and tell him to stop being so difficult!'

Valerie was enraged. 'I'll do no such thing! Ross is a fine businessman and I wouldn't dream of interfering in the way he does things. He is the one who makes such decisions and I'm sure he wouldn't welcome my dabbling into that side of his life.'

Gloria stood up. 'I see I've wasted my time. I'd have thought you would have wanted what was best for the company, after all, it's your living as well as the rest of ours.'

'Perhaps I think Ross's decisions would be better for the company. Have you ever considered that he may be in the right?'

Her mother-in-law just glared at her and walked out.

Valerie drank the coffee, fuming to herself, *That old harridan! How dare she interfere?* It made her even more determined to help Ross start his own business and when he came home that evening, she told him of his mother's visit.

He was livid! 'You see what I'm up against don't you?' He poured himself a drink. 'Well that's it! Tomorrow, I'll make a determined effort to find office space!'

He caught sight of the painting. 'When did that arrive?'

'This morning. Max was just leaving and met Gloria on the doorstep. She didn't like it, of course, and told me as much.'

He stood for a while studying it. 'You're right you know, the way he's caught the evening light is really quite special. I'd say this was a good investment. It should be worth something in time.'

Valerie was appalled. 'I'd never ever sell it!' she proclaimed. 'You bought it for me as a gift and I'll keep it, thank you!'

'All right darling, I was only making an observation.'

Later as they sat down to dinner, Valerie questioned him further about moving his office.

'Will you take your clients with you?' she asked.

'I'll give them the choice, of course, but I doubt I'll lose any of them. They won't want to start all over again with someone new. I really want to get into corporate litigation. Dad wouldn't hear of it, but that's where the money is to be made.'

'You'll need more staff won't you?'

'Yes, of course. Once I've procured my office space, I'll advertise but . . .' he hesitated.

'What?'

'I know one or two of the younger members in Dad's office are chomping at the bit to move on and I do believe they might be interested in coming with me.'

Valerie grimaced. 'That will put the cat among the pigeons!'

'What on earth does that mean?'

Laughing she explained. 'It's a British saying meaning, that will cause a furore.'

'It's been on the cards for a while really, but Dad will be surprised. He only wants to see what he wants. The fact that I might leave, I don't suppose has ever entered his head.'

'Your mother will have a fit! I wonder what she'll have to say?'

But Gloria Johnson, unable to get Valerie to intervene, had another plan. She was determined as always to get her own way and she put her plan to work the following morning after her visit to Valerie.

Ross was working on his papers for an approaching court case when his secretary rang his intercom.

'What is it?' asked Ross

'Miss Laura Kennet to see you, sir.'

He frowned. *Whatever did Laura want?* 'Show her in,' he said.

Laura, dressed immaculately, sauntered into the room,

smiling and walking round the desk, kissed Ross on the mouth – to his surprise – then sat down.

'Good morning, Laura. This is a surprise. What can I do for you?'

She gazed coyly at him. 'So very formal darling!'

'You've come to see me at my office, Laura, so I assume you want some advice?'

She crossed her legs, hoisting up her skirt just enough to be provocative. 'In a way, I suppose I do. I want us to be friends again, Ross.'

He looked somewhat puzzled. 'I don't understand.'

Letting out a deep sigh she said, 'I can't believe you've forgotten already just how close we used to be. I miss you, darling.'

He became impatient. 'For goodness' sake, Laura, that was quite some time ago and you seem to have forgotten I'm now married!'

'You don't have to pretend to me, Ross. We all make mistakes. I can forgive yours!'

His eyes narrowed and he stared at her with disbelief. 'You are wasting your time and mine. I have a wife I adore, believe me she is no mistake but the best thing that's ever happened to me.' He shook his head. 'You don't fool me for a minute. Mother put you up to this! She'll do anything to get her own way. She may run my father's life but she certainly doesn't run mine. How pitiful!' He pressed the intercom.

'Will you please show Miss Kennet out, she's leaving!' He sat and glared at Laura as his secretary appeared at the door.

With as much dignity as she could muster, Laura rose to her feet and left the room.

Ross sat back in his chair, fuming, then he picked up the phone and dialled.

Chapter Eight

Ross had found his office space. He'd been incensed by his mother's interference and had searched fervently for new premises and found space in an office block in the financial district, which was well located near City Hall and the Law Courts. He took Valerie to look at it.

It wasn't at all what she'd expected. She'd envisaged a floor with small offices set up ready instead of a whole open floor space without furnishings of any kind.

Seeing her dismay, Ross explained. 'I can set up my own offices to my own specification this way, which means I'll have control and choice.'

'Oh, I see, well that makes perfect sense. Have you worked it out?'

'Indeed I have, here take a look.' He produced a rolled-up paper and laid it flat. Then he showed her the plans. 'The reception area here, my office there . . .'

'You need potted plants to soften the place,' she suggested.

'I've already got that in hand,' he said, 'and I can move my paintings from my present office and hang them here too. That will help to dress the place.' He pointed to a wall. 'Your painting would be just right over there.'

She looked at him to see if he was serious and was furious when she realised he was.

'Ross! That is *my* painting, a gift from you!'

He saw he'd made a mistake. 'I was only joking,' he said.

'No, Ross you were not! But let's get one thing straight, no one moves it anywhere at all, except me!' But she was disappointed in him. There was a touch of his mother in him after all, determined to get their own way. It could be a good thing sometimes but Valerie found it disconcerting in this instance.

'How long before this space will be ready for business?' she asked.

'About three weeks, then of course I'll have to move all my papers over.'

'When are you going to tell your father?'

'This weekend. I'll have to give him notice, and my clients, of course, and on Monday there is an annual general meeting, so it will be out in the open for all to know. But it's only fair that I tell him privately first.'

'He won't like it!' she warned.

'Probably not, but then he won't work the business the way I want to, he's determined about that. It's the only way really.'

'Of course, you're right but please don't ask me to come along. You need to see him man to man. This won't be a social meeting.' Secretly Valerie thought, *I don't want to be around when the balloon bursts.* She was sure that Gloria would have something to say about it and she didn't want to be there.'

Her supposition was correct. Ross went along to the penthouse and asked his father to step into his study, as he wanted to talk to him, and when he told Leo of his plans, his father blew his top. Then he went storming into the living room to tell his wife what had taken place. She was livid.

'You've never been the same since you came home,' she accused. 'That English wife of yours is behind all this, I know!'

'This wasn't Valerie's idea, Mother, but as it happens, she agrees with me.'

'Of course, she does. She wants you as far away from your family as possible. That's what happens when you don't marry one of your own! Now if you and Laura had married . . .' She got no further.

'Enough!' Ross was doing his best to hold his temper. 'When will you get it into your head that a future with Laura was only your idea and not mine? I'm not interested in Laura that way, never was. I'm sorry, Dad but I am stifled working with you. I see a different future for the firm and you won't be moved, so I have to go my own way. I'm sorry but that's how it is. I'll see you at the meeting on Monday.'

* * *

When he returned home, he told Valerie what had transpired, not holding anything back.

She just raised her eyebrows and said, 'Your mother has always made it clear that she didn't agree with our marriage and she'll hate me even more so now. But Ross, that doesn't bother me, you have to do what's right for you, but I do hope in the future you and your father will be friends again.'

He shrugged. 'That'll take some time darling, but hopefully one day . . .'

Later that evening the phone rang and Valerie answered it. It was Bonny.

'Hi Valerie. Wow! What an eruption there was at our mother-in-law's. It was like the A-bomb going off! Leo rang Earl to tell him the news. Well, good for Ross I say. Bet the old bitch didn't like that?'

'No, Bonny, but are you surprised? Anyway, Ross can now run his business his way. But I'll be looking over my shoulder for a while,' she laughed.

'So you know how unpopular you are?'

'I was before but now even more so, but it's water off a duck's back, it runs off.'

'You have the cutest sayings. How about lunch next Monday? Whilst they have their AGM, we can celebrate. What do you say?'

'Excellent.' And they made a date.

The air was stormy at the AGM on the following Monday morning. Leo, flushed with anger, made his statement.

'Before we start our business gentlemen, I have an announcement. Ross will be leaving the company and setting up on his own!'

There was a buzz around the table.

'He doesn't agree with the way things work around here, things that have suited the company for many years and successfully, so he's leaving.'

The few diehards that had worked with Leo for many years looked at Ross, their outrage obvious to see, while the younger members brightened, but kept their opinions quiet.

'This being the case gentlemen, I have no choice to ask him to leave the room during our discussions.' He glared at his son.

Ross gathered his papers and left the room. He returned to his office and dictated letters to his clients, telling them of his plans and asking them what they wanted to do. Stay with the firm or continue with him at his new offices?

When he'd finished his secretary looked up and asked, 'Have you advertised for a new secretary, Mr Johnson?'

Shaking his head he said, 'No, Jane, I haven't. Why do you ask?'

'Then I'd very much like to come with you, if you have no objection?'

He smiled at her. 'I have no objection at all, if you're sure you don't mind the move.'

'I think it's exciting. You are the future Mr Johnson, whereas Mr Leo is the past and I want to be part of the future.'

'Then you shall be, Jane. You are good at your job and I'd be happy for you to come with me.' He shook hands with her. 'But keep this to yourself for the time being. My father is already outraged, we don't want to give him a heart attack!'

As he left the building that evening, two of the younger lawyers stopped him.

'Got time for a drink, Ross? We would like to talk to you,' one said and they went to the nearest cocktail lounge.

It transpired that they too wanted to be part of his new company, which was no surprise to Ross. He told them of his plans and this excited them. They discussed salaries and a starting date, shook hands all round, drank up and left.

Ross drove home a happy man.

While Ross had been dealing with his affairs, Bonny and Valerie had enjoyed a lunch together. Bonny, delighted with the news of Ross starting his own company, insisted they have a glass of champagne to celebrate.

'Listen, Valerie, had I not been adamant with Earl about stepping back from the family, Gloria would be still running our lives! Thankfully, Earl listened to me. So what are you going to do with your spare time when Ross is working?'

'I'm still exploring the city,' Valerie told her.

Bonny searched in her handbag and produced a folder. 'Here, I wondered if you would be interested in this?'

Valerie looked. It was a programme about a drawing class, opening in the village. Valerie was puzzled.

Bonny looked at her. 'I heard about you buying a painting and when Ross first came home and told us about you, he mentioned that you liked sketching.'

Valerie remembered that Ross had seen some of her drawings when they'd started seeing each other. She looked at the details – it looked interesting, especially when she saw that it included a class for watercolour.

'Thanks, Bonny. I'll look into this. It's just what I need to keep me busy. Without a green card I can't work.'

With a broad grin, Bonny said, 'You don't have to work! For goodness' sake, the Johnson family are wealthy,' she chuckled. 'We can meet up regularly and you can tell me about England, I've never been and would like to take a vacation there in the near future. You can help me choose the places to visit.'

When Valerie arrived home, she put away the programme and started to prepare dinner and when Ross walked through the door soon after, he was so full of what had happened during the day that she forgot to mention it to him. However, the following morning, she decided, she would go to the Village and find out more about the classes on offer.

The studio was large and light, she discovered. The person in charge was taking bookings and when Valerie told her of her interest in the class for watercolour, she enthused about the tutors.

'We are so lucky,' she said, 'the tutors all give their time voluntarily. They are all professionals, so we are extremely lucky.' She gave Valerie a list of things she would require and the address of an art shop where she could purchase her canvas and paints.

'Then you'll be ready to roll!' she said.

Valerie thanked her, signed on for the class, paid the fee and, holding the list, found her way to the shop and came away with a huge bag, filled with the necessary items. The first class started the following week.

Chapter Nine

Gracie Rider was in her element, settling into her new home. She'd scrubbed every room from top to bottom, been to Woolworth's, or the five-and-dime store as it was known in the States, to purchase bright cushions to liven the furniture, bought pretty ready-made curtains and a bunch of flowers.

She and Jeff had sat down to work out their finances and she insisted on having a weekly housekeeping allowance. Then they put aside rent money and cash to cover the bills. Jeff wasn't earning a large wage, but it was enough for them to live on and, if they were careful, they could save a little towards their own home. He hadn't been too happy with the arrangement.

'My father didn't do this,' he complained. 'My mother asked for money when she needed it.'

But Gracie was adamant. 'Well I don't want to keep

coming to you for money, I want to know exactly how much we have so eventually we can save to buy our own home and the only way to do that is to budget.'

Seeing the determined look in her eye, Jeff gave in, after muttering, 'It doesn't seem manly to me.'

'That's the way we do it back home,' she insisted. 'In fact my father hands over his pay packet to my mother unopened and she doles out the money.'

That was too much for him. 'Well that ain't going to happen in this house!'

She laughed at his outrage. 'No Jeff, that's not what I asked for, we will do things our own way.'

'Your way you mean,' he muttered as he walked outside and lit a cigarette. He sat on an upturned case. Things hadn't worked out the way he expected, he mused. He thought they'd stay with his parents, which wouldn't have cost much and save until they could buy a house, but Gracie had changed all that and now, she was taking over again. It was an alien concept to him. Men had always been in charge and the women had to go along with it. He was finding his new wife's ideas hard to stomach and his ego was badly dented, but then he gave a smile of satisfaction. It wasn't all bad. Since they'd moved, his sex life had vastly improved. Without his parents in the next room, Gracie hadn't felt inhibited in bed, so it had its compensations.

Having cleaned the apartment, Gracie set about painting the walls in the living room. She moved all the furniture into the middle of the room and started. She was pleased to have something to fill her days now that they'd moved into their own place as it stemmed the feelings of homesickness, which sometimes overwhelmed her. She missed familiar surroundings, her friends and family. Things were so different here and it was taking her some time to adjust. Yes, she was happy with her husband and her marriage, but most of all she missed the camaraderie of her friends. Here she hadn't any and she wondered how she was going to fill her time when the decorating was done.

Three days later, the living room was finished. Gracie looked around and decided to rearrange the furniture. With much pushing and shoving, she eventually stood back to admire the new look and decided it was a great improvement. She quickly ran a bath and washed the paint out of her hair, then changed into clean clothes and started to prepare the dinner, excitedly wondering what Jeff's reaction would be when he walked in that evening. But she was disappointed.

Jeff walked in to the apartment, went straight to the fridge, took out a can of beer, opened it, flopped onto the settee, kicked his shoes off and let out a deep sigh.

'I'm bushed. What's for dinner?'

Gracie just stood and stared at him, speechless. After working so hard, Jeff's lack of appreciation was just too much.

'What?' he looked puzzled. 'Why are you looking at me that way?'

She could feel the anger slowly rising within her. 'Perhaps when you've had your fill of beer, you might take a minute to look at your surroundings!' she snapped.

He did so, but it took several minutes before it registered with him. 'You've moved the furniture round.'

She placed her hands on her hips. 'And?'

'For Christ's sake Gracie, I'm far too tired for twenty questions.'

'You're bloody tired! I've been painting all day *and* cooked a meal, but obviously I need not have bothered. You wouldn't care what the place was like as long as there is a meal on the table!' She stormed off into the kitchen.

Jeff then took a closer look. 'Looks great,' he called. She didn't reply.

He slowly got to his feet. *Women!* He thought. Then he walked into the kitchen and standing behind Gracie put his arms around her, encircling her breast as he did so.

She shook his hold off. 'You stink of beer! Sit down, it's time to eat.'

The atmosphere was decidedly cool as they both ate in silence until Jeff spoke up.

'I'm sorry honey. I know how hard you've been working on fixing the place up, but I've had a hell of a day and didn't notice, but the room looks lovely, honestly.'

She wasn't that easily mollified and didn't reply and, when the meal was finished, she took the dirty dishes into the kitchen, closed the door and washed up with tears of frustration trickling down her cheeks. Later in bed, when Jeff put his arm round her, she stiffened like a board until he turned away from her.

* * *

The following day, she started on the bedroom, and as lunchtime drew nearer she felt really hungry but didn't feel like preparing something to eat, so she walked down the road to the diner and ordered ham and eggs . . . sunny side up. She was learning.

As she tucked into her meal, a voice made her look up.

'Hi there Gracie! All alone?' Rick settled himself opposite her, grinning broadly.

'Oh Rick. Hello, I didn't see you come in.'

'You were too busy tucking into your food. What are you doing eating here?'

'I've been painting the bedroom and was too tired to cook, so here I am.'

He reached out and touched her hair. 'You've got paint all over you.'

Laughing she said, 'Well I've been painting the ceiling and it isn't easily done without a few splashes.'

The waitress came over and he ordered a club sandwich.

'What's that?' she asked.

'A double-decker toasted sandwich with chicken, bacon and salad,' he explained. When it arrived she was fascinated to see an orange stick keeping the layers together. It looked delicious, she thought, and stored the information away for next time.

Rick was easy to talk to, she found. He was bright, funny and good company. He encouraged her to try the apple pie, saying it was the best in the area. Then they had coffee to follow.

'So how's my brother treating you, Gracie, is he looking after you well?'

'Yes, he's fine . . . we're fine,' she said, with feeling.

He seemed amused. 'Take it easy, I only asked. Had you said he wasn't then I'd have had words with him. He's a lucky guy, I only hope he appreciates it, that's all I'm saying.'

She cast a suspicious glance at him.

'No need to look at me like that, Gracie honey. You're a member of the family now, so I must make sure you're happy.'

'That's nice of you Nick, but what I do is not really any of your business, you know that.'

He laughed loudly. 'You're a smart girl; there's no fooling you. I just want you to know if things go wrong, I'm always around to pick up the pieces.'

'Yes I bet,' she said sarcastically. Getting up, she said, 'Must get on, I need to pay my bill, then it's back to work.'

'I'll pick up the tab,' he said. 'A treat for all your hard work.'

'There's no need for that,' she argued.

'My pleasure. When it's all done, do I get an invitation to see the place?'

'If Jeff invites you, yes.'

With an enigmatic smile he said, 'We both know that's not going to happen.'

'Thanks for the meal,' she said and left the diner.

Gracie had a bounce in her step as she walked home. It was nice to have company for a change. She knew that there was trouble between the brothers, which was a shame because Rick seemed like a nice person. A little dangerous perhaps, which if she were honest, added to the pleasure of his company. But she wouldn't mention meeting him to Jeff, especially after their spat last night. It would only enrage him and that she didn't need.

Rick sat and finished his coffee, musing over his conversation with his new sister-in-law. Cute girl. Smart, he liked that in a woman. Much too good for his brother who wouldn't appreciate Gracie in the same way that he would. His brother was much too staid. Gracie was a girl who could be great fun and Jeff had never had a sense of humour. As for spontaneity, he wouldn't understand it. Such a waste for such a girl, she definitely married the wrong brother! Then he chuckled softly. He'd bide his time, but he intended to get to know Gracie better. Much better.

When Jeff came home that evening, Gracie greeted him without rancour, for which he looked relieved. But when he sat down to dinner he looked at his plate and asked, 'What's this dish then?'

Gracie had been cooking all the British dishes she was used to, as often as she could and today she'd made another.

'It's made with minced beef and mashed potatoes on the top. At home we call it cottage pie.'

He picked some up with his fork and tasted it. He saw the expectancy on her face.

'It's nice,' he said, not wanting to upset her further. 'Don't suppose there's any cornbread to go with it?'

His mother had made and served cornbread with every meal, Gracie remembered. She'd not liked it much.

'No, but there's plenty of vegetables and I've made

an apple pie for desert.' She glared at him, daring him to complain. He didn't.

After the meal, Jeff rose from the table and put on his coat, which surprised Gracie.

'Where are you going?' she asked.

'Me and some of the boys are meeting up to play poker,' he explained. 'Before you came out here, we used to meet every week and they asked me along tonight to make up the numbers.'

'But poker is played for money!' she exclaimed.

Laughing he said, 'Of course it is.'

'But Jeff, we're saving for a house! You can't afford to go. What happens if you lose?'

The smile left his face. 'Now you listen to me young lady. I've gone along with your money schemes. We could have saved much more had we stayed with my parents, but no, you had to move out. But you can't have everything your own way. Tonight's for the guys and I'm going to enjoy myself!' He slammed the door as he left.

Gracie sat stunned at this turn of events, then she remembered that today was payday and he'd not given her any money!

It was almost midnight when Gracie heard her husband return. There was much banging and clattering in the living room and she wondered what on earth he was doing, but when he eventually staggered into the bedroom she realised why. Jeff was drunk and legless.

He looked at her with an alcoholic grin. 'Gracie honey! Did I wake you?' He made his way unsteadily to his side of the bed and with great difficulty, removed his clothing. Then he crawled in beside her.

He reeked of beer as he turned towards her, 'Come to Papa.' His speech was slurred.

She was livid! 'Get off me,' she cried. 'You're drunk!'

'Aw, come on honey, I've just had a few drinks with the boys, now be a good wife. Come on, do your duty.'

She flung back the covers and got out of bed. 'Duty? How dare you! Yes I am your wife but I am nobody's duty! That's disrespectful. You can damn well sleep on your own!' She grabbed a blanket off the bed and went into the living room. Within minutes she could hear loud snoring coming from the bedroom.

Gracie made a cup of coffee to give herself something to do, then sat alone on the settee, tears brimming in her eyes. This was not how she had envisaged married life at all.

It was bad enough living with his mother and she'd hoped that on their own it would be better and, in time, they'd have a home of their own and a family, but she now wondered if her dreams of the future were futile. If her husband was a gambler, that was really bad news. She had enough money for the week ahead from what they had saved, but if this happened often . . . she didn't dare think about the consequence. She curled up on the settee, covered herself with the blanket and eventually fell asleep.

The following morning when the alarm clock rang, Gracie was already up, preparing breakfast but, not hearing the sound of movement in the bedroom, went in. Jeff was still sound asleep. She shook him violently until he opened his eyes and gave her a bleary look.

'Get up Jeff! It's time to get dressed for work!'

'He winced. 'Do you have to shout so loudly?' He reluctantly put his legs over the side of the bed. 'Oh my head!'

Gracie ignored him, returned to the kitchen and made some strong coffee and when Jeff did appear she made him eat some porridge to line his stomach. He didn't have the energy to argue. When eventually he put his coat on to leave for work she spoke. 'Before you go, I'd like my housekeeping money please. We can sort out the rest tonight.'

He paused by the door and took out a few dollars from his pocket and handed them over.

Gracie looked at them. 'What's this, it isn't nearly enough!'

With a sheepish look he said, 'Sorry Gracie, that's all there is. I had a bad night last night. I lost the rest.'

She was speechless with rage and he took that moment to make his escape.

'Got to go I'm late, we'll talk tonight.' The door was quickly closed behind him.

Chapter Ten

In the financial district of New York City, Ross Johnson, walked around his new offices with a smile of satisfaction. The large space had been turned into separate offices for him and his two lawyers who'd moved with him. A reception desk was situated just inside the entrance and the central part was laid out in an open plan for the secretaries to work, separated only with partitions, which made the area light and airy.

The walls had been painted in the palest green which offset the potted plants very well. There was a water cooler and coffee machine in one corner and copy machines on another wall. It was all very attractive and workable, and the staff were delighted. They were now open for business.

All Ross's clients had followed him, as had the clients of the other two lawyers, but Ross had set up appointments to see one or two large firms, hoping to convince them that moving their business to him and his associates would be to their advantage. To his delight, one had accepted, bringing a million dollars a year into their coffers.

He was delighted with his success as this had been what he'd wanted his father to do and had been sharply rebuked for such ideas. Leo hadn't wanted to extend his business into corporate litigation. The idea unsettled him. He'd forged his own way of doing business for years and he was scared of changing to such a degree, but now Ross was ecstatic with his new client. All law firms had their own grapevine and Leo Johnson soon heard about Ross's new client. He was scathing in his opinion.

'That boy comes home from the war filled with new ideas, but he's taken on more than he can handle now. Before very long he'll come unstuck; well he'd better not come running to me for help. When he walked out of the family business, he shut the door very tightly behind him!'

Whilst Ross was busy, Valerie had joined the art class and was learning how to use watercolour. She was delighted with the result and had set up their spare bedroom as a studio because the light was so good. She had rediscovered her love of drawing and when she had any free time, she would take her canvas and easel with her, find a scene that was interesting and paint. One morning she wandered into Central Park, settled in a quiet corner and lost herself in her work. She was used to people stopping and watching. Sometimes they would comment, other times just walk on, but it didn't distract her. She was pleased to talk to those who wanted to chat and often it would lead to really interesting conversations.

'I have to say Mrs Johnson, that you have grasped the use of watercolours extremely well. That is delightful!'

She looked up and saw Max Brennen looking over her shoulder.

'Max! What a surprise! How are you?'

'Very well, thanks. Tell me, when did you start using watercolours?'

She told him about joining the art class in the Village. 'You were right of course, it does give my drawing more depth, brings them alive really.'

He knew about the class as it wasn't far from the gallery where he displayed his own paintings and his apartment. 'You know, Valerie, you have a real talent, you should hold an exhibition of your own.'

She felt her cheeks flush at the compliment. 'Oh I don't know about that, but the class is holding an exhibition in two weeks' time and a couple of my paintings are among the exhibits.'

'That's splendid. I'll make sure I come along. I have to fly I'm afraid or I'd invite you to come for a coffee somewhere. See you soon.'

Valerie was thrilled that he liked her work. As for giving an exhibition of her own, she felt that was a step too far, but she was excited at the thought that he would be at the class exhibition because she so admired his work. She also wanted Ross to see how she'd improved. He'd never come into her studio and seen anything she was working on. Whenever he came home, he relaxed with a drink and a meal and then most evenings he brought work home with him. She'd not complained, knowing how hard he was trying to build his own business and she so wanted him to succeed, just to prove to his family that his ideas for the future had been solid.

Two weeks later, Valerie was standing nervously looking at her paintings on the wall in the hall of the art class, which had been set up for the evening's viewing. She stood back and eyed them critically. She thought she couldn't have improved them in any way, but as usual, she was fearful of failure. She so hoped that Ross would be impressed.

The doors opened and people started to arrive. To everyone's delight, it was very well attended. Valerie was helping to hand out the glasses of wine and chatting to various people who were enquiring about the paintings and the class. She kept glancing at her watch. Ross was late!

A hand held her arm gently. 'Hello Valerie.'

'Max! You came.'

'But of course, I told you I would so why are you so surprised?'

Shrugging she said, 'Oh I don't know, I thought you might be too busy.'

'What nonsense. Come on, show me your work,'

They stood in front of her paintings. One was of an

old woman, sitting on a stool with a knitted shawl around her shoulders, feeding the birds – the lines on her face and hands, clearly depicting her age. It was a simple picture but it had an honesty about it. The second was of a view of Central Park with two children feeding ducks. Valerie had cleverly caught the delight on the faces of the children. It was charming.

Max looked at both for a long time in silence, then looking at Valerie he said, 'I had no idea you did portraits too. The sketches you showed me in your apartment were scenic. These are quite extraordinary!'

She frowned. 'In what way extraordinary?'

Laughing, Max said, 'Relax! That wasn't a criticism. What is so impressive is the detail. First, the old woman's face. Every line shows her age, the hands too. You've caught her spirit. The same with the children. Here is the innocence of the young, clearly depicted.'

Valerie was at a loss for words. She painted because she loved it.

Max looked at her and smiled. 'You know the best thing of all? You have no idea just how good you really are.'

'I don't know what to say,' she murmured, overcome by his praise.

'Come on, let's look at the rest of the exhibits.'

It was like a lesson to Valerie. Max talked to her about several of the paintings, discussing the finer points of some and how others could be improved and how to set about it. Eventually it was time to close.

'Your husband not here?' asked Max.

Valerie looked at her watch. 'He said he was coming but . . .'

'Right!' Max took her by the arm. 'I'm taking you out to dinner and we'll have a glass of champagne to celebrate your success.'

She was so disappointed that Ross hadn't showed up that she didn't hesitate to accept.

He took her to a Greek restaurant and introduced her to their particular cuisine. The owner knew Max and chatted with them, making Valerie blush when he complimented Max on his beautiful young companion. They drank wine and champagne and, at the end of the dinner, the waiters and the owner lined up and danced to Greek music, eventually calling on the customers to join in. Valerie and Max included. It was great fun.

When the music stopped, Valerie and Max returned to their table, breathless from the dancing and the laughter.

'Oh, Max, that's the best evening I've had since I arrived in New York!'

'Really?' He looked surprised. 'Then you have been sadly missing out. This city is built to be enjoyed. I'll just have to show you how I guess.' He held her gaze, waiting for her reaction.

Filled with bonhomie, wine and champagne, Valerie returned his gaze. 'I'd like that very much!'

They left the restaurant and he put her in a taxi and insisted on paying the driver. 'I'll be in touch,' he said and waved her off.

When she arrived home, she found Ross sitting at the dining room table, working.

'There you are!' He looked at his watch. 'You're home late.'

'You didn't come to my exhibition!' she exclaimed angrily.

He dismissed her lightly. 'Sorry, darling, I really couldn't spare the time. I wanted to finish this tonight.'

'You couldn't spare an hour for your wife? Was it really that important? Couldn't your work wait just an hour longer?'

He could see the anger in her eyes. 'Well, darling, it's not as if the exhibition was professional. It was just a display of the school's students' work.'

'It was important to me! You expect me to show you a hundred per cent loyalty and you get a hundred and fifty, but you couldn't spare an hour to give me the same. To you my work is just a hobby, something to keep me from getting bored. Nothing of any consequence – you have no idea!'

She swept out of the room and into the bedroom, undressed and stood under the shower until she'd calmed down, then went to bed.

When Ross climbed in beside her and put his arm around her she moved away.

'Don't touch me!' she cried.

When Valerie rose the next morning, she found an empty apartment. Ross had left early and she was glad. She was still seething from the previous night's scene. As she ate her toast, she vowed to show him. Max said she had talent. Well she'd work hard until she was good enough to hold her own exhibition, then Ross would see she was serious about her work. She took Max Brennen's card from her handbag and rang his number.

Later that afternoon, Valerie rang the bell at Max's studio and was greeted warmly.

'Valerie, come in.' He offered her a seat and with a smile asked, 'What can I do for you? You said you wanted my advice.'

'Yes, Max I do. You say I have real talent; well, I want to learn more. I want to do this seriously, not as a hobby. Do you think that's at all possible?'

He looked delighted. 'Without a doubt! You have the talent, I've told you that. All you need is more technical know-how. These things have to be taught. But yes, I'd say you were more than halfway there.'

'Who would you recommend as a teacher?'

He laughed. 'Are you kidding? I'll teach you then, when you are a success, I can take some of the credit!'

'Are you serious?'

'Absolutely!'

'But you have a job to do, apart from that you have your own pictures to work on, you don't have time.'

'We'll work out a schedule. As you know, I'm able to work from home, it's not as if I'm stuck in an office from nine to five. It would be a privilege and a pleasure. I'll make some coffee and we'll work out a plan.'

During the following two months, Valerie still attended the art class but three afternoons a week, she and Max painted

101

together. Sometimes in his studio, sometimes out in the open. They travelled to various parts of the city, armed with canvas and paints, where they would settle together and work. He would stop her and show her how to improve or change the light or shade of her scene, how to use various ways with her paints, to improve the depth or to lighten the sky to enhance the weather. She had never been happier.

Ross had no idea that this was taking place. Indeed he hardly asked how she spent her day, so involved was he in his business. Before long, Valerie realised that he was just like his father in this regard. But she didn't care because it was Max who encouraged her, who was interested in her and who understood her needs.

Then one evening when Ross was away on business, Max invited her round to his studio to dinner, saying he had a proposition he wanted to put to her. Alone and intrigued, she agreed and made her way to the Village wondering what he was going to say.

When she arrived she saw that he had laid the table, lit several candles, which filled the room with a soft scent, and was busy in the kitchen.

'That smells good,' she said as she took off her coat.

He poured her a glass of wine. 'It won't be long,' he promised.

He served her a delicious beef stew on a bed of rice, followed by profiteroles, which he admitted to buying ready-made. They drank red wine and talked. Valerie was so relaxed in his company and found him easy to talk to. But they never mentioned her husband.

At the end of the meal, Max made some coffee and they

sat on a settee to enjoy it. It was then that he told her the reason for his invitation. It took her breath away.

'I'm holding an exhibition of my own work in the gallery you came to and I would like you to exhibit with me.'

Valerie was speechless for a moment. 'You can't possibly be serious!'

'Why ever not? You're ready, believe me.'

'But my pictures alongside yours! People would laugh!'

He raised his eyebrows in surprise. 'I can't believe you just said that! If I didn't think they were good enough, would I ask you to show them?'

Her hands were shaking and he took her coffee cup from her. 'For goodness' sake woman, calm down. Lovely Valerie, you have a God-given gift and you still don't realise it. What do I have to do to convince you?'

She just sat shaking her head. He took her hands in his. 'You said you wanted to be a professional, well here's your chance.'

Looking into his eyes, she asked, 'Do you really think that my pictures are good enough?'

'Yes! Your paintings have an honesty about them. You see things in a different way and that shows in your pictures. It's really refreshing and different. The public will love them. Trust me. Come along and I'll show you the ones I have chosen.'

Valerie had stored her paintings in Max's studio as there was more room and now she followed him and saw the six he had chosen. Recovering from her shock, she looked carefully at them and was pleased with his choice. Slowly she began to feel more confident. These were good, she knew that, but were they good enough? She supposed if Max thought so, she would have to trust him. Then he showed her the publicity poster.

She couldn't believe what she read. It gave the name of the gallery, the date, the time and underneath . . .

An exhibition of Max Brennen's paintings and introducing Valerie Johnson, an exciting new talent.

She looked at him. 'I don't know what to say.'

He gazed back at her and said, 'If I'm not very much mistaken, Valerie, your life is about to change. It will be a pleasure to stand back and watch.' He leant forward and kissed her softly. 'I am going to be so proud!'

'Oh, Max. I owe it all to you. If you hadn't asked to see my work, I wouldn't have started drawing again, let alone use watercolours.'

'Fate is a very strange thing, Valerie. We were brought together for some reason, of that I'm sure.'

There was such affection in his look, that Valerie felt her legs weaken and she hurriedly said, 'I must go. Will you call me a cab?'

'If we walk outside I'm sure we can pick one up. Come on a short walk will do us both good.'

They walked hand in hand to Columbus Circle. The April night air was balmy and several people were out for a stroll. He hailed a cab and put her inside.

'See you tomorrow afternoon as usual.'

Valerie sat in the back of the cab lost in her own

thoughts. *An exhibition! Would Ross bother to come to this one?* she wondered. She looked at the poster Max had given her.

An exciting new talent! Well, that would show him. She would just leave it on the table for him to see when he returned.

Chapter Eleven

Gracie tidied away the table and washed up the breakfast dishes, all the time trying to decide what to say to Jeff when he came home. She couldn't believe he'd been stupid enough to lose most of his wage packet. Surely when he'd started losing he could have quit before it became serious, he knew they had a budget to keep to. She remembered him saying that he used to play poker before she came out to the States, so this might have been a regular thing. It wasn't that she minded him having a night with the boys, she thought that was a healthy thing to do, but not when it meant losing the money they had to live on.

She was so upset that the thought of staying inside to continue decorating the house was the last thing on her mind. She needed space and time to think, so she left the apartment and walked until she found a quiet park at the far end of the town. Here she bought a coffee from a diner and sat down upon a bench to gather her thoughts.

Jeff hadn't taken to the idea of a budget; he'd found the whole idea repellent. It seemed to him to take away his manhood and she wondered what his reaction was going to be when he came home tonight. He'd looked shamefaced when he left but he didn't take kindly to being told what to do and Gracie knew that she had a difficult time ahead of her. What if it all went wrong? Here she was, stuck in a foreign country with no way of getting back to Britain, if things didn't work out. Without money she couldn't leave. Her family couldn't afford to send her enough for the fare, so there was no one she could turn to if things went pear-shaped. She walked slowly home.

In the general store where he worked, Jeff Rider was also wondering what would happen when he went home after work. He knew he'd let his wife down by losing at cards last night, but he'd been sure that if he doubled up on the next hand and the next he would recover his losses, but of course the cards hadn't been kind to him. Eventually he'd quit, but far too late.

Nevertheless, he'd enjoyed the camaraderie of his male friends. He hadn't met up with them since Gracie had arrived and he'd taken a lot of ribbing about this from them.

'Under the little woman's thumb are we?' one jibed.

'Not your own man any more, Jeff?' asked another.

He'd laughed, but they had made their mark. His father had ruled his household. His word had been law and, as a boy, Jeff knew that if he crossed him the feel of his belt would be suffered for days after. He didn't rule his house and he didn't like it, not one bit. He needed to regain his position.

Gracie was in the kitchen preparing the dinner when he eventually arrived home. She had decided not to confront him but to wait and see what her husband had to say first and take it from there. She placed the chicken dish and vegetables before him and sat down.

Jeff sat and ate, without saying a word. She waited. He finished what was left of the apple pie, got up from the table, took a can of beer out of the fridge, picked up the local paper and sat down.

She was astonished. There was not a word said about the food, nor of the previous evening's happenings. Nothing! She walked over to where he sat and stood in front of him.

'Did you enjoy your dinner?' she demanded.

He looked at her with surprise. 'Yes it was fine.'

'Yet you didn't think to say anything, just took it for granted.'

He gave her a thunderous look. 'It's what wives do, they look after their man after a day's work.'

'Even when their man has lost nearly all his weekly wage playing poker?' There was a note of steel in her voice.

'For Christ's sake, Gracie! So I lost at cards, that's hardly a crime!'

'It is a crime when it takes food out of our mouths, stops us for saving for the future, the future you brought me across an ocean for!'

His eyes blazed. 'The trouble with you is that you don't

108

give a man any room to manoeuvre, to spend time with his friends. You are all about saving. Where's the fun in that?'

She was taken aback. 'I thought you wanted your own home? Well, that's what you led me to believe. A home of our own, a family. That's what you promised me, have you changed your mind? If so, don't you think you should have told me?'

'Yes, of course I still want those things, but I'm prepared to wait for them – but not you! You want everything now. You might as well get used to the idea, Gracie, I enjoy a night with my male buddies and I will continue to do so.'

She tried to reason with him. 'I don't mind you enjoying such a night, Jeff, but if you lose more money we'll never have a home to call ours. But if you must play poker, then we'll allow a certain amount for you to play with.'

This was too much for him. 'You make it sound like giving pocket money to a small child! I will take what money I want and don't you dare try to interfere. I'm the wage earner in this house and in future I'll be the one to say how it will be spent!'

Gracie was seething now. 'Fine! If there isn't enough money for food, you won't eat. If the bills aren't paid. I'll refer the suppliers to you. I will be sleeping in the spare room from now on. You may decide how to spend your money but I decide who I will share my bed with!'

She removed some of her clothes into the spare room. Quickly washed and got undressed, but before getting into bed, she pushed the back of a chair under the knob after locking it from the inside. No way was she letting her husband in. He had to learn that she too had choices to make, but she knew he'd be angry. Jeff was a highly sexed man and he wouldn't be happy being shut out of the bedroom.

An hour later, Gracie heard him moving around, he stopped outside her door and tried the handle. She heard him curse when he found it locked, but to her relief he moved on to the main bedroom. She wondered just how long that would last? But she was determined to stay there until things returned to normal.

The week passed with hardly a word exchanged between them and when Friday night came, Jeff ate his dinner, donned his coat and left the house.

Gracie said nothing. She'd been wracking her brains wondering just how to make some money. Money that she could save and book a passage back to England. Jeff, she'd decided was not the man she'd believed him to be. When they met, he'd seemed reliable, caring and fun. Here in his own environment, he was different. They didn't go out often, except to a movie or a meal but, other than that, when he came home from work he ate, read the paper, watched TV and went to bed. It was almost as if he didn't have to try anymore. Gracie was there to see to his needs, pleasure him in bed and do as she was told. That was no life for her!

Whilst Jeff was out playing poker, Gracie cleared the dishes away and tidied up, had a bath and went to bed early with a book. She didn't want to be around when her husband returned in a drunken state and she was therefore surprised to hear him return earlier than the previous week.

There was no banging about and she found she was holding her breath wondering what was going on. Then she heard him walk past her door, go to the bathroom and eventually shut the door to the main bedroom. It was more unnerving than when he'd returned legless!

The following morning, after eating his breakfast, Jeff threw a handful of dollar bills onto the table. Gracie looked at them with surprise.

'Now you've got nothing to complain about,' he said. 'There's the equivalent to three weeks' money there. You see poker isn't always a bad game, you just have to learn to take the bad with the good.' He put on his jacket and turned to her.

'When I come home, I expect to find you have moved back into our bedroom.'

She glared at him. 'I am not a prostitute! You can't buy sex with me. I am your wife!'

'Then behave like one! You will be in my bed tonight or there will be trouble!' He left, slamming the door behind him.

Gracie sat at the table with a cup of coffee, wondering what to do for the best. She would not be treated like a chattel by anyone, least of all her husband, but she'd never seen Jeff as angry as he was when he'd left for work this morning. How would he behave when she defied him, because no way was she returning to their bedroom until things were settled between them. She needed the security of knowing there was a regular amount of money coming in, that wouldn't be frittered away every Friday night. But she would hide some away that he'd given her this morning. She had come with a small amount of savings, a little of which she had spent when they had moved into the apartment, but she'd some left and she would add part of Jeff's ill-gotten gains to it. It would be a start towards going home. Her own private little fund. She'd stow away the odd dollar whenever she could. But now, she'd walk to the local grocery store to stock up for the week.

Gracie didn't see Rick, Jeff's brother, until their shopping carts collided as they emerged from two adjacent aisles. She looked up to apologise then realised who she was about to talk to.

'Hi Rick, sorry about that.'

Laughing he said, 'There you go, you haven't yet learnt to drive on the right-hand side!'

She laughed back. Rick always seemed to make her smile and at this moment in her life, she needed that. 'Don't tell me you've moved out into a place of your own,' she teased.

'Nah! Ma asked me to pick up a few things for her that's all.' They walked up and down the aisles together and eventually out to the car park.

Rick pointed to the diner opposite. 'Fancy a coffee, Gracie, before we go home?'

She nodded, 'Thanks, that would be great.'

They settled in a booth and Gracie asked after Rick's mother.

'She's fine thanks, you know Ma, she never changes.

How about you, Gracie, how are things with you?'

Without meaning to, she hesitated and then said, 'Fine, just fine.'

Rick's eyes narrowed and he looked at her as he said, 'You're not telling me the truth, young lady.' She looked away but didn't answer. He caught hold of her hand. 'What's wrong, honey? Is there anything I can do?'

The sudden kindness caught her unawares and she fought to stop the tears brimming, but to no avail. She brushed them away hurriedly.

Rick took a paper napkin out of the holder on the table and handed it to her. 'Now wipe your tears or else people in here will think I've made you unhappy and I'll probably get lynched for nothing!'

She smiled at him and wiped her cheeks.

'That's better. Now, Gracie, out with it. What's wrong?'

'Do you play poker?' she asked.

'No, not me, I'm never going to throw away my hard earned cash that way . . . but my brother used to.' He studied his companion. 'He's started playing again would be my guess. Am I right?'

She nodded. She didn't want to say more, she'd said too much already, this was Jeff's brother after all.

'Did he lose his money, is that why you're upset?'

Despite everything she found herself telling him what happened. 'He did the first time, but on Friday he won a small stack, but what if he keeps losing, what will happen to us then?'

His gaze was full of sympathy. 'Gee, Gracie I'm real sorry to hear this. Jeff always liked a gamble and that's fine when you are a single man, but now he has responsibilities and it's not right.'

She looked at him in surprise. 'I didn't expect you to think like that,' she confessed.

He raised his eyebrows and with a wry smile said, 'I guess you thought I was irresponsible, right?'

She shrugged. 'I suppose I did and for that I apologise.'

'Don't beat yourself up about it honey. I am a free man and I like a good time but I'm no fool. I have my own plans for the future, I just keep them to myself.'

Intrigued she asked, 'What are they, these plans?'

'I aim to open a small workshop, repairing cars and trucks. I trained as a motor mechanic and now I want to work for myself, be my own man.'

She hid a smile. 'Leave home? Get away from your mother?'

He laughed loudly. 'Something like that. Ma's alright but she treats me like a child, which believe me I'm not and I need my own place so I can live and breathe.'

'When is all this going to happen?'

'Next month. I've got a place lined up. A small garage with living accommodation over the top. I'm hoping to get it all signed up in a couple of weeks.'

'That's great!' Gracie enthused. 'I hope it all works out for you.'

'Thanks, but that doesn't solve your problem, Gracie. What are we going to do about my brother?'

Gracie felt her heart beat faster. There was already trouble between the brothers, she didn't want to make it worse. 'You don't do anything!' she said. 'This is my problem. We'll work it out, you'll see. Please don't interfere, you'll only complicate matters.'

He studied the worried expression on her face. 'Fine, if that's what you want, but promise me one thing.'

'What's that?'

'If things get really bad between you, you'll come to me.'

'Why would you want to be involved with my problems?'

'Because I admire the way you left your family to come to a strange country. That took courage and I can't sit back and see you treated badly. You are stuck here whether you like it or not and that isn't fair.'

Gracie was overcome by his kindness. 'Thanks Rick, but I'm sure I can work things out. If only I had a green card I could work.'

'You can apply for one, you're entitled to one, because you married an American.'

She looked at him in surprise. 'I didn't know that!'

He scribbled a number onto a piece of paper. 'This is the phone number at home until I move, should you want me. Keep it and use it if you ever need me. Promise?'

'Your mother would really be furious if I rang and asked for you!'

'My parents hardly ever answer the phone at night,' he told her. 'It's usually me that does, so don't you worry none.'

She rose from her seat. 'Thanks, Rick. I've got to get back.'

'You made a serious mistake, Gracie honey.'

'I did?'

He grinned broadly at her. 'You sure did. You married the wrong brother!'

She laughed at him. 'You are outrageous!' Still laughing she left the diner.

But as she walked home, she still had tonight to face. Jeff would expect her to move back into their bedroom and she had no intention of doing so and that would cause trouble. But she was determined. There would have to be a compromise before she would even consider doing so and he wouldn't like that. Not one bit!

Chapter Twelve

Ross Johnson was due home from his business trip and Valerie was buzzing with excitement. She had now accepted the fact that she was good enough to exhibit her paintings and had been working hard, both at the art classes and under Max's tuition. Her renewed belief in herself had given her a real drive to succeed and Max had been so pleased with her work that he'd included two more of her paintings in the viewing, which was taking place the next evening.

Valerie had prepared a special dinner for her husband, the table set beautifully, candles waiting to be lit, wine opened and breathing ready to be poured. Beside Ross's plate was the small poster advertising the exhibition. She could hardly wait for him to see it.

When he eventually arrived, Ross put down his case, kissed Valerie briefly and said, 'I need a shower before dinner, if that's alright with you?'

'Of course,' she said. 'I'll pour you a drink.'

She pottered in the kitchen until Ross emerged in slacks and a shirt. He walked into the kitchen, kissed the back of her neck, saying, 'That smells delicious. It's good to be home.'

'It's nice to have you back. How was your trip?'

He began to tell her in detail what had transpired. As they sat at the table and she served the meal, he was still talking. He pushed the poster aside without even looking at it.

Valerie hid her disappointment but as a dutiful wife she listened until he'd finished.

'What have you been up to?' he asked.

'I've been painting,' she said.

'Oh good,' he broke a piece of bread. 'How is the art class going?'

She felt the excitement building inside her as she said, 'Fine, but I've been taking extra lessons.'

'Really?'

He continued to eat and Valerie felt he was just being polite; there was no real interest in his voice. She felt her anger growing.

'Yes, Max Brennen has been teaching me.'

Now she'd caught his interest. Ross looked up. 'How did that come about?'

She explained how they'd met in Central Park and how he'd offered to teach her then she pushed forward the poster. 'Here,' she said . . . and waited.

Ross read the poster, twice as if he couldn't believe what he was seeing, and then he looked up. 'You agreed to this?'

This was hardly the reaction she was expecting. 'Yes, why do you ask?'

'But this man is a talented artist!'

Valerie felt as if he'd slapped her. 'You don't think that I am, is that it?'

'Well darling you draw very well – but you're hardly in his class!'

She was enraged by his condescension. 'Of course I'm not but Max likes my work. He thinks I'm someone with a special talent, that's why he asked me to share his exhibition. But you don't have to come along, after all you didn't come to the last viewing!'

He realised his mistake. 'Of course I'll come along. If the great man thinks you have talent then who am I to say differently?'

'Who indeed!' She rose from her chair. 'I'll just get the dessert.'

The art gallery was ready and Valerie and Max, having arrived early, viewed the paintings on show. He complimented her on her attire.

'You look lovely,' he said, 'you have such an air of elegance about you that is captivating!'

She was wearing a simple but expensive black dress, which showed her slim figure off so well. In her ears, a simple pair of diamond earrings and a matching brooch. Her blonde hair swept up in a sophisticated style. She had taken great care with her appearance not wanting to let herself or Max down.

'Why thank you,' she said.

She'd been surprised to see the wall showing her work. There was a banner with *Valerie Johnson, a bright new talent* across the top. She didn't know what to say when she first saw it and had looked at Max with a worried frown.

'Trust me, Valerie. I know what I'm doing,' and he'd squeezed her hand. 'Is your husband coming this time?'

She gave a wry smile. 'Yes, although he thinks this,' she indicated towards her work, 'is a big mistake!'

'Then he's in for a shock. Are you ready for the consequences I wonder?'

Before she could ask him what he meant, people started arriving. Max took her by the arm. 'Come, there is someone I want you to meet.' He walked her over to a tall distinguished looking gent.

'Carl, how good of you to come. I'd like you to meet Valerie Johnson, my protégé. Valerie, this is Carl Blackmore, a friend of mine.'

The man shook her hand. 'Mrs Johnson. I've heard a lot about you from Max.'

'You have?' She didn't know what to say, other than, 'Can I get you a glass of champagne?'

'Thank you, I'd love one.'

She took one off a tray that a waiter was carrying, gave it to him and left as Max led him over to her paintings. She watched from a distance wondering just who he was.

The room was filling up when she saw Ross arrive. He saw her and walked over.

'Good turn out,' he said then added, 'but of course, Max is pretty well known.' He helped himself to a glass of champagne and said, 'Well, let's look at your paintings.'

Just as a parent would say to their child on a school night she felt, but when he stood before the wall and looked at the eight pictures on show, his demeanour changed.

'These are really quite good,' he said with some surprise.

'Your wife has a great talent, Mr Johnson!' Max stood beside him.

'Well, she paints quite well,' Ross answered.

'Rather more than that, if I might contradict you!' Valerie turned to see Carl Blackmore standing next to Ross.

'Carl Blackmore is the art critic for the *New York Times*,' Max told Ross quietly.

Valerie wasn't sure who was the more surprised she, or her husband!

'Your wife has a unique quality about her work that really excites me,' the man said. 'You must be very proud of her?'

'Yes, yes I am,' Ross stammered.

Max looked at her and winked, she hid a smile.

'Sorry Ross,' Max said, 'but there are people I want Valerie to meet, who will help her in her career, excuse us?'

'Career, what career?' Ross asked but he was now alone. He stood in front of the paintings but now he studied them more closely.

The evening was a resounding success. Several of the glitterati of New York had been invited, as had several reporters, all of whom wanted pictures of Valerie and Max together and Valerie alone. There was an air of excitement about the place as people viewed the work of this new artist, the discovery of Max Brennen – noted artist in his own right.

It had been a good night for sales too. Several of Max's sold and all eight of Valerie's at prices set by Max himself. Valerie had thought them far too expensive but he had explained his reasoning to her before they opened the gallery.

'Tonight is going to be special for you. It's your first showing and if it goes as well as I think it will, people will rush to buy because very quickly the price will be sky high. Tonight they'll feel they have a bargain.'

She'd just laughed at him but now, after all the interviews, the pictures and the accolades, she was starting to believe him.

Ross, who had been observing how things were going the whole evening, was suddenly realising that his wife was about to become a celebrity. Once he'd got over his surprise, he began to scheme how this could help him business wise. If she did become a success, she'd maybe be mixing with folk who could become prospective clients. He suddenly brightened and at the end of the evening, he walked over to her and kissed her cheek.

'Well done, darling. I had no idea you were so clever. I'm so sorry I didn't take your work more seriously.'

Max watched and listened. He didn't like Ross Johnson! He didn't think for one moment he was being sincere and he wondered what was behind his change of heart.

Ross shook Max by the hand. 'I can't thank you enough for helping Valerie. It was very kind of you.'

'Kindness didn't come into it!' Max stated rather sharply. 'I saw real talent, talent that was being wasted and I wanted to bring it to the fore and I did tonight, as you saw.'

Valerie interrupted. 'Max is not only going to be my teacher but he's going to be my agent too.'

'I don't understand,' said Ross.

Max glared at him. 'Tonight is only the beginning, we have a long way to go now, but it's late, I think we all need a good night's sleep.' He leant forward and kissed Valerie on the cheek.

'Well done. I'm really proud of you. I'll see you tomorrow.' He nodded to Ross and walked away.

Valerie took her husband's arm. 'Come on Ross, I'm beat! Let's get a cab and go home. I need a hot bath and my bed.'

On the way home, Ross was silent for which Valerie was thankful. Tonight had been so exciting, an unbelievable success and she still couldn't quite believe it had happened. Sitting quietly in the cab, she went over the whole evening in her mind and was awash with happiness. She would never be able to repay Max for nurturing her and making her a better artist.

Once they were in the apartment, she ran a bath and luxuriated in the warmth and the scent of the bath oil she'd put into the water. All she wanted now was to sleep. But Ross had other ideas.

'Sit down, darling,' he said as she emerged from the bathroom. 'We must make plans for your finances.'

'My what?'

'Well, your paintings all sold tonight. You made an amazing amount of money, we must decide how best to deal with it.'

'No need,' she told him. 'Max is taking care of

everything.' She walked towards the bedroom. 'Goodnight, Ross, as I'm sure you can understand, I'm really tired.' She left him sitting in the living room, a look of surprise on his face.

When Valerie woke the next morning, she looked at the clock on her bedside table and was shocked to see it was ten o'clock. She climbed out of bed, put on a dressing gown and walked into the kitchen. On the side were a cup and saucer and a plate that Ross had left after his breakfast. She made herself a coffee and sat down on the settee, just as the phone rang.

'Hello?'

It was Max. 'Good morning, have you read today's issue of the *New York Times*?'

'Good heavens, no! I've only just woken up.'

'Right! I'll buy some croissants and come over. You must see this, it's terrific,' and he hung up.

Valerie quickly washed, changed into a pair of trousers and sweater, brushed her hair and applied her lipstick just in time to answer the doorbell.

Max stepped into the room, lifted her off her feet and swung her round. 'You are a star!' he said. He then led her to the settee and opened the paper. 'Here is the art column. Read it!'

She read the headline. A NEW TALENT EMERGES. It was written by Carl Blackmore. She slowly read his words of praise for her work and could hardly believe it.

The article ended by saying, *Valerie Johnson has an honesty about her work. The portraits capture the character of the person with every brush stroke in a way I've not seen before. I was fortunate enough to purchase one of her paintings last night, before the art world discovers her and the price rises astronomically.*

'He bought one?' She looked at Max, hardly able to believe what she'd read.

He grinned broadly at her. 'Yes, the one of the old lady, feeding the birds.'

She was so overwhelmed, she could feel the tears brim in her eyes.

'Hey, come on now.' Max put his arms around her. 'No tears, this is a day for great joy!'

'I am happy, honestly. It's just so much more than I ever imagined.'

He stood up and pulled her to her feet. 'Come on, we're going to celebrate. Grab a jacket.' He picked up the bag of pastries. 'We'll take these with us.'

They left the apartment, running out of the entrance hall, laughing and holding hands, much to the surprise of the guard on the desk.

Chapter Thirteen

As Gracie prepared dinner, she felt tense, knowing that tonight was not going to be pleasant. Jeff had made it very clear that he expected her to return to their bedroom tonight and resume the physical side of their marriage. She was equally determined that before she did so, he had to compromise.

Her stomach tightened as she heard him enter the apartment. To her surprise, he was quite affable. 'Hi, honey, I'm home!' He walked into the kitchen. 'What's for dinner?'

'Roast beef and sponge pudding with custard,' she replied.

'I'll just wash up then.'

She laid the table and served the meal. 'Had a good day?' she asked.

'Yep! Been real busy, looking forward to a good evening,

then bed.' He gazed at her and she saw the look of desire in his eyes.

She said nothing until she'd served the pudding and Jeff had finished his meal. They sat in comfortable chairs to have their coffee. Gracie took a deep breath.

'Jeff, I need to talk to you about things . . .' she began.

His eyes narrowed and his jaw tightened. 'What kind of things?' he asked.

She tried to explain how she felt without upsetting him. 'I know we think of things in a different way sometimes, that's because you've been brought up one way and I've been brought up another—' He just stared at her but said nothing.

She continued. 'I have to feel secure. I can't live without certainty.'

'Nothing in life is certain, Gracie, you know that.'

'Yes to a degree, but after all, we have a nice flat, you are working and earning, but I have to know we can meet our bills every week, otherwise I worry.'

'Oh, we're back on my playing poker again!' She could hear the anger in his voice.

'Play poker, if that's what you want, but before you do, please make sure I have the housekeeping and money to cover the bills – that's all I ask.' Before he could answer she continued. 'I don't want this to come between us. I want us to be happy. Remember when you first took me to that hotel in Bournemouth? You were so kind, so understanding but now, we seem to be at cross purposes and I wonder what happened to that lovely man I knew back in England.'

His expression softened. 'Yes, I remember. But times have changed Gracie, now we are here and life is different. I don't want you to be unhappy, honey, but you must let me be a man in my own house. I had enough of obeying orders in the army!'

'I'm sorry if I seemed to take charge, it's just that I want us to have the things we planned for.' She paused. 'I've been thinking, I could get a job, that would bring in more money. I've applied for my green card, which being married to you I'm entitled to, apparently.'

The idea seemed to please him. 'I think that's great! After all, when you've finished decorating, what then? Working would give you something to do.'

And money, I can save, she thought, *just in case things don't work out.*

The tension in the air lifted. Jeff read the paper whilst Gracie cleared away and eventually when it was time for bed, she looked at her husband.

'So do you agree with what I said earlier?'

Jeff realised that if he didn't, he'd be sleeping alone and, as he gazed at his wife, he felt the ache in his loins. He smiled at her. 'Yes, honey. Let's put this all behind us and start again.'

They lived in harmony for the following weeks. Jeff handed out her money on Friday before he went to play poker and was able to give her a few extra dollars the first week, but nothing the second. She thought he'd probably lost, but didn't ask. In the meantime she'd applied for her green card and had asked around at the various stores to see if they needed any staff, but as yet had not succeeded in finding work. But several weeks later, on the day her card arrived, she waited until Jeff left to play poker and then rang Rick's number, her heart beating in case her in-laws answered. To her relief it was Rick's voice she heard.

'Hello Rick, it's Gracie.'

'Is something wrong?' she heard the concern in his voice.

'No, no everything is fine, only I've now got my green card and I wondered if you knew of a job going anywhere.'

He let out a sigh of relief. 'I can ask around if you like. Give me a couple of days. Where's Jeff? I assume he's out or you wouldn't have called.'

'Yes, he's out for the evening.'

'Playing poker?'

'Yes, with his friends. But I don't want to talk about that.'

'Meet me in the diner on Monday morning,' he said, 'around eleven o'clock and I'll see what I can do, OK?'

'Thanks Rick, I'll do that.'

On Sunday morning, Jeff announced they were going to his parent's house for lunch. 'Ma's complaining that she hasn't seen us since we moved.'

Seen you, not me, Gracie thought. She couldn't refuse so, with a sinking feeling, she left the apartment, dreading the next few hours.

Velda barely greeted her when they arrived but,

thankfully, Ben was more welcoming. 'How are you settling in, Gracie?' he asked.

'Fine, thanks. It's all a bit strange. I've just about got used to American money and walking around a grocery store, helping myself instead of going into the shops and being served. I'm also surprised at all the packets of cake mix. At home we don't have that, we make our cakes from scratch.'

'Are you saying that they aren't as good?' Velda took her remark personally.

'Not at all. I've never tried one, I cook the way I've been taught.'

'Then perhaps you should before you make such remarks!'

Gracie didn't argue. If Velda wanted a fight she'd have to have one on her own.

The following three hours were difficult. Velda made a point of spoiling her son, piling food on his plate and inferring that he wasn't being fed properly since leaving home. To his credit, Jeff praised his wife's cooking, which didn't sit well with his mother, and Gracie was relieved when it was time for them to go. Rick hadn't made an appearance and she wondered where he was, but his name wasn't mentioned and she didn't ask.

On Monday morning, Gracie rushed around tidying the house, then set out for the diner to meet Rick. They met at the door. He kissed her and held the door open for her. They both had a club sandwich and coffee.

'I hear you came to lunch with the folks,' he said.

Gracie pulled a face. 'Yes, your mother really wanted to see Jeff not me.'

'She's certain you're starving her boy, you know?' His eyes twinkled with amusement.

'Oh yes, she made that perfectly clear.' She bit into her sandwich. 'This is so good,' she remarked.

He started laughing. 'Yes, indeed and it doesn't come out of a packet!'

'Oh, she told you about that too!'

'Yes, then I took off. I know Ma too well, she'd have carried on and on. Don't let her get to you honey, she's an embittered old woman. Anyway I have some news that'll cheer you up.

'What's that?'

'I've found a job for you, if you're interested. The wife of a friend of mine has a clothes store on the other side of town. Goldstone Parade, do you know it?'

Gracie did, it was in a more upmarket part of town and she'd seen it when she'd been driving around in the car with Jeff.

'Yes, of course, it's the smarter part, with small exclusive stores.'

'True. But this store sells T-shirts and shorts, shoes and accessories, a little quirky but very popular and they're looking for someone. She thought an English girl would be interesting, you know how we Yanks love to hear the English accent?' He took a card from his pocket. 'Here, give her a call. She's a nice woman and you two should get on. You can catch a bus right to the door.'

She read the card. 'Thanks Rick, I'm really grateful.'

'Just promise me one thing, Gracie.'

'What's that?'

'Do you have your own bank account?' When she shook her head he said, 'Then open one and put your wages in it, don't let Jeff get his hands on it, please.'

'Why are you saying that?'

'You don't want your earnings to end up on a poker table do you?'

She looked at him in horror. 'Do you think that's a possibility?'

'Don't you?'

She knew he was right. The money she still had from her savings and the few extra dollars she'd been given when Jeff won money, she'd hidden. A bank account would be safer. 'Yes, I'll do that.'

'Good. Are things alright at the moment?'

'Yes,' she said. 'We've come to an arrangement and so far it's working.'

'Don't hold your breath honey, I know my brother. Look, I've got to go. Good luck and I'll see you again soon to see how you make out.' He kissed her, paid the check and left.

Gracie ordered another coffee and read the card again. A job would be a lifesaver. It would fill her time, she'd meet more people, maybe make friends, but what was more important, she could begin to save for a rainy day. But as her mother always said, *It's mad money, love. When you get mad, you've got money to go where you like.* Well this would be hers!

* * *

Two days later, Gracie was on the bus, on her way to her interview. Her heart pounding, nerves tense, praying she'd be successful. The bus stopped at the parade as Rick had said. She was a little early, so she walked the length of the shops, loving what she saw. There were small stores selling furniture, another electrical goods, a couple of dress shops and eventually, *Milly*, the one she was looking for. In the windows were T-shirts, handbags, jewellery, sports shoes, sportswear, blouses, all manner of unusual bits and pieces. She loved the look of it and opened the door.

The young blonde woman behind the counter looked up. She was dressed in a T-shirt with *I Love the Rockies* emblazoned on the front, a pair of shorts and her blonde hair tied back with a daisy on a band, and her long nails painted different colours. Gracie took to her immediately.

'Hi,' said the girl, 'are you Gracie Rider?'

'Yes I am.'

'Come on in, I'm Milly Roberts. It's an English name, my husband's great grandparents came from the old country.'

'Really? Do you know where from?'

'Some place called Coventry, do you know it?'

'No, but it was badly bombed during the war.'

The girl frowned. 'Gee that's awful.'

The two of them talked, Milly showed Gracie all the things in the store, took her to the stock room, explained how they liked to work, then asked how she liked living in America.

133

'It's very different of course, but I expected that,' she told her. 'But I need to work, I can't sit around all day doing nothing.'

Milly listened closely. 'Gee, I love the way you Limeys talk,' she said. 'My customers will love you. When can you start?'

Gracie was delighted. 'Next week if you like!'

They discussed a salary and Milly said she'd pay for her bus fares as well. They had a coffee in the back room to celebrate.

'I'm sure glad Rick mentioned you were looking for a job.'

'Do you know him well?' asked Gracie curious to know about their friendship.

'He's a friend of my husband, Chuck. They've know each other since their school days.'

Gracie rode home on the bus, thrilled to know she would be earning her own money. She'd taken her savings to the bank the previous day and opened an account, taking Rick's advice.

When Jeff came home that evening, she was full of excitement and told him about getting the job and how much she was looking forward to it, what the shop was like and how she and Milly got along so well.

'Milly? Not Milly Roberts?'

'Yes, do you know her?'

'We went to school together, she married a friend of Rick's.'

'Really, what a coincidence. She didn't say she knew

you.' No way was she going to tell Jeff how she got to know about the job. She knew that would only start another row. If he knew she'd seen his brother and that he'd helped her, he'd blow his top.

The next Monday morning, Gracie dressed in a pretty blouse and skirt and set off for her first day of employment in a foreign country.

Chapter Fourteen

Valerie wasn't the only one reading the *New York Times* that morning, Gloria Johnson was leafing through the paper whilst having breakfast when she saw Valerie's name. She put down her toast and read the art review. Then she read it again and rose from the table, walked over to the telephone and rang her son.

'Hello Mother, what can I do for you?'

'Have you read the *New York Times* this morning?'

'I have and I imagine you have too?'

'What does it mean? I had no idea that Valerie was an artist. You never mentioned it to me!'

He could hear the indignation in her voice and smiled to himself, knowing how this would annoy her. She liked to be in touch with everything that was going on within the family, so she could orchestrate things.

'I knew she liked sketching,' Ross said, 'but to be honest

I thought it was just a hobby. But she's been attending art classes and Max Brennen has been giving her lessons too. She's actually very talented and I didn't realise this myself until last night.'

'This article is by Carl Blackmore! You know who he is don't you?'

Ross lit a cigarette, knowing Gloria he knew this was going to be a long conversation. 'Of course, I do. I spoke to him at the viewing, he praised Valerie's work, in fact he bought one of her paintings.'

'Actually bought one . . . for money?'

'Yes, Mother, American dollars!' He tried not to laugh. It gave him a certain satisfaction to find his mother so disconcerted.

'What are you going to do about all this?' she asked.

'Absolutely nothing! I will, of course, encourage her to continue. Valerie's a success and will be continuing to paint. She's going to be a star in the art world and that has to be a good thing for both of us. Perhaps now, you will show her a little more respect!' He could hear Gloria blustering over his remark, but before she could say another word he said, 'Sorry, but I have to go, I've a call waiting,' and he hung up.

He sat back in his chair with a feeling of great satisfaction. Of course, he'd encourage Valerie. He saw last night the people who were interested in her work, folk who were wealthy and who might need a good lawyer in the future. Nothing but good could come from this. He would make sure he was around, so she could introduce him to her patrons. Not once did he think what a talented wife he had and how happy he was for her.

In the meantime, Max and Valerie were out celebrating. They took a buggy ride around Central Park while eating their pasties, talking about the previous evening.

'What happens now, Max?' Valerie asked.

'I suggest you leave the art class. Continue with your watercolours, whilst I teach you how to paint in oils.'

This really excited her and she loved the idea. 'That would be wonderful, I have always admired that medium, but will you have the time?'

With a broad grin he said, 'I'll make time. Apart from which, I'll expect you to accompany me to other venues as we need to publicise your pictures.'

'Other venues? You mean viewings?'

'In a way, fashion shows, first nights, we need your picture in the papers. Give you a public image. There is a charity auction next week at the Waldorf Astoria; we'll go to that. Formal wear, so dig out a fancy gown. There will be a dinner first, then the auction. You don't have to buy anything, just show up. I'll buy the tickets.'

'Oh, Max let me buy them out of the money I made the other evening. It will be my way of paying you back.'

'No, this is my treat. I hope your husband won't mind you coming?'

With a naughty twinkle in her eye, she said, 'I don't really care if he does, it'll teach him not to be so condescending about my work.'

'That's my girl! Come on, we'll have lunch at the Tavern on the Green and celebrate.' He instructed the driver of the buggy and they moved off.

When that evening Valerie told Ross she would be going to a charity dinner at the Waldorf Astoria, he was delighted. 'I'll get my tux cleaned,' he said.

'That won't be necessary, Ross. Max is taking me; he's bought the tickets. It's for publicity, of course,' she added, secretly enjoying the moment.

'Oh, I see, yes, of course.' Ross looked surprised, but there was nothing more to be said.

'In the meantime, I'll be working, building up my stock as it were, for the next exhibition,' she said casually.

'When will that be?'

Shrugging she said, 'I don't know, but Max will arrange it when the time is right.'

'I hope you're not letting Max Brennen take over your life.' he said somewhat tersely.

'Like your mother, you mean? No, but he's the reason for my success don't forget and he's my agent after all.'

And I'll make damned sure that's all he is, Ross thought angrily. He didn't like not being in charge, but here he had no choice and knew, if his wife was to be a success, she needed Max and, if he wanted to profit from it, he needed him too, but he wasn't happy about the situation.

The charity evening was a glittering affair. Outside the hotel was a red carpet and news cameras, vying for position with those from the *WNBT New York* television station, for those who had sets in their home.

Max, resplendent in a dinner jacket, held Valerie's arm as they posed for the cameras. She was dressed in an emerald green gown, which was simply cut, just off the shoulders, the bodice swathed across her body, with a flowing skirt that showed her slim figure and décolletage to perfection. She wore a pair of long diamond earrings and her hair was dressed in a chignon. She was a picture of elegance and the reporters loved her. She turned this way and that at their request, before thanking them politely and walking into the hotel.

Max squeezed her arm. 'You look amazing Mrs Johnson and I feel a lucky guy to be your escort for the night.'

She was delighted. 'You look pretty good yourself, Mr Brennen. I think we make an impressive couple.'

They checked the table list and made their way across the dining room. Many people greeted Max as he passed; he smiled and waved in return until they reached the table. Valerie was surprised to see Carl Blackmore sitting there. He rose from his seat.

'Valerie, my dear, for your sins, you're placed next to me.'

'How marvellous! I'll love that,' she said and sat down, Max sat beside her.

He grinned at her and said, 'An English rose between two thorns!'

The evening was a great success. The meal was fabulous, the champagne flowed and after the meal, the auction began. Valerie was filled with excitement as she listened to the prizes on offer. A week in the Bahamas, a weekend in

Las Vegas, theatre tickets, a car, credit at Sak's Fifth Avenue and so on. She couldn't believe the huge amounts of money being offered.

Seeing her delight, Max leant towards her and softly said, 'There, didn't I tell you this city was the place to have fun?'

'Oh, Max you did and when I'm with you it's always fun.'

He looked at her, holding her gaze with his. 'I'm so pleased you feel that way because when we're together, I feel the same.'

It suddenly felt as if there was no one else in the room, just the two of them caught in a moment of time.

'Five hundred dollars!' Carl Blackmore boomed, making a bid, bringing them both back to the present.

As they left the hotel, Max said, 'I don't want to go home yet, do you? I'm too pumped up.'

'I feel just the same,' she agreed. 'Tonight was so exciting I don't feel at all sleepy.'

Max hailed a passing cab. 'Come on, we'll go to a nightclub to round up the evening.'

When they arrived at their destination, they were ushered to a table in a roomful of customers. The place was lit with soft lighting, busy waiters and a four-piece band was playing for those who wanted to dance. Max ordered a bottle of champagne and then led Valerie onto the floor. Glenn Miller's *String of Pearls* was being played as he drew her into his arms.

She melted against him as they traversed the floor, neither of them speaking. Valerie closed her eyes as they danced. She felt at ease and comfortable, as if it was right being there with this man who was about to change her life. The scent of Max's aftershave wafted between them and she could feel the warmth of his body against hers and thought it felt good.

Returning to their table, they drank the champagne and made plans.

'How do you fancy appearing in *Vogue* magazine?' he asked.

'What?' She couldn't believe she'd heard correctly.

'I had a call yesterday from the editor, she wants to do an article and pictures, featuring you.'

'*Vogue*? Are you crazy?'

He found this amusing. 'No, I'm serious. Valerie, you are a beautiful woman, apart from which you have such an air of elegance that the editor was really excited about doing a fashion shoot with you. It would give you publicity that some women would die for!'

She started laughing.

'What's so funny?'

'I'd love to do it, not for the publicity, which would be marvellous, but just to see my mother-in-law's and Ross's ex-girlfriend's faces when they saw it!'

'Yes, Mrs Johnson senior has quite a reputation as a harridan. She's involved with several committees and isn't particularly popular – but her money talks.'

'When do they want to do it?'

'Next week, then it can go into the following month's issue, but I have to let her know in the morning, they're holding the pages until then.'

'Then tell them yes! I'd like to keep this a secret from Ross, if you don't mind. It'll be a surprise for him too.'

Max topped up their glasses. 'Are you happy in your marriage, Valerie?'

His question took her by surprise and she hesitated. 'I do love Ross and, although I admire his drive and ambition, he has too much of his mother in him for my liking, if I'm honest . . . And if I'm being completely honest, I've been disappointed by his reaction to my work. I thought he'd be really proud of me.'

'But I'm sure he is,' Max protested, 'how could he not be?'

She tossed her head. 'He sees me as a good introduction to wealthy clients for his firm.'

'You can't mean that!' Max was appalled.

'He hasn't said in so many words, but I know him very well. It has been an eye-opener I must admit, and one I'm not at all comfortable with. I'm not a business commodity, I'm his wife for goodness' sake!'

Max looked thoughtful. 'Your success could come between you, are you ready for that?'

She looked down at her hand nestled in her lap and twisting her wedding ring, said, 'Yes, I am, but I've decided that I'm doing what I want to, thanks to you, and I have to feel fulfilled. If Ross can't accept that and still be the man I thought he was, then . . .'

'Do you believe in fate?' Max asked.

'Yes, yes I do and I realise that things are going to change, I'll just have to wait and see how much.'

* * *

A little later, the cab took the two of them back to Valerie's apartment. Max told the driver to wait and walked Valerie to the door. As they waited for the guard to open it, he took her into his arms, kissed her cheek and said, 'You have no idea how proud I am of you and I can't wait to see your talent grow even more. This is just the beginning.'

He watched her safely inside then climbed into the cab and was driven home. Once there, he removed his jacket and bow tie, made a pot of coffee and sat down. He had told Valerie her life would change, but he also knew his had done so from the moment they had met. He got up and walked over to his studio, uncovered the canvas on the easel. It was a portrait of his protégé, painted in oils. He was pleased with it, felt he had caught her gentle character, her composure, her elegance and, as he stood back and looked at it, he knew he'd fallen in love with her.

Chapter Fifteen

It was three weeks now since Gracie had started work and she felt really happy for the first time since she'd moved to America. She loved being in the shop, surrounded by bright clothing, summer shoes and hats, it brought life and colour into her world. She was no longer lonely. Milly's customers were very friendly and plied her with questions about England. She was amazed at the ignorance in that direction, from many of them.

'Do you know the King and Queen?' one asked.

It took a second or two before Gracie realised the woman was serious. 'Good gracious no,' she replied. 'I've only ever seen them on the newsreels.'

When another heard she was from Southampton, she was thrilled. 'My brother was there during the war, before being shipped out, maybe you saw him,' and she hastily showed Gracie a picture.

'No, I'm afraid not, there were thousands of troops passing through before D-Day, so I wouldn't have met any of them, unless they were stationed there and went to the local dances. That's where I met my husband,' she told her.

She and Milly got on well together as she knew they would.

'You and Jeff must come over to dinner one night,' Milly suggested.

'That would be lovely,' said Gracie. They arranged an evening the following week.

Jeff had readily agreed to go when Gracie mentioned the invitation and so a week later, after she'd arrived home, Gracie showered and changed then they set off in Jeff's father's car, which he'd said they could use.

Gracie was really looking forward to it, as she and Jeff didn't go out much, so this felt rather special.

Jeff had met Chuck, Milly's husband years before it seemed and, of course, Milly and Jeff talked about their schooldays, laughing as they recalled various incidents of their childhood. Chuck and he talked about their war days and how lucky they were to come out of it alive when many of their buddies had fallen. It was a very convivial evening until Milly told Jeff how delighted she was that Gracie was working for her.

'She's a great asset to me,' she told him, 'my customers love to hear the English accent too, I'm sure it helps with sales and Gracie is a great saleswoman!'

This pleased Jeff. 'Glad to hear it, I must say she's seems much happier living here since she started work.'

'I can't thank Rick enough,' said Milly. 'But for him, I'd never have known she was looking for work.'

'Rick? What's Rick got to do with it?' The atmosphere changed immediately.

Milly knew that something was wrong but had no idea what it was. 'He told me Gracie was looking for work,' she said tentatively.

Jeff turned to his wife and glared at her. 'How did my brother know this?'

'We bumped into each other in the grocery store and he asked me how I was doing and I told him. He said he might be able to help,' she said quietly.

'And?' he demanded.

'He said to meet him the following Monday and he might have some news for me.'

'Meet him? Where?'

'Only in the diner opposite the grocery store, that's all.'

Milly rose from the table. 'I'll make the coffee,' she said.

Chuck very quickly changed the subject but the evening was ruined, and all the way home in the car Jeff railed on about his brother's interference.

Once they arrived home, Gracie blew her top. 'Well thanks for ruining a perfectly good evening!'

He stormed back at her. 'I don't want my brother anywhere near you, understand?'

'For goodness' sake, Jeff, he only tried to help, that's all! The way you're going on, you'd think we were having an affair!'

He grabbed her arm. 'Don't think that hasn't crossed

his mind. I saw the way he used to look at you when we all shared the same house.'

'Now you are being ridiculous! Rick was kind enough to help me and I'm grateful. I'm really happy working for Milly, so don't you go spoiling things or I'll never forgive you!'

They went to bed in silence.

When she arrived at work the following morning, Milly came over to her immediately.

'Gee, I'm sorry if I said anything wrong last night, Gracie. I didn't mean to cause trouble for you.'

'It's alright,' Gracie assured her, 'it's just that there are bad feelings between the brothers, but you weren't to know. I'm sorry the evening was spoilt as I was really enjoying myself.'

'Anything I can do to put things right?'

'No really, everything's fine.'

Two nights later, Jeff went to play poker straight from work, as he had to put in a couple of extra hours, stocktaking. Gracie didn't mind, their relationship was still somewhat strained and she welcomed a quiet night alone, but when Jeff returned, she saw from the look on his face that he'd had a bad night. She didn't say anything, just made him a coffee.

He pushed it aside and got a can of beer from the fridge, lit a cigarette and sat down.

Gracie decided to go to bed, to get out of his way, she didn't want another argument. She gathered her things together and looked at him.

'I'm tired, so I'm going to bed,' she said, 'but before I go can I have the housekeeping and money for the bills?'

He looked at her with distain. 'There is no money, I lost it all!'

'You what?' she was shocked.

'I lost it! You can pay this week from the money you've earned from the job that my brother helped you to get.'

Gracie was furious. 'No way am I working to pay for your gambling Jeff Rider! I work hard for that and I will not see it wasted because you don't know when to quit.'

He laughed at her. 'Suit yourself. Go to my beloved brother, I'm sure he'll be only too happy to help you out!'

'At least he doesn't waste his money, he's got more sense!'

It was the worst thing she could have said. With a roar of anger, Jeff hurled his can of beer across the room, the contents spilling all over the newly painted walls. He grabbed her and she thought he was going to hit her.

'Don't you *ever* compare me with him. Not ever,' and he sent her flying across the room.

Gracie hit her side on the corner of the table and cried out with pain, but she managed to keep on her feet, determined not to let Jeff see how scared she was.

'That's the last time you manhandle me! You do it again and I'll pack my bag and leave.' She hobbled towards the spare room, where she sat on the bed.

'Bastard!' she muttered. 'No man will ever raise his hand to me and get away with it!' Angry tears brimmed in her eyes and she brushed them away. She decided then and there that her marriage was over, but she still didn't have enough money to pay for a trip home, so what was she to do? The first thing she did was lock the door and put the chair by it. If her husband couldn't show her respect then she would not be a wife to him. Tired from work and now this confrontation, she undressed and climbed into bed. She'd sort out what to do tomorrow, she couldn't think straight now. She looked at her hip, it was red and she knew that tomorrow it would start to bruise.

In the morning, Gracie dressed for work as Jeff was just about to leave. He just glanced in her direction, but she ignored him and he walked out of the door. She quickly made some tea and a piece of toast, then left to catch a bus.

But as the day progressed, Gracie's hip really started to hurt and when she accidentally knocked it against the counter, she let out a cry of pain.

'Whatever's the matter?' asked Milly.

Gracie tried to pass it off. 'Nothing. I banged my hip last night in the kitchen and I just knocked it again in the same place.'

Milly said nothing but looked concerned.

At the close of day, Gracie took the bus home and pottered in the kitchen preparing dinner. She was determined not to contribute to the housekeeping from her own money, so warmed up some stew that was in the fridge, adding fresh vegetables. This she put before her husband when he sat at the table, having not said a word to him when he arrived.

Jeff looked at the plate before him. 'We had this two nights ago,' he remarked.

'Yes, that's right. It needs using up. We can't afford to waste food, especially this week.'

He cast an angry glare in her direction. 'So I lost the money! You can buy food from the extra dollars I gave you when I won a couple of weeks ago. It's called taking the good with the bad!' He was unrepentant.

'Yes, I could, but that doesn't excuse you from losing every cent of your wages. You do that this week but what happens when this occurs again and there is no extra to draw on?'

'Then you use your money. After all we're both earning now.'

'I've already told you, Jeff, the money I earn is certainly not there to cover your gambling losses. You lose, you have to make do!'

His smile was full of mockery. 'You have become very independent all of a sudden.'

'Fortunately I'm in a position to be so, no thanks to you. The way you are carrying on, we'll end up in debt and I have never been in debt. My mother taught me if you can't afford it you can't have it. It's called being responsible.'

'Don't preach to me, Gracie.'

She didn't know how to get through to him. She tried to reason with him. 'I crossed the Atlantic Ocean to be with you. I left my family, my country and all my friends behind because I loved you and thought we could have a good life together, but I'm beginning to think I made a mistake. I thought you wanted a home and a family, now I don't know what to think.'

Caught on the back foot, his ego wouldn't let him admit

he was in the wrong. 'Think what you like!' He pushed his plate away. 'I'm going out!'

As Jeff walked down the street to the nearest bar, he was in turmoil. He did love Gracie and he did want the same as her, but poker was in his blood. He knew it was dangerous, but the adrenaline that flowed through him when he was holding a good hand of cards was like a drug – a drug he couldn't resist. But what stuck in his craw was the fact that Rick had interfered in their lives. He had no right to do that. No right at all!

Gracie tidied the house, washed up and went to bed. She had no idea what was going to happen between her and Jeff but she was determined to make a stand. Then, when she'd saved enough money, she'd book a passage home. America was not for her!

The weekend passed quietly but Gracie was pleased when Monday arrived, at least she had a pleasant day ahead of her at Milly's shop.

The day was busy and just before closing Gracie was surprised to see Rick walk in.

'Hello,' she said, 'what on earth are you doing here?'

'Just thought I'd check up on you to see if you're happy in your work,' he explained. 'How about a quick coffee in the diner across the road before you go home?'

Rick always made her smile and she was so grateful to him for finding her a job, she didn't hesitate. 'Thanks that's a great idea.'

They settled at a table in the window and ordered. 'So how's it going?' Rick asked.

'I can't thank you enough for introducing me to Milly. I love my work and she's a lovely woman. We get on really well.'

He beamed at her. 'That's great! They're a really nice couple, I knew you'd do well. How does Jeff feel about you working?'

'Oh, he's pleased. He says I'm so much happier since I've been there.'

'But not happy that I was the one who found the job for you.'

She looked at him in surprise. 'How did you know that?' Then she thought for a moment. 'You couldn't unless Milly told you.'

He gazed at her and frowned. 'Yes she did tell me, she's worried about you, she thinks things are not going well between you and my brother. Is that right, Gracie? Please don't try and cover for him.'

Letting out a sigh she admitted that when Jeff had found out he was furious. 'What is it with you two? Why don't you get along?'

Rick looked amused. 'I was the baby and I guess a bit spoilt, but I was better at everything than he was. I was in the school football team, you know, American football and I was good. I was more popular than he was. I had more girlfriends than he did. I do believe he was pleased to go into the army. There he felt he'd done something I hadn't.' He sipped his coffee. 'We just never got along and . . . I hated his gambling. When he lost, he was mean and when he won he couldn't stop crowing about it, waving his winnings in my face.'

Gracie nodded. She had seen both of these moods and didn't like either.

Then Rick surprised her. 'You thinking of going home, Gracie?'

Looking at him, she didn't see why she should lie. 'Yes! I'm saving every penny and when I've got enough, I'm off.'

'Does my brother know this?'

'We're not really speaking at the moment, but no, I've not said so.'

'Then my advice to you is keep it to yourself. Why aren't you speaking, did he lose at poker again?'

'Yes, every cent of last week's wages.'

Rick looked furious. 'Don't tell me, he expects you to cover the bills with your wage?'

'Yes, but I flatly refused. I'm not working to cover his gambling losses and told him as much.'

Rick ordered fresh coffee. 'You see now why I told you to open your own bank account.'

'Yes, it was good advice but I'm so sad, Rick. I came here with such high hopes and dreams. I really loved Jeff.'

'You said, loved, in the past tense, are you saying you no longer love him?'

'He's not the man who left me in Southampton with so many promises. That man I adored. I'd have followed him to the ends of the earth.'

He took out a paper and pen and wrote something, then handed it to her.

'Look this is my new place, I open next week and I've moved into the accommodation already. If you ever need me, day or night, promise me you'll call me.'

She took the piece of paper. 'Thanks, Rick. I promise, but I'll be fine.'

He walked her to the bus and when it arrived he kissed her on the cheek. 'You take care, you hear.' He watched until the bus pulled away, unaware that Jeff was sitting in his car, watching both of them.

Chapter Sixteen

When Valerie told Ross she was to be featured in *Vogue*, he was delighted, knowing just how important was the invitation. To be in *Vogue* was a real coup. Only prominent people were ever within the pages of *that* elitist magazine. For once, he was really thrilled for his wife. He drew her into his arms.

'Darling, that's wonderful and you'll do them justice. I'm so proud of you.'

Valerie felt really happy to hear these words, as she'd waited so long for him to say them. 'Are you really, Ross?'

'But of course, how could you have ever doubted it? Besides it will be great publicity for you and that will be great for us both.'

She felt suddenly deflated. Couldn't Ross for once be pleased for her alone without seeing the dollar signs maybe creeping into his firm through her contacts? The fact that he was so dedicated to building his business was to be admired, but the ruthless way he was using her was more than distasteful.

The following morning, Valerie made her way to Max's studio. At least there she was relaxed and happy. With her tutor, there was no hidden agenda.

Max greeted her warmly and kissed her cheek. 'Have you recovered from last night?'

'Just about. Oh Max, it was great fun, I really enjoyed myself.'

'Did you tell Ross about being in *Vogue*?'

'Yes I did.'

Max started setting up their easels for work as he spoke. 'I bet he was thrilled for you.'

'Yes, he was,' was all she said.

The next two hours they worked side by side, as Max taught her how to get the best effect with oils. Valerie was lost within the world they both loved and this new medium thrilled her as she became more adept. Watercolours were gentle but with oils, there was a strength, depth, an excitement that thrilled her artistic soul.

They stopped for lunch and made their way out into the street, where they sat outside a cafe and ate sandwiches and drank beer, watching life pass by in the Village, discussing the mishmash of cultures that survived in New York City.

Valerie sat back in her seat. 'I love this city,' she declared with a happy smile. 'There is such a buzz about it. I know every metropolis is that way but here, somehow it seems different. I love the smell of the pretzels on the cart over there, the hot-dog stand, the way women dress. The exuberance of the people. The whole attitude of the place. I just love it!'

Max looked delighted. 'I am so pleased you feel that way, because it shows in your work. But never ever lose you Englishness, if there is such a word, because Valerie my dear, that is an important part of your charm.'

Laughing she said, 'Oh Max, flattery will get you everything!'

He grinned broadly. 'I'm banking on it! Come on, back to the grind.'

The following week, Max accompanied her to *Vogue*'s office for the photo shoot. It was a long, tiring day for Valerie, but she enjoyed every moment. The hairdressers and make-up artists did their work and Valerie was photographed in various designer gowns, draped amidst different settings. She had a natural elegance and poise, which pleased the professional photographers and when they showed her the rushes, she was amazed at the results.

Max was looking at the photographs over her shoulder. 'Didn't I tell you Mrs Johnson that you were a beautiful woman? When this issue hits the news stands, your name will be on everyone's lips.'

The editor, picked up one photograph and said, 'We'll put this on the cover.'

Valerie gasped. 'The cover? I'm going to be on the cover of *Vogue* magazine, you're kidding!'

'No way,' said the editor. 'Take a good look, this is a superb picture.'

It showed Valerie in a sumptuous evening gown sitting in front of an easel, a paintbrush in her hand as if she was working.

'We'll publicise you as the new find in the art world. I expect it to increase our sales.'

A while later, Max and she left the offices, Valerie still in a whirl, unable to believe what had happened. Max hailed a taxi and took her to the Plaza Hotel to celebrate.

They sat at a table, ordered a meal and drank champagne.

As she lifted her glass, Valerie looked across the table at her tutor. 'How can I ever thank you, Max? All this has happened because of you.'

He took her hand in his. 'No, my dear, this has happened through your God-given talent. I'm the lucky one to be part of your success.'

'But where is this going to lead and where will it end? It's far too good to be true, it's bound to end at some time and that will be so sad.'

'Hey! That's no way to talk. You are at the start of a great career, which can continue as long as you want to work.' He hesitated. 'The only thing that might suffer is your marriage, if I'm honest with you.'

'How do you mean?' She asked with some trepidation.

'Ross will have to get used to the idea that your work is important and will take up much of your time. He will also have to get used to the fact that you will no doubt become somewhat of a celebrity. The male ego can be unpredictable. Could he handle that?'

Valerie laughed with delight. 'Oh, Max, I really think you are putting too much store at my becoming that well known.'

He sipped his drink. 'Time will tell,' he said.

Three weeks later, the issue of *Vogue* magazine hit the news stands and bookshops. Valerie stopped on her way to the studio and bought a copy. The man behind the counter glanced at the cover then at Valerie.

'Geez, honey, that's you! Holy cow!'

She laughed with delight. 'Yes it is.'

'Hey!' he said to the customer waiting, 'This girl is on the cover, take a look!'

The man did and smiled at her. 'Great picture, you are a very beautiful woman.'

Feeling embarrassed she thanked him and hurried away. When she walked into the studio and told Max he burst out laughing.

'There you go, that's just the beginning!' He then picked up the copy he'd bought earlier. 'I shall keep this and start a scrapbook of my protégé and when I'm an old man, I'll sit in my rocking chair and reminisce.'

'Don't be ridiculous,' she chided, unable to cope with any more compliments. 'I'll make us some coffee and get down to work or they'll be nothing to show for all this hype!'

* * *

The following day, Gloria Johnson and Laura, Ross's ex-girlfriend, were out shopping when they saw the copy of *Vogue* displayed on a bookstand in one of the stores. Gloria did a double take as she caught sight of the cover and grabbed Laura's arm.

'Am I seeing things? Is that Valerie on the cover of *Vogue*? No, it can't be!'

They both stopped and looked closely. Laura's face paled. 'Yes it's her! I can't believe it, what's she doing there?'

'There's only one way to find out!' Gloria snapped and bought a copy. The two women went into the coffee shop in the store to look inside. As they poured over the pages, both were speechless.

'How on earth did she manage this?' Laura was candescent with rage. 'She must know someone.'

'A new find in the art world,' Gloria quoted. 'Well, I know she showed some of her paintings and was written up in the *New York Times*, but this . . .' She was at a loss for words.

She wasn't the only person to be surprised. Gracie Rider spotted the picture in the news stand in the parade where she worked. She stopped, made sure it was Valerie whom she'd met as a GI bride and had shared a cabin with. When she realised it was, she bought a copy and rushed to show Milly.

'Look! This is my friend Valerie. We came across to the States together!' They sat down and read all about her.

'She's doing really well,' said Gracie. 'I'm so pleased, she was a lovely woman. Her husband is a lawyer, they live in New York and she's still there, it says so.'

'Why don't you look up her number and give her a call,' Milly suggested.

'I don't think I can do that, she'll think it's because she's important.'

'I thought you said she was nice?'

'She is, honestly. She came from a well-to-do family, but she didn't have any airs and graces.'

'There you go. I'll find her home number and one evening you can call her. Listen, she'll be pleased to hear from someone from her own country.'

That night, Gracie went home with the copy of *Vogue* and Valerie's home number, which she put in her wallet.

Ross was sharing the limelight with his wife, showing the copy of *Vogue* to all his staff, saying how well she was doing, how proud he was of her and bathing in her glory! He bought a huge bouquet of flowers to take home that evening and booked a table at Sardi's for dinner.

When she arrived home, she was overwhelmed by his attention and delighted that he was taking it all so well.

'Well honey, Sardi's is where all the stars dine so I thought it a fitting place to take you to celebrate.'

She was deeply touched at his thoughtfulness and took care dressing for the evening. When they arrived at the restaurant, the manager was more than welcoming.

He complimented her on the cover. She thanked him, somewhat puzzled as to how he knew, but then Ross explained.

'I told him when I booked the table. After all honey, you are going to be someone and I wanted them to know who you were. One day a picture of you could join all these.' He pointed to the walls covered with signed copies of movie stars and other public figures.

She was angry. 'Oh for goodness' sake Ross, I thought we were going to have a private dinner to celebrate without all this fuss. Don't do that again if we go out or I'll get up and leave!'

He looked nonplussed. 'I don't understand you at all.'

'That's becoming obvious to me as each day passes. Well let me explain. I love my work and as it happens so far I have met with a little success, but don't let it go to your head. I don't want all this fuss, I just want to get on with my life, as quietly as possible!'

'Are you crazy? Do you realise just how hard it is in this city to get recognition for anything? People have to slug their guts out to get where you are today, yet you dismiss it so readily. I would give my right arm to have your exposure!'

'That's where we are different, Ross. I paint for the love of it and nothing more. You are ambitious and that's your way, and in your line I can see you must be in order to succeed, but I'm not like you in that respect!'

The waiter came over to take their order but there

was a tense atmosphere between them for the rest of the meal and as they ate, mostly in silence, Valerie remembered that Max had predicted that their marriage might suffer. She couldn't help but think he was right in his assumption.

Two months later, Max arranged another viewing, but this time solely of Valerie's paintings. There were several watercolours she'd painted earlier and three of those worked in oils. In the foyer of the art gallery was a blown-up photo of her on the front cover of *Vogue*.

This time it was Ross who accompanied her, resplendent in a dinner jacket, delighted that he would be recognised as her husband, his arm round Valerie's waist to emphasise his position. Charming those who were introduced to him.

Max walked over to them, shook Ross by the hand, kissed Valerie on her cheek and, making excuses to Ross, led her away to talk to the reporters. This time the price of her paintings had skyrocketed. She hid a smile as she looked at the price tickets beside the label with the title of the painting, inwardly doubting that anyone would pay that much.

She was so busy during the next hour, she didn't see Ross to talk to, but as her last client walked away, she glanced over to him and was puzzled when she saw him handing a business card to a gentleman to whom he was chatting. The smug grin on Ross's face made her walk over to him.

'What was that all about?' she asked.

'I think I've just got myself another client!' he declared, smiling at her.

'You what?' She was furious. 'Have you been touting for business at my exhibition?'

'What better place? There are rich pickings here, honey.'

Trying to keep her voice low she raged at him. 'How dare you! How dare you use me in this way. It's like a form of prostitution and you working as a pimp! This is the last time you will be invited to any of my viewings, understand?'

He looked surprised. 'You can't mean that?'

'Indeed I do! I will make sure you are refused entry to another!' She walked away, fuming.

Max had been watching this scene from across the room. Taking two glasses of champagne from a tray, he wandered over to her. 'You look as if you need this,' he said and handed her a glass.

Her eyes flashing she turned to her mentor. 'You won't believe this but Ross has been touting for business. Here! Tonight! I won't have him use me this way. I've told him he will never come to another viewing of mine!'

Max was silent. It didn't surprise him. He didn't like Ross Johnson, never had and he could well understand Valerie's distress and anger. Once again, Ross had let her down.

Valerie looked at him. 'Get me out of here Max before I explode!'

He took her glass and put it on a table with his, held

her arm and led her out of the building through a back entrance, hailed a taxi and took her to his apartment.

When they arrived, Valerie threw off her wrap, lit a cigarette and walked up and down the room fuming. Max ignored her and made some coffee then he led her to the settee and sat her down, the coffee placed on the table in front of them. He drew her into his arms and held her close.

'Calm down,' he said softly. 'What's done is done, it's over. He won't be able to do that again if he is barred from any further exhibitions. Now just relax.'

Tears of frustration trickled down her cheeks. She looked up at Max. 'How could he do such a thing?'

Max gazed at her tear-stained face and slowly leaning forward, he kissed her. For just a moment her lips remained closed, but then she returned his kisses willingly. There was a hunger in both of them and the need within them grew until they both rapidly removed their clothing, Max lifted her naked body into his arms and carried her into the bedroom.

There was almost a savagery about their lovemaking at first, but then they took their time, pleasuring one another, leading each other to a height of ecstasy until eventually they lay in each other's arms, replete . . . and in love.

Valerie stroked Max's cheek. 'I have been a complete fool not to realise what you mean to me,' she told him.

'I fell in love with you the day we met at the coffee shop, remember?'

'Yes, I do. I was studying a map of the city and you offered to show me round. Oh dear Max, what do we do now?'

'What do you want to do?'

'I want to paint and be with you,' she replied without hesitation. 'When we are together, I'm happy, I feel alive – but I'm married to Ross.'

'Then you have to make a decision. Do you want to stay married to him?'

She put her hand over her eyes and rubbed them. 'No, I don't love him any more. He's not the man I thought I knew and, after meeting his family, I can see why. His father lives for his business and Gloria is a ruthless manipulator. He takes after them both. It's not how I want to live.'

'If you leave him, there may be a scandal now you're getting well known. It could harm your career.'

She started to laugh. 'I don't care about my career! I just want to paint, that's all.'

'On the other hand,' he said chuckling, 'you know what they say, any publicity is good publicity and to be honest darling, your talent will carry you through. If not, I'll have to keep you!'

'Oh, a kept woman, how decadent! I kind of like that, it sounds exciting.'

He drew her nearer and with a sigh said, 'I guess we should get dressed and find a cab to take you home.'

'I don't want to go home, Max, I want to stay the night with you,' she whispered.

'If you do, there will be trouble, you know that?'

'Do you want me to go?'

He pushed a lock of hair out of her eyes and kissed her. 'Are you crazy?'

'I think I must be, but I love it. Max darling – put the light out!'

Chapter Seventeen

The following morning, Valerie, woke and went to stretch, but Max had wrapped his arms about her as they slept, he stirred as she moved.

He rubbed his eyes sleepily. 'Good morning,' he said quietly and gave her a leisurely kiss. 'Sleep well?'

Now she was able to stretch. 'Mm, like a baby.'

'Would you like some coffee?'

'Not yet,' she murmured and wound her arms around his neck, snuggling closer, feeling his bare flesh against hers.

They made love slowly, enjoying every move, every touch, lost to their need for one another, luxuriating in their newfound intimacy – loath to spoil the moment – until they both were satisfied.

Max kissed her forehead. 'Now I think we could both do with a cup of coffee.' He climbed out of bed and pulled on a pair of trousers, at the same time tossing her his dressing gown.

'I'll take a quick shower whilst you're doing that,' she said and made her way to the bathroom. As she stood beneath the warm flow of water, she remembered vividly how his hands had covered her body, how he had made her feel, how he'd brought her to a climax, how she'd felt loved and cosseted for the first time in months. She also knew that staying the night with Max would change everything. Her marriage was over and Ross would be ruthless when he discovered her infidelity. But she didn't care. She was in love with Max Brennen and wanted to share the rest of her life with him, she would just have to face the consequences. She stepped out of the shower, dried herself, put on the dressing gown and went into the kitchen.

Max had been busy. He'd cooked eggs and bacon, poured glasses of orange juice and made toast. When Valerie looked surprised at the spread, he laughed.

'Sex always makes me hungry,' he explained. 'Come on tuck in.'

As they ate he said, 'I'll come back to your apartment with you.'

'Whatever for?'

'I don't want you to face Ross without me. I need to be there.'

'Ross will have gone to the office by now and although I appreciate your offer Max, I need to handle this alone.'

He looked concerned. 'I want you to move in here. You can't stay with Ross when he knows you spent the night with me. That's even if he agrees to let you do so.'

'I'll pack my things today, but I'll have to wait until he comes home to talk to him. I can't just walk out.'

'Of course you can't. Are you sure you don't want me with you to give you support? I'll do so willingly.'

She looked lovingly at him. 'Thank you darling but seeing you would be like a red rag to a bull as far as Ross is concerned. It's best I do this on my own. Don't worry, I'll be fine. I'll be back later tonight.'

After eating, Valerie donned her evening dress and borrowing a raincoat from Max, put it on. It made it a little less obvious that she was inappropriately dressed for the hour of the day. Later, when she stepped into the cab Max had called, the driver took one look at her and smiled to himself, but didn't pass any remark, for which she was grateful.

Valerie walked into her apartment and gazed around. When she'd first arrived here, she'd been full of hope for her future with the man she'd married but now, just months later, she was about to leave it all behind. She lit a cigarette and walked outside onto the balcony and looked out over the city. She was leaving her husband but she was so very pleased she wasn't leaving New York. This city soothed her soul, made her feel she'd come home. She'd never felt this about any other country she'd visited through her father's work, but here was where she belonged. The ring of the telephone interrupted her thoughts and she walked into the room and picked up the receiver.

'Hello, this is Valerie Johnson,' she said.

'Valerie, it's Gracie Rider, I don't know if you remember

me, but we met at Tidworth Camp, then came over together on the *SS Argentina*.'

'Gracie! Of course I remember you, how are you?'

'Fine, I saw your picture in *Vogue* and thought I'd give you a call. Obviously everything is fine with you. Congratulations!'

Valerie didn't contradict her. The two of them chatted for a long time, neither confessing their true situation. They exchanged addresses and promised to talk again soon.

Hearing another English voice had cheered Valerie and she was pleased that all seemed well with her friend and thought how great it would be if they could meet up in the future. But her frame of mind was spoilt when the telephone rang once more.

'Hello, Valerie Johnson.'

'Oh Valerie!' her mother-in-law's imperious voice echoed in her ear.

'Gloria! This is a surprise, what can I do for you?' She frowned wondering the reason behind the call.

'I saw your picture in *Vogue*,' she began . . . Valerie smiled to herself . . . 'I'm going shopping and wondered if we could meet for lunch?'

'Sorry, Gloria, but I'm tied up all day.'

'What about tomorrow? I have a meeting in the morning, we could meet after that.'

'I am sorry, Gloria, but I'm not at all sure of my movements over the next while so I'm not able to say when I'll be free.'

'Oh I see! Very well.' She replaced the receiver without saying goodbye.

'Rude woman!' Valerie slammed the receiver back in its cradle and went into the bedroom to change and pack. She then prepared a chicken salad and put it in the fridge, grabbed her sketchbook and left the apartment. She needed to keep calm waiting for Ross to return and the only way she could do so was to work. She walked until she found a restaurant with outside tables, ordered a coffee and started to sketch.

She drew the shops with their colourful blinds, the goods on display outside. The different people from different cultures. The street musician. The small child, dancing to his music. She loved every minute of it, breathing in the life that was being lived around her.

Later she moved on, went into a drugstore, sat in the snack bar and ate a sandwich, sketching the people sitting at other tables until she was tired – then she walked home.

As the time for Ross's arrival drew nearer, her whole body tensed, knowing that their meeting was not going to be enjoyable. Three suitcases were already downstairs behind the reception desk for her to take when she left. She made herself another cup of coffee and waited to hear Ross's key in the door. And eventually, the moment arrived. She sat in a chair and waited.

Ross entered the apartment, threw his keys onto the table in the hall and walked into the living room. When he saw Valerie, he stopped.

'So you decided to come home at last!' The anger in his tone was not wasted on her. 'Perhaps you'd like to tell me where you spent last night?'

Taking a deep breath she replied, 'I stayed with Max Brennen.'

He gave her a look of disdain. 'Why doesn't that surprise me?' He crossed to a small table and poured himself a drink from the selection of bottles of liquor.

'I couldn't stay a moment longer after I saw you touting for business at *my* exhibition. How could you *do* such a thing?'

'Well darling, I'm sorry if that upset your sensibilities, but you still haven't grasped the American way of life. We business men never let an opportunity pass by, that's why we are successful.'

'It's not the way I want to live!' she exclaimed, horrified at his arrogance.

He laughed loudly. 'Really? I didn't notice you being uncomfortable as your paintings were being sold at exorbitant prices!'

'That was different,' she protested. 'People bought those because they liked them; no one was coerced into doing so. There was no hard sell. No American way of life. It's called art appreciation. All you can ever see is the dollar signs. Money seems to be your God! Don't misunderstand me, Ross, I admire your tenacity in business and fully agreed with you starting up on your own,' she hesitated, 'but now I realise that money is more important to you than anything else!'

'That's simply not true!'

'Yes I'm afraid it is, you just can't see it!' she rose to her feet. 'Not once have you been pleased for me as your wife to have proven herself. Not once have you shown that you might be proud of me for what I've achieved. All you saw was an opportunity to find new clients and fill your coffers!

Well, I can't go on like this. I'm sorry Ross, but I'm leaving. I don't have a choice, you have changed beyond belief from the man I first met and married. We want different things out of life.'

His surprise was evident. 'Are you crazy?'

'No! It isn't how I saw our lives. I expected to be happy with you, building a home, a business, then a family. I really loved you, wanted to spend the rest of my life with you.' Her voice was choked with emotion. 'I just can't live with your ruthless ambition.'

He was furious. 'I suppose Max Brennen is behind all this. I was afraid he'd take over your life. But don't be fooled for a moment, he sees you as a way to make money!'

'Like you, you mean? You couldn't be more wrong. That's the difference between you two. Money isn't his priority. He has the soul of an artist and luckily for me, he saw something in my work that interested him. Money didn't enter his head!'

'You slept with him didn't you?'

'Yes I did. We didn't mean it to happen, but . . .'

He stood up and glaring at her said, 'Then go to your bloody artist! I'll file for divorce and name him as correspondent and take him for every cent he has!'

'You must do what you think is right.' She opened the door, took the elevator to the ground floor, collected her cases from reception and calling a cab, she walked out of her marriage.

Ross picked up his glass and threw it against the wall, smashing it into pieces. He then picked up an ice pick from the table and ripped the canvas of the painting by Max Brennen that he'd bought for his wife.

As Valerie's cab drew up outside the studio, Max came running down the steps.

'Are you all right?' he asked, his voice full of concern.

Climbing out of the cab, she waited for the driver to remove her cases from the trunk.

'I'm fine,' she assured him, 'but I could do with a stiff drink!'

Once inside the studio, they put down her cases and Max drew Valerie into his arms, holding her tightly. 'Any regrets?'

'No,' she replied, 'but it wasn't nice as you can imagine. Ross was furious and he had the right to be really.'

Max released her and poured them both a glass of whisky. 'Here, drink this.'

Valerie told him what had transpired. 'I'm worried about you, Max. Ross will try and ruin you. He said he'd take you for every cent. I didn't mean to bring you any trouble.'

'Darling, there's trouble and there's trouble. This kind I can handle as long as you're happy.'

'I am a bit fraught, but I *am* happy. I can't be myself as Ross's wife. His needs are all financial. He'd never understand my world and the two would clash and eventually destroy us anyway . . . as you predicted.'

They sat on the settee. 'Why don't we take off for a few days?' he suggested, 'take our paints with us. Get away from here and all that it holds. A break would do us both good and will give us time to plan a future.'

To Valerie it was a wonderful idea although it sounded like running away, yet it really appealed to her. 'Where do you suggest?'

He thought for a moment. 'We need a different kind of landscape, something to excite us, something new.'

'How about Colorado?'

'Where did that come from?' he asked with surprise.

'I had a call today from the girl I made friends with before coming here. We travelled together and she rang me out of the blue. She lives just outside Denver.'

'Well that certainly is different. Colorado is arid, with cacti that stretch to the sky once you leave the city behind. It nestles in the Rockies which are beautiful in themselves.' He paused, 'I guess you'd like to visit with your friend too?'

'Oh Max, that'd be wonderful. When I heard her voice it made me a little homesick if I'm honest, not that I want to go back permanently, but it made me feel very nostalgic.'

'Then that's what we'll do. We'll fly out there and hire a camper and tour. Stop where we like, when we like. What do you say?'

'I think it's an inspired idea.'

Whilst Max and Valerie were making their plans, Ross had gone out to dinner. He saw the chicken salad in the fridge then closed the door. He needed to get out of the apartment, away from the marital home. Away from the feminine touches that Valerie had made to the furnishings, which reminded him his wife was with another man.

He sat at a table in a corner where he ordered a drink

and a meal, although he'd no appetite. He couldn't yet believe that his marriage was over! Valerie had encouraged him to open up his own firm, had been a great support, so how come she couldn't understand his looking for business among her wealthy clients? It was a heaven-sent opportunity. Why couldn't she see that and help him instead of blowing her top? Well she'd made her choice.

Max Brennen of all people! What the hell did she see in the guy? OK, he could paint and he had a certain charm, but he'd never amount to anything, well not by his standards.

All these thoughts went through his mind as he drank his wine and pushed his food around his plate. But even when he paid the bill and left the restaurant, he still couldn't understand.

Chapter Eighteen

Whilst Valerie Johnson was starting a new way of life, Gracie Rider was trying to cope with hers. The atmosphere at home was increasingly tense. Jeff was moody and drinking heavily when he came home at night and she couldn't understand why. Eventually she decided it was time to find out. When he arrived home that evening, before he took his first can of beer from the fridge, she faced him.

'I want to know what's wrong!' she demanded. 'For the past week, you've hardly spoken to me, all you've done is drink until you go to bed and I want to know what the hell's going on.'

He glared at her. 'Well how strange you should use that choice of words because that's exactly what I've been wondering.'

He wasn't making any sense. 'I've no idea what you mean.'

'What's going on between Rick and you is what I mean!'

She looked puzzled. 'Nothing's going on, I don't know what you are driving at.'

He opened his can of beer and looked at her with eyes flashing in anger.

'Don't take me for a fool, Gracie. I saw Rick meet you from work the other day, walk you to the bus and kiss you!' He sat down in the chair and waited for her reply.

There was relief on Gracie's face. 'Oh, for goodness' sake is that all? He came into the shop to see if I was doing all right. Yes, he walked me to the bus, but that was a brotherly kiss on the cheek, nothing more. How could you even think such a thing?'

She then realised her husband must have been watching them, which chilled her bones. Jeff was becoming obsessive to have done such a thing. She turned away to the oven and took out two plates of food and placed them on the table.

'Come and sit down.'

He ignored her. 'You don't expect me to believe that Rick was just checking up on you, do you?'

Gracie was scared of the belligerent tone in his voice and thought she'd try and cajole him out of his mood. She walked over to his chair and knelt down beside him.

'Jeff why on earth would I be interested in your brother when I have you?'

This took him by surprise. 'I can't imagine!'

She took hold of his hand. 'I know we've had our ups and downs lately but I do love you, you should know that. If we really want it, we can still have a happy marriage. Look, why don't we eat our meal and maybe go for a drive somewhere? It would be lovely to spend an evening out of the house, maybe walk around, stop for a coffee or a drink, spend time together, just the two of us. What do you say?'

His shoulders relaxed, his anger abated and he looked at her. 'Do you really mean what you said about still loving me?'

She smiled with relief. 'Of course I do, how could you doubt it?'

He hesitated but only for a moment, then getting to his feet he said, 'Right, then we'll do what you said, eat and go for a drive.' He helped her to her feet and sat at the table.

She watched him eating and wondered what happened to the man she'd fallen in love with? There was not a shred of him in the person sitting opposite her and she knew that now, she was just playing a game. She had to keep things on an even keel until she had enough money for a passage home, then she would be away from this claustrophobic relationship. Apart from his gambling and drinking, Jeff's jealousy of his brother was the final straw. Gracie was now concerned that in his drunken anger, Jeff might become physical and she was frightened of him.

It was a warm evening and they drove out of the town into the countryside. Gracie could never get over the power that the Rocky Mountains seemed to exude. There was a splendour about them but at the same time they made you very aware of the power of nature. The mountain range always overwhelmed her but at the same time held a deep fascination for her.

They stopped the car beside a small river, sat on an upturned log and lit a cigarette. It was peaceful among the pine trees.

'This is such a huge but beautiful country,' she said. 'So very different in every way to England. It has a wildness, a raw feel to it. I expect renegade Indians to come whooping round the bend, looking for scalps!'

Jeff started laughing. 'That's Hollywood movies these days, however many years ago it was different. Life was tough for the early settlers. They came out looking for gold, living in tents, trying to make a living without any amenities. They had the terrain and the Indians to cope with.'

'It's not so easy now when you consider the war, Jeff. Look how that changed so many lives.'

They sat talking for some time then Jeff suggested they look for a place where they could get a drink or a cup of coffee, so they moved on.

When eventually they returned to the apartment, Gracie thought how sad it was that tonight, for a while, she'd been with the old Jeff – the one who had been such a pleasure. But she knew now that such days wouldn't last.

The trip out that evening seemed to have settled Jeff's suspicions and his manner was different towards

Gracie. There had been no poker for a couple of weeks as two of the men were away and another taken poorly, therefore no money was lost and harmony reigned within the household, so much so, that Gracie wondered if it was all going to work out after all. Then, she had a call from Valerie telling her that she would be in the area and wanted to see her – she was delirious with happiness.

Valerie and Max had flown to Denver, hired a camper van and driven into the mountains where they spent many happy days, painting, trying to immortalise the beautiful scenery on canvas. The roads here were quiet, so unlike New York, and there was a calm about the place, a wilderness where wild life abounded, unfettered by human habitation.

Away from the bustle of the city, they both found inspiration for their work, often without conversation. Yet there was a closeness between them that made chatting irrelevant as they lost themselves in their own worlds. At night they would park beneath the trees, light a fire and cook over the flames, then they would talk and later make love. It was a time without worry and they savoured every moment, knowing that when they did return, there would be situations to be faced that neither of them were looking forward to.

Valerie had contacted Gracie and arranged to meet her in Barton where she now lived. Both the women were looking forward to the meeting; both grasping what to them would be a touch of home. There was a camping site on the edge of town that Gracie had advised them of, so they could park the camper van and she and Jeff would drive out and meet them.

The day arrived and Gracie had been given a day off work by Milly, who was delighted for her, and Jeff had taken a day's vacation so he too could be free. They drove out in the morning so they could have a whole day together.

Gracie could hardly contain her excitement as they neared the site and as they drove in, she spotted the camper van and Valerie standing beside it with a man.

'There, there she is!' she told her husband.

'Fine, honey, I can see,' he replied smiling at her enthusiasm. 'Calm down or you'll explode!' He pulled the car in beside the visitors.

Gracie got out of the car and the two women rushed into each other's arms.

'Oh Gracie, I never thought we'd see each other ever again!' Valerie exclaimed. 'Look at you, you look so well!'

'You too!' said Gracie and turned to introduce her husband. 'Jeff, this is my friend Valerie.'

He shook her hand. 'Howdy, good to meet you. Gracie has been like a scalded cat ever since she got your call.'

Laughing Valerie said, 'I know, I've been just the same. This is Max, my friend, agent and my mentor.'

Max stepped forward.

Both Jeff and Gracie looked surprised, they had imagined Valerie was with her husband.

'We've come out here to find other vistas to paint,'

she explained. 'We thought the Rockies was just what we needed.' She gazed at Gracie. 'To be honest it was knowing you were here that decided where we'd come. We thought we could see you and paint as well.'

'We thought you'd be with your husband,' said Jeff.

'No, he's back in New York and is far too busy to take time off,' Valerie explained, but there was something in her voice that made Gracie wonder.

There was a small table and chairs set out in readiness and Max said, 'I'll go and make some coffee whilst you two catch up.' He looked at Jeff. 'Would you like to see inside the camper? I think we both might be in the way out here?' he said laughing.

Jeff agreed and stepped inside. He was surprised at how roomy was the interior and said so.

Max filled a kettle from the tap in the small but compact kitchen area. 'Yes, it's really well designed.'

There was a settee in the window with a table, a small toilet with a shower and at the back another settee, both which could be turned into beds. Jeff looked around with interest.

'Is it easy to drive?'

'No problem at all. The only problem is finding enough space to park,' Max told him, 'but we can park on the street if we like. But out here in the mountains, space isn't a problem.'

'You an artist too?' Jeff asked.

'Yes, it's my life really. But I work from home in New York in advertising too.'

Whilst the men were getting to know one another,

outside the girls were catching up. At Gracie's insistence, Valerie was telling her how she started painting again after meeting Max, about her exhibition and about her cover in *Vogue*, which Gracie had asked about.

'When I saw you on the cover I couldn't believe my eyes!' Gracie exclaimed.

'I couldn't believe it when they asked me to do it,' Valerie confessed. 'Now tell me, are you happy. Did it all turn out well for you?'

Gracie hesitated. She hadn't anyone to share her worries and now Valerie was here it was as if one of her own was asking the question.

'Not really,' she said quietly, 'but I can't say any more just now.'

As she spoke the two men emerged with the coffee.

The next few hours passed in easy conversation until lunchtime when Valerie said she'd prepared a cold lunch and they sat outside and ate that. Afterwards, Valerie said she'd leave the men to clear away as she and Gracie would take a walk.

Once they were clear of the men, she and Valerie found a wooden bench and table in a picnic area and sat down. 'Now Gracie, tell me what's wrong.'

It was like offloading a huge weight as she explained to her friend what had befallen her since her arrival and how she was determined to save enough money to go home.

Valerie was full of sympathy and told Gracie about *her* situation. 'Fortunately I'm making money from my paintings and now I have Max.'

186

She saw the bewilderment on her friend's face.

'We are in love, Gracie. I've left Ross and am living with Max. Ross is going to file for divorce, which will be unpleasant. But I have found real happiness, just sadly not with the man I married!'

'Will you stay out in the States?' Gracie asked.

'Oh yes. I love New York, I'm happy there and at the moment my work has met with success, so I'd be foolish to move away. Are you certain you want to go home Gracie?'

She nodded. 'Jeff will always be a gambler and when he's been drinking, he scares me if he's been losing. Today he's like the old Jeff, but it won't last once he starts playing poker again.' She then told Valerie about the bad feeling between the brothers and how Rick had helped her find a job – and the consequences.

'Oh, Gracie I am so sorry. We and the other GI brides came out here with such high hopes. I wonder how many made it work?'

With a sigh, Gracie said, 'It couldn't go wrong for everybody I'm sure, but who knows?' The two walked back together.

During the afternoon, Max and Valerie showed their visitors the work they had done during their time in the mountains. Both were very impressed.

'These are beautiful,' said Gracie as she looked at the canvases, filled with awe at the artistry.

'Valerie has a great talent,' Max stated. 'I see her becoming a major name in today's art world.'

'How does your husband feel about that?' asked Jeff, staring across at Valerie. 'Does he mind?'

Gracie looked appalled. 'Jeff! What a question!'

'That's all right,' Valerie assured her, 'it's a valid question, but answer me this first Jeff. Why would he mind?'

'Well, after all, he's the man of the house, doesn't he object to your certain notoriety?'

She started to laugh. 'I'd never thought of it as notoriety, Jeff. That sounds a bit naughty. Wouldn't you be pleased if this was Gracie, making a success of her life?'

He looked scornful. 'Gracie's success is she's married to me!'

Max intervened. 'There you go! What greater vocation could there be?'

Jeff missed the mild sarcasm of the remark. 'Got it in one!'

Gracie just looked at her friend with an expression of resignation on her face. She looked at her watch. 'I think we should make tracks,' she said reluctantly. 'We both have to be up early in the morning.'

Jeff was ready to leave. It had been a pleasant change but he'd had enough. He shook hands with Max, thanked Valerie for the food and walked towards the car. Valerie slipped a card into Gracie's hand.

'This is my address at Max's. I'll let you know when I'm back. If you need a bolthole, Gracie, we have a spare bed any time. You can call me for a chat whenever too.' She hugged her friend and walked with her to the car and waited until they drove away.

Max came and put his arm round her shoulders.

'Lovely lady your friend, but unless I'm very much mistaken, she's in a mess of trouble with her man.'

Gracie blinked away her tears as they drove away from the camping site. It had been wonderful to meet up again with her friend and to be able to share her troubles, but even after a lovely day, Jeff had spoilt it with his male domination theory. She was sorry Valerie's marriage had broken down but Max seemed a lovely man and she was happy, she was glad of that. It made her all the more determined to go home and lead her own life.

Jeff's voice interrupted her thoughts. 'Sorry, what did you say, I was miles away?'

'I said a strange set-up there with her and her . . . mentor, wasn't that what she called him?'

'What do you mean?'

'Oh come on, Gracie! He might be her mentor but he's also her lover! Who did your friend think she was kidding?'

'Why do you say that?' Gracie was not going to let her husband know the true situation.

'What woman would leave home to paint with a man other than her husband and share a camper? You can't tell me that is just a professional arrangement, no way! I wonder if her husband knows?'

'I'm sure he does, in any way it's none of our business and I don't want to hear any more. I've had a lovely day with my friend so don't you go and spoil it!' *But*, she thought, *you spoilt it anyway.*

* * *

Rumours had started to circulate within the New York art community when it was known that Valerie and Max had taken off together, and eventually it was mentioned in print in a gossip column in one of the newspapers.

Is Ross Johnson, the eminent lawyer, feeling lonely now his beautiful English wife has taken off with Max Brennen, supposedly on a painting trip?

Gloria Johnson saw the article and read the words whilst she was having breakfast. She immediately picked up the phone and rang her son in his office.

'Good morning Mother and how are you?'

'More to the point, how are you?' she asked.

With a puzzled expression he said, 'Fine, why wouldn't I be?'

'You obviously haven't read any papers this morning.'

'No, I've been too busy, why, what's that got to do with my health?'

She read the article to him.

'So what the hell's going on, Ross?'

He figured there was no point in lying now. 'Valerie has left me and gone to live with Max Brennen.'

'She *what*?'

He let out a sigh, this wasn't going to be easy, his mother would be like a dog with a bone until she was satisfied she'd heard everything.

'It seems she doesn't like my work ethic, thinks I'm only

interested in money, not making a life with her, so she's left!'

He sat back and listened to the diatribe from his mother until she'd run out of steam.

'So what are you going to do about it?' she demanded.

'I'll sue for divorce and name him as correspondent of course.'

'There! You wouldn't listen to me. Oh no, you had to go your own way and marry a foreigner, not one of your own!' Her strident voice echoed in his ear.

'Now don't start that all over again, I don't want to hear it. My marriage hasn't worked out, end of story and I'm busy. I'll talk to you another time.'

'Is there anything I can do, Ross?'

'Yes, Mother. Leave me alone!' He put the receiver down, wondering how much time it would take before the news spread – knowing the city, it wouldn't take long. He was correct in his assumption. By the afternoon, everyone in his office knew. Word soon spread among his peers and when his father arrived home that evening, Gloria showed him the article.

Leo Johnson sat reading the paper. 'Well, that's another mistake he made! I'm sure that woman was behind his leaving our company. Yes she was charming and beautiful, but we obviously misjudged her. Imagine leaving Ross for that artist. She must be out of her mind!'

'I met him once at their apartment,' said Gloria. 'She said he was there to hang a picture Ross had bought for her. Now I wonder . . . Has Laura seen this do you think?'

'Now Gloria! Don't start interfering with this. Let Ross sort out his own mess!'

But later that evening, Gloria went to her bedroom and picked up the phone.

Chapter Nineteen

The following morning, Gracie was regaling her meeting with Milly, who was anxious to know how things had gone.

'Oh Milly, you should have seen the paintings they had done. So clever, I was frankly in awe of their talent but you know, Valerie hasn't changed a bit.'

'Gee, that's great, I'm so happy for you, but who is this Max?'

'He's the artist who discovered her and now he teaches her and acts as her agent. He said she's going to become really important in the art world. Imagine that!'

'Wow! You never know what life is going to throw at you, do you?'

'No, we wondered how the other GI brides made out. Some I expect are fine but some I suspect will have been in for a bit of a shock,' Gracie said, thinking of her own experience.

'Did Jeff enjoy the day?'

'Yes, it made a nice break for the two of us. It was so peaceful at the camping site and their camper is great. Mind you, it's a bloody great thing. I wouldn't like to have to drive it!' She started to sort out some summer tops.

'Have you heard anything from Rick?' she asked Milly. 'He's starting his own business in a couple of days.'

'I haven't, but Chuck met him for a beer last night. He has already got some jobs lined up, he said. Rick's all right you know. He used to be a bit wild but he's settled down some now. What he needs is a good wife and a couple of kids.'

This amused Gracie. 'Rick married? I don't think he's ready for that for a while yet. I think he's still out looking for a bit of fun.'

They started to be busy so no more was said about her brother-in-law. But towards the end of the day, the telephone rang. Milly answered it then held out the receiver to Gracie.

'It's for you,' she said.

'Hello.' Gracie couldn't imagine who would call her here.

'Hi! How's my sister-in-law?'

'Rick! Why are you calling me?'

'Chuck told me you were off to meet your friend from England yesterday, I wondered how it went?'

She enjoyed telling him about her meeting. 'She's

happy in New York and doing really well with her art.'

'And you, Gracie? How are things with you?'

'Fine at the moment, thanks.'

'Fancy a coffee after work?'

'No, no thanks Rick. Jeff saw us last time and you can imagine what trouble that caused. He almost accused me of having an affair with you! It took some time to talk him round.'

She heard him chuckle. 'An affair? Now that's a thought!'

'You behave! Look I've got to go, we have customers and you'll get me the sack. Goodbye.' She walked away grinning to herself. Rick always made her smile.

'What are you looking so happy about?' asked Milly.

'It's Rick, he's outrageous really, but he always makes me laugh.'

Milly looked thoughtful. 'Jeff was a nice boy but always a bit dour, even at school,' she told Gracie. 'He wasn't often a barrel of laughs. There was always something deep inside him that stopped him really letting go. On the odd occasion when he did, when we were getting up to something naughty, he was like a different boy, but that didn't happen often. I blame his mother!'

'Really, why?'

'She's such a miserable woman as I'm sure you discovered for yourself, but of course, her husband rules the house, so maybe she hasn't had a chance.'

Gracie grimaced. 'We didn't get along at all, that's why I found an apartment so we could move out. I am certainly not popular with Velda Rider! But you know, when I first met Jeff, he was a different man.'

'Probably because he was away from here and that old biddy,' Milly declared.

As she went about her work, Gracie thought her mother-in-law would certainly be delighted when she returned to England. After seeing Valerie, she'd felt really homesick. Colorado was beautiful, but she longed for the verdant English countryside, rain, a ride on a tram, the news being read over the wireless in a clear educated English voice, fish and chips, a walk on the pier overlooking the Solent, her family. She found herself blinking back the tears as she wallowed in her nostalgia.

Still feeling unsettled, she suggested to Jeff when he returned home that they go out to a diner. It wouldn't cost very much, the food was good and she didn't feel like cooking.

'Not tonight, Gracie, it's Friday, I'm off to play poker. The guys are together again, so I'm looking forward to it.'

Filled with trepidation at the return of his Friday night's entertainment, she cooked something for him, but when he'd driven away, she locked up the apartment and went for a walk, taking a magazine with her. She didn't want to spend the evening cooped up inside, wondering what sort of mood her husband would be in on his return. It was a warm evening but there was a light breeze. She walked towards a park thinking to sit quietly and read. She missed a garden, like the small one at home, but the apartment was on the first floor, so there wasn't one where she could relax.

Lost in thought as she walked, she didn't hear a car pull alongside her until a voice called, 'Want a lift lady?'

She turned and saw Rick, grinning broadly at her. He stopped the car. 'Where are you off to?'

'Just out for a walk, that's all.'

He thought for a moment. 'Of course, it's Friday, I guess Jeff is playing poker, right?'

She nodded. 'Right.'

'Then get in and I'll take you for a drink. Now don't say no. Jeff will be out for hours, we'll have plenty of time to get you home.'

Feeling as down as she was, Gracie didn't hesitate and climbed into the passenger seat. 'Where are we going?'

'Away from here, we don't want anyone to see us together and go running to my brother or he'll go nuts.' They drove out of the town into the arid countryside and stopped at a bar, went inside, where they sat in an alcove and ordered beer.

'Well, Gracie, this isn't something I expected to do this evening, but I'm sure glad I saw you.' He clinked his glass with hers. 'Let's enjoy it whilst we can.'

They talked again about Gracie seeing her friend. 'Did she make you feel homesick?' asked Rick.

'Oh yes she did. Not that she's going home, she's happy in New York, but to hear an English voice made me long for home, everything that was familiar. America is so big! I come from a small island in comparison, life is gentle, people are more conservative.'

'Are you saying we Yanks are brash, Gracie?'

She flushed with embarrassment. 'If I'm honest, then, yes. You Americans are so outgoing. At first it was overwhelming, don't get me wrong, it wasn't unfriendly, just strange. During the war I suppose we were used to the GIs in the town who seemed to us a bit wild, but they were just passing through. Truth to tell, I suppose I don't feel as if I belong here!'

'You would if you were happy in your marriage.' He stared at her. 'You could be happy with me.'

She was startled by his declaration. 'No, I could not and don't you start getting ideas Rick Rider. I'm already in enough trouble! I shouldn't be here now. If Jeff found out well . . . I don't know what he'd do.' The very thought made her tense. 'I want you to take me back – now!'

No way could Rick change her mind. In the end he picked up the tab, paid and walked her out to the car.

They drove in silence until they arrived at the point where he had first seen her.

'I'll drop you here, then no one will be any the wiser,' he said, 'but before you go . . .' Before she knew what he was doing, he put his arm around her, pulled her close and kissed her.

She was so surprised she didn't struggle to remove his hold and before she realised what she was doing, she was kissing him back. Suddenly she pushed him away.

'That was really stupid,' she said and went to open the car door.

'I thought it was kind of nice,' he said with a grin.

She looked at him. 'You had better keep your distance

Rick. Because you are going to get me into trouble and I don't need it!' She closed the door and walked away.

Back in Greenwich Village, Max and Valerie had returned home and were unpacking the camper van before Max drove it back to a nearby garage. They had been so happy during their time in Colorado, but now had to return to reality.

Valerie opened the window to let in some fresh air, picked up the pile of mail from the mailbox in the entrance and was sorting through it when Max returned with the groceries they'd bought on the way home.

'I'll make some coffee,' he said.

Valerie didn't answer. She was reading a letter from Ross's lawyer telling her that her husband had filed for a divorce. She handed it to Max.

He quickly read it. 'He hasn't wasted any time,' he remarked.

'No,' she agreed, 'but it was expected. Have you got a lawyer?'

'Oh yes.' He put the letter down. 'I'll make an appointment for us to see him later this week. Come and drink your coffee, then we'll unpack. After, I'll shower and then we'll eat.'

She gazed at him with a worried frown. 'He's going to be very difficult, you know that don't you?'

'Of course, but we expected that. Come on darling, we'll meet all that when we have to. Life goes on.' He kissed her forehead and then poured the coffee.

As they sat at the table Max said, 'You do realise that

when this divorce is made public, the press will be on to it in a flash, don't you?'

With a look of surprise she asked, 'Why would they be interested?'

'Because the Johnsons are amongst the A-list in this city and because you, darling, are also very much in the news. The reporters will have a ball! If I'm right, they'll be photographing our every move. Scandal sells papers, Valerie.'

The idea appalled her. 'Isn't there anything we can do about it?'

'You're kidding right? No, we'll just have to behave in a civilised manner, but there's no way we should hide from them. You had your reasons to leave Ross, which will come out in court. I'm afraid we'll just have to face them.'

Nothing is hidden in a city like New York and pretty soon Max was proved right, as one morning they left the apartment to find a photographer outside. The flash of his camera caught them by surprise. The photographer just grinned at them and walked away.

Max took her hand as they made their way to the shops. 'It's started,' he said.

During the following weeks, pictures of Valerie and Max were often in the papers and those of Ross, leaving his office, entering his home – always alone. He made certain of this as the pictures of his wife were usually of her with Max. It strengthened his case he thought and so was careful to seem to live a solitary life. To be the victim. His family's money and position helped too. The Johnson family had some pretty heavyweight friends in high places, so the press trod very carefully when handling them.

News filtered down to Barton where the New York society news was reported and Jeff very soon caught wind of what was happening. At dinner one night, he read the society column and looked at his wife.

'Didn't I tell you that your friend the artist was having an affair. It was blatantly obvious.' He cast the paper aside. 'Imagine coming here with her lover, that's pretty low.'

'I don't know why you're so worked up about it, it's none of our affair!' snapped Gracie.

'I guess not, except she's a friend of yours. Didn't she tell you about it when you went for your walk?'

'No, she didn't,' Gracie lied. 'Why would she?'

His eyes narrowed as he looked at her. 'I don't believe you.'

She glared at him. 'Please yourself.'

He stood up and took her arm in a vice-like grip. 'Just as long as you don't take it into your head to do the same. You double cross me, you'll be sorry you did!'

'Now you're being ridiculous!' She shook off his hold and went into the kitchen so as not to let him see she was shaking. If he knew she'd had a drink with Rick . . . well, she didn't know what he'd do. She would keep well away from her brother-in-law until she could leave this godforsaken country and go home. The longer she stayed in this loveless marriage, pretending to be the good wife, in bed and out of it, the harder it was becoming every day, especially now that Jeff was back to his old ways of gambling.

Chapter Twenty

It was now late September and somewhat cooler temperatures had replaced the searing heat and humidity of New York. It was the beginning of fall, as the Americans called autumn. Having lived in Singapore in her youth, Valerie had taken the heat in her stride, thankful for the air cooler in Max's apartment, but she welcomed the change even so.

They had both been to see Max's lawyer, but had been advised that Ross held the upper hand in the divorce case, even though Valerie had stated that she'd left him because of his attitude to all things financial, which made living with him untenable.

'But unfortunately, Mrs Johnson, you immediately moved in with Mr Brennen, so your husband has sited him as correspondent. Had you set up a home on your own, it would have been different.' The lawyer raised his eyebrows and shrugged. 'You don't have a leg to stand on, I'm afraid. He can have you for adultery.'

As they left the office, Max put an arm round her shoulders. 'Never mind, he didn't tell us something we didn't already know. There's no point us going to court to defend the case, we'll just have to take what comes.'

'He'll claim damages and court costs,' she said.

'Then you'll be free, that in itself is worth every cent. After, we can get on with our lives.'

Ross, too, was anxious to get things settled. He was sick of seeing photos of his wife with Max Brennen in different locations. The press had been relentless in their pursuit of them and to a lesser degree with Ross himself. But to his great annoyance his mother had been very vocal whenever a reporter had questioned her about her son's marriage.

'Well you know how it is,' Gloria had told one reporter, 'these boys go to war fighting for their country, putting their lives on the line. They get stationed in Britain waiting to fight, feel lonely, and marry in haste to some woman who is entirely unsuited to life out here!'

'But your daughter-in-law has had great success in this country with her paintings,' the reporter had persisted, 'and I believe she comes from a wealthy family. He father worked in Singapore for the British government.'

Gloria floored him with an icy glare.

'That maybe so, but she doesn't understand the American way of life, so she was unsuitable as a wife for my son!'

The reporter watched her stormy exit with a grin. 'Hell, I'd hate to have her as my mother-law,' he muttered to himself.

When Ross had read the report in the paper, he'd rung his mother, furious at her intervention.

'I have asked you not to say a word other than "no comment", Mother!'

'Maybe so, but it makes me so mad when I see pictures of her with *that* man!'

'I don't give a damn about that. Just keep out of my business! You are not helping!' He slammed down the receiver.

That evening he was going to a dinner given by the law society at the Plaza Hotel on Central Park. He had mixed feelings about it. It was an event he needed to be seen at as a lawyer of repute, but his father would also be there and they hadn't met since he'd set up on his own. The two other lawyers who had left to join him would also be with him and Ross wondered what kind of reception he would get if he bumped into his father.

He found out as soon as the three of them arrived and walked into the foyer. Leo Johnson was standing there, talking to another man, but saw Ross enter the hotel. They looked at one another. It was Ross who made the first move. He walked over to him.

'Good evening, Father,' he said.

'Evening Ross!' he said gruffly. The man he was talking to walked away.

'You're looking well,' said Ross.

'I'm fine, not pleased with all the gossip in the papers

about your divorce. Not good for the family name and reputation!' he stated bluntly.

'Yes, well there's not much I can do about that. However, the case comes up next month so then it'll be over.'

His father glared at him. 'Pity! I rather liked Valerie. I thought she'd have been an asset to you. She had style, you could tell she came from a good background – pity you couldn't have made it work.' He turned and walked away.

Ross felt like a child who'd been chastised, which didn't sit well with him and made him feel irritable all through dinner and then after. When he was at the bar, he was suddenly faced with Laura, his ex-girlfriend, who flung her arms around him and kissed him soundly, just as a photographer was on hand to record the incident. Ross was furious! He pushed her firmly away.

'What the hell do you think you're doing?'

Taken aback by his anger, she looked startled. 'Why Ross, I was just so pleased to see you, that's all.'

'You stupid bitch! Don't you know I'm suing Valerie for a divorce? A picture of us kissing is the last thing I need!'

She was so angry, she threw the contents of the glass of wine she was holding in his face. The flash from the photographer caught the scene beautifully.

Ross, dripping wet, glared at Laura and walked out of the hotel.

The incident made the news the next day, to Valerie's great amusement. She showed the pictures to Max. 'Well it's his turn now,' she said with much hilarity. 'Bet he'll be livid!'

She was right. Ross stormed around his office after reading the paper and the headlines. *Eminent lawyer Ross Johnson gets soaked by ex.*

If any of my clients see this picture they will not be pleased, he thought. Especially the big company he was dealing with who were about to sign a contract the following week.

When days later they backed out of the deal, Ross was in a murderous mood.

He picked up the phone and rang Laura. When she answered he railed at her.

'Your stupidity the other night, cost me an account that would have brought a lot of money into my business. Just keep away from me in future. Understand?'

'I wouldn't have you, Ross Johnson, if you were the last man on earth!' she screamed down the phone. 'No wonder your wife left you, she has my deepest sympathy!'

He was left holding the receiver as she rang off.

Despite the imminent divorce hanging over them like the Sword of Damocles, Max and Valerie were living together, happily. They had so much in common. They visited museums and art galleries, had heated discussions about a number of subjects and they shared the special world of the artist, working together in the studio or out at some location where they could find a different perspective for their paintings.

Valerie became a favourite with the local store owners, who loved to hear her accent and where her natural charm endeared her to them. She in turn, depicted them on canvas, showing the everyday life in the village.

Carlo was delighted to see himself and his store featured in one scene. 'Senora, this is *bellisimo*!' he cried. 'You make me look very 'andsome, no?'

Laughing she said, 'But Carlo, you are! I paint what I see.'

He clapped his hands with joy. 'Anything you want, any time, you come see me!'

Max had overheard his comment and smiled. 'I can see I'll have to watch my back or that man will be making a move on you!' He looked at the canvas. 'That's really good. I love the detail of the passers-by.'

Valerie had caught the feel of the Village with its inhabitants. The smiling black woman with her small child, the lanky young man on his roller skates, the headband he wore, keeping his long hair under control as he sped along the sidewalk. The elderly man slightly bent with age, the woman beside him, helping him manage the step into a nearby grocery store. The colourful display of goods outside the small shops. It had a warmth about it, a sense of belonging.

'This is one for the next viewing, definitely,' Max declared. 'The public will love it!'

They had discussed when to hold another display of their work. Neither could decide whether it would be wiser to wait until after the divorce, or before. Would the press activity before the divorce work for them or against? It was a difficult decision; after all, their livelihoods depended on it.

'You lose the affection of the public, you're finished in

any business,' Max had said. In the end, they decided to wait. Time was on their side and it meant they would have more paintings to show.

Valerie was secretly pleased as she felt that any sales she made would go towards whatever cost would be incurred when the divorce went to court, knowing that Ross would do his utmost to make them pay.

In the home of Gracie Rider, money wasn't a problem at the moment. Jeff seemed to be on a winning streak, so he was in the best of spirits, which made life for Gracie more than pleasant. She quietly slipped a few of the dollars Jeff had thrust at her every time he won into her bank account towards her fare back to England. She was still enjoying working for Milly, but she knew that this *joie de vivre* couldn't last for ever.

As the month of September slowly passed, the temperature slowly cooled. Milly had warned her that the winter could be severe with heavy falls of snow and she didn't relish the thought, having experienced snow on her arrival in the country. She remembered the extreme cold.

Milly told her. 'One year we had six feet of the darned stuff!'

'Yes I remember. I arrived here last January. Jeff kitted me out in warm clothes because of the cold.'

A week later, Jeff's run of luck ran out! He came home in a foul temper and started drinking.

Gracie tried to talk him out of his mood. 'You've had a

good run,' she said, 'you're bound to have a setback now and again.'

'Since when did you become a specialist on poker?' he sneered.

'You know I'm not. It's just common sense.'

He refused to listen and as he drank more and more, Gracie decided to go to bed out of his way.

How long she'd been asleep she didn't know, but she woke when Jeff staggered into the room and undressed. She pretended to be asleep as he reached for her, but he wasn't fooled.

'I know you're awake baby, come to papa.'

His stale breath made her feel nauseous and she pushed him away. 'Not tonight,' she said, 'I can't stand the smell of beer, and you reek of it.'

But he would have none of it. He gripped her breast so hard it made her wince.

'Jeff, you're hurting me!' she cried.

He ignored her. The next twenty minutes would be forever carved on her soul as her drunken husband forced himself on her. When she struggled, he hit her so hard she saw stars. Eventually to evade another blow, she lay still until he'd finished invading her body with some force, then he turned over and went to sleep.

For a while, Gracie couldn't move. Every bone in her body seemed to hurt. Her right eye was closing. She felt violated! She slowly climbed out of bed and went to the bathroom. Soaking a flannel in cold water, she held it over her eye, but when she went to the toilet, she found she was bleeding. She started to cry.

She sat like that for a while, but the thought of seeing Jeff in the morning was terrifying. What if he was still in a bad mood? She made her way downstairs, reached for her handbag, took out a card and picked up the telephone, praying there would be an answer.

'Hello!'

'Rick! Rick!' she started crying. 'I need your help,' she managed to say.

'Gracie where are you?'

'I'm at home, Jeff's drunk and asleep. Help me Rick!'

'I'll be there in ten minutes,' he said and put down the phone.

She grabbed her bag and a rug from a chair, put it round her shoulders, opened the front door and waited.

Rick came flying up the stairs, two at a time until he saw her. 'Christ!' he said. Then closing the door, he picked her up in his arms, took her downstairs, put her in the car, started the engine and drove away. When he reached his place, he helped her out and once again carried her inside, sitting her gently on a couch.

'Oh, Gracie honey! What the hell happened?'

Between sobs she told him. But when she told him she was bleeding, he rang for a doctor, holding her and trying to comfort her whilst they waited. When the doctor arrived, Rick told him quickly what had happened.

The doctor examined Gracie and turning to Rick said, 'We must get her into the hospital. We need to find out if she has any internal injuries.'

'I'll drive her there,' said Rick.

The next few hours passed in a haze to Gracie. She was aware she'd been examined, had an X-ray and put into a hospital bed. Rick stayed with her all the time, saying little, just holding her hand.

The hospital doctor told them that apart from some tearing, fortunately Gracie wasn't injured internally. She was badly bruised and they wanted to treat the swelling round the eye, to make sure there was no damage.

'I'm going to give Mrs Rider a sedative so she'll get a good night's sleep. I suggest you come back in the morning,' he told Rick.

He started to argue but Gracie, who had recovered enough to understand, urged him to go home. 'Please, Rick. You get some sleep too. I can't thank you enough for getting me out of that place.'

Taking her hands in his, he said, 'You will *never ever* go back to my brother, understand?'

Tears filled her eyes. 'Thank you. I don't think I could face him again.'

He leant forward and kissed her forehead. 'You get some sleep, you hear. I'll come by tomorrow morning.' He reluctantly left her to the care of the hospital staff and drove home, seething with rage.

Early the next morning, Rick drove to his brother's flat and stood with his hand on the doorbell, keeping it there until he heard footsteps.

With bleary eyes Jeff opened the door. When he saw his brother standing there he was not pleased.

'What the hell are you doing here?' He had hardly got

the words out when he was sent flying backwards as Rick punched him on the nose.

'You son of a bitch!' Rick yelled at him before hitting him again. 'I had to take your wife to hospital after you beat her up.' He held Jeff by the throat. 'You go near her again, I'll kill you!'

Chapter Twenty-One

Gracie spent the next three days in hospital. The swelling around her eye was going down. Fortunately there was no damage done to her sight but she was badly bruised. The hospital staff were very solicitous, treating her kindly as she was so shaken mentally by the attack and terrified in case Jeff came to the hospital to see her. Rick soon put a stop to that by informing the hospital reception that Mr Rider was not in any way allowed to see his wife. He wanted Gracie to report the incident to the police, but she refused.

'I don't want to have to go to court and face him,' she said, 'I couldn't do it.'

Rick assured her if that's what she wanted it was fine with him. 'You'll come and stay at my place,' he told her.

'Won't that cause more trouble?'

'Jeff won't bother me I can assure you!'

The venom in his tone made her question him.

'How can you be so sure?'

'Because I called on him and gave him a taste of his own medicine,' he said. 'He won't want more of the same.'

'Oh dear, Rick, that wasn't very wise, it will only make things worse between you.'

With a derisive laugh he said, 'I never got on with him so he's no great loss.'

'What about your family?'

'Now you listen to me, Gracie honey, stop looking for trouble. We need to get you well, that's more important.'

She lay back on her pillows, exhausted, wondering what would happen when she'd recovered. She certainly didn't want to stay around Barton. She wanted to get as far away as possible, but she still didn't have quite enough money to get her home. But Rick came up with a solution.

'When you're better, why don't you go visit with your friend in New York? Take a break away, give you time to think?'

She loved the idea but knew, having read the newspapers, that Valerie was going through a divorce and this was not the time to accept her invitation, she thought. She'd wait until her bruises had gone and she'd recovered, then she'd think about it again.

The day his brother had given him a hiding, Jeff called his employer saying he was unwell. He was sporting a black eye, his face was cut from the punches he'd received and his ribs were sore. He bathed his face in cold water and filled a bag of ice, holding it over his eye. He realised that he was in trouble. He didn't remember what had happened, he'd been too drunk, but Rick had made everything very clear and when he'd had time to think, he was full of remorse. Poor Gracie, she hadn't deserved that. He knew his gambling was addictive, he'd often tried to stop, but the draw of the cards had beaten him every time.

What would Gracie do? Would she come home? He doubted it, why would she? But in his heart he knew where she would find comfort – with his brother! During the many spats he and Rick had in the past, Jeff had never ever seen him so angry and he knew it would be most unwise to cross him again. Jeez, he'd threatened to kill him and Jeff was convinced he meant every word.

During the two weeks convalescence, spent with Rick at his apartment over the garage, Gracie gradually recovered. Rick had insisted she sleep in his bed, whilst he slept in the spare bedroom. Not once did he make a pass at her, just made sure she was comfortable, took the tablets the doctors gave her and made sure she ate. She was overwhelmed by his kindness.

Milly had been told what had happened and helped Rick choose some clothes for Gracie as she'd left her home with just a nightdress and a blanket. She called on Gracie with a further selection of clothes a couple of times, bringing flowers and cookies as well. She'd made no comment about Jeff or what had transpired, but had just sat drinking a cup of coffee and chatted.

'Gee, Gracie, we all miss you in the shop. All my

customers are asking when are you coming back, I don't know what to tell them,' she said. 'They think you've not been well, that's all.'

'Thanks for that,' said Gracie, grateful for Milly's diplomacy. 'I'm thinking of going to New York to see my friend for a few days, but after that I don't know.'

'You know that Rick's in love with you don't you?' Seeing the surprise on Gracie's face she chuckled. 'I'm surprised you didn't guess. I've never seen him like this with any woman. If you leave for good, you'll break his heart!'

After Milly had gone and she was alone, Gracie thought back to the beginning when she'd called Rick for help and the days that had followed and realised that he had shown how he felt about her in a million little ways and she'd been too blind to see. This only complicated matters even further. She needed to get away to give herself time to sort out her future . . . away from here. She found Valerie's telephone number and called her.

Valerie had been delighted to hear from her. Gracie had been completely honest and told her what had happened.

'Oh Gracie, how dreadful! Of course you must come. Max and I aren't planning to be away for some time, we'd love to see you – especially me! Let me know the date you are coming and what time the train arrives and I'll meet you at Grand Central Station.'

'I can't thank you enough, Valerie. I know you've got your own problems. I read about you in the papers.'

'Damned press!' Valerie exclaimed. 'However they have left us alone at last. As for my problem, it pales into

217

insignificance against yours. When we get together, we'll try and sort out your future.'

Gracie felt as if a weight had been taken from her shoulders, remembering how very capable her friend was. Her spirits lifted immediately.

When Rick had finished work, Gracie told him of her plans as they sat down to a meal. 'I just have to book a train ticket and she'll meet me.'

'I'm happy for you honey. I know how fond you are of your friend, she's just what you need right now, a touch of home.' But there was such a look of sadness in his expression that Gracie was filled with concern.

'What's the matter?'

'I just have this awful feeling I'm losing you. I know you won't want to stay around here and I wonder just where you'll settle. I'm gonna miss you so much.'

She looked over at him with an overwhelming feeling of tenderness. Rick had been wonderful, he'd treated her with gentleness and understanding, had cared for her every need and she suddenly realised she'd miss him too – and told him so.

'His eyes brightened and he smiled. 'Honestly? You wouldn't kid a boy, would you lady?'

'No, I wouldn't. I don't know what I've had done if you hadn't been around.'

'I'd kinda like to be around permanently, how does that appeal to you?'

What could she say? If things had been different, if he had been the GI she'd met in Southampton . . . but he wasn't.

'Oh Rick! Another time, another place, maybe we could have had a future together, but here in Barton, it would never work, there are too many complications.'

He looked disappointed but he didn't press her further. 'I guess we'd better fix your train ticket then,' was all he said.

A week later, Rick drove Gracie into Denver. He'd insisted on paying for her fare.

'You need whatever money you have for your stay in the Big Apple. Just give me a call when you get to your friend's house so as I know you've arrived safely.'

He walked her to the train and found her a carriage, put her case on the rack then, putting his hands on her shoulders, he drew her close.

'You take care, you hear!' Then he gave her a long lingering kiss. 'I've wanted to do that from the moment I picked you up all bruised and battered,' he said.

Gracie just looked at him, her emotions in turmoil. 'Oh, Rick, it all could have been so different!' She gently held his face and kissed him before he left the carriage, and as the guard's whistle blew, she leant out of the window and waved goodbye, wondering if she'd ever see him again.

Rick walked out of the station, feeling desolate. He'd never felt like that about any of his many girlfriends. He'd always declared forcibly that marriage was for fools, but now he'd just said goodbye to the only woman with whom he'd love to spend the rest of his life. His hatred for his brother swelled inside him like a balloon.

When he arrived back in Barton, he drove to his

mother's house and walked into the kitchen to see Velda.

She was surprised to see him. Since he'd moved out, his visits had been infrequent.

'Well, the prodigal returns,' she said sarcastically. 'Where have you been?'

'I've just put your daughter-in-law on a train to New York,' he told her, 'and I'll doubt she'll be returning! And before you start cheering, Ma, you might as well know that your beloved son Jeff put her in hospital.'

'Hospital? What are you talking about?'

'He forced himself upon her and beat her up. He's darned lucky she didn't report him to the police. Had it been my choice, I'd have seen him up in court and paying for what he did.'

'I don't believe you!' She glared at him. 'You're making this up!'

'Believe me, I'm not, but he didn't enjoy a taste of his own medicine I gave him I can tell you, and if he ever crosses my path in the future, he'll get the same again, you best tell him so!' He walked out of the house, slamming the door behind him.

Gracie's journey eventually was at an end and as the train pulled into Grand Central, she grabbed her case and stepped onto the platform, slowly walking towards the exit, searching for a familiar face.

'Gracie! Gracie!' Valerie came running towards her and the two women embraced.

'How are you?' Valerie asked quickly. 'Are you completely recovered?'

'I'm fine,' she replied. 'God! You've no idea how wonderful it is to hear an English voice!'

'Come on, we'll get a cab and go home. You must be feeling weary.'

'Where are you and Max living?'

'Greenwich Village, it's quaint, you'll love it!'

As they were driven through the city, Gracie remembered spending her first night in America here, with Jeff. It seemed such a long time ago.

Max greeted her warmly when they arrived at his apartment. He'd obviously been working and his clothes were splashed with paint.

'Come on in, Gracie, it's good to see you. I've got some coffee on the go, or would you like something a bit stronger?'

'Oh, Max, a drink is just what I need right now.'

He poured her a gin and tonic with ice and lemon, then discreetly left the two women alone to talk. Gracie told her friend her sad tale and how Rick had cared for her.

'He sounds a really nice man,' Valerie remarked.

With a slow smile Gracie spoke. 'He wanted to be around permanently, but I can't stay there with him, not with Jeff still around, I'd be a nervous wreck!'

'What do you want to do?'

With her voice trembling with emotion, Gracie said, 'I want to go home, but I haven't enough money saved yet to pay for the fare.'

'Are you sure this is what you want do, Gracie?'

'I've never been so certain of anything in my life. I want

to see my family, my mother and leave all this behind.' With a grimace she added, 'Before I got married, Mum asked me if I was really sure I wanted to go ahead with the wedding because, as she said, living with a man is very different to being courted. How right she was!'

With a shrug, Valerie agreed. 'Those were wise words, however, we didn't know did we? I too found that out, but I'm so lucky to have met Max. At least I know where my future lies – after the divorce.'

Max reappeared and said if the girls would like to wash up, he'd prepared a meal.

Valerie grinned broadly. 'I'm only with him because he can cook!'

Max looked at Gracie and pretending to be mortified said, 'Sadly this is true!'

The evening was a joyful one with much laughter and banter and for the first time in an age, Gracie relaxed. It thrilled her to see just how close and happy were these two together. But the long journey had taken its toll and after a meal and a few glasses of wine, Gracie asked to be excused.

Valerie showed her to her room and the bathroom saying she was to sleep in and not rush to get up in the morning. 'Max and I will be working so just wander in when you're ready.' She gave Gracie a hug. 'Sleep well,' she said and walked back into the living room.

She and Max discussed Gracie's situation. 'She just wants to go home, that's all but she doesn't have enough for the fare, so I'm going to get her a passage out of here, after she's enjoyed the city for a few days. It's the least I can do for a friend.'

Gracie had a shower then slipped beneath the sheets with a sigh. 'Thank you God,' she said quietly and immediately fell asleep.

When she woke in the morning, she was surprised to see it was past ten o'clock. She stretched then lay still, thinking of Rick. Then she sat up remembering she'd forgotten to phone him to say she'd arrived. Gabbing a dressing gown she ran out of her bedroom in search of Valerie.

'Whatever is the matter?' asked Valerie seeing the look of alarm on the face of her friend.

'I forgot to call Rick! I promised to do so when I arrived. Oh Valerie, how could I do such a thing?'

Relieved that it wasn't something serious, Valerie showed her where the phone was. 'There, make your call and I'll fix you some breakfast.'

Left alone, Gracie dialled the number and was relieved to hear Rick's voice on the other end.

'Rick! I'm *so* sorry! In all the excitement I forgot to call you!'

She heard him chuckle. 'There you go, you've forgotten about me already.'

'No I will never forget you, it was just that I was tired, then seeing Max and Valerie . . .'

'It's fine, Gracie honey. I guessed that was the reason. Is everything OK with you?'

'Yes thanks. It was lovely to see Valerie, and Max cooked us a meal, but when I went to bed I think I died!'

'Don't you dare go and die on me, you hear? We have unfinished business.'

'What do you mean?'

'I mean that I'm not going to let you walk out of my life, no how! I'm not sure just what I can do about it, but I aim to find a way.'

With a deep sigh she said, 'That's a wonderful thought, but it's just a pipe dream.'

'Ah well honey, if you don't have a dream, you ain't living! Let me know your plans when you've made them will you?'

'Yes Rick I will, I promise.'

'Just remember that I love you. Call me again soon.'

Gracie replaced the receiver, her mind spinning. Rick loved her! What a hell of a time to be told that!' She wandered into the kitchen in a daze.

Max had already eaten so the two women sat and ate breakfast together. It was then that Valerie told Gracie of her plan.

'The *Queen Elizabeth* has just sailed but she'll be back in New York in two weeks. I plan to book you a passage on that ship.' At the look of amazement on Gracie's face she said, 'Don't worry, I can well afford it and it'll give us two weeks together in this wonderful city. What do you say?'

Gracie was too shocked to speak for a moment. 'I don't know what to say,' she eventually blurted out.

'You don't have to say anything, just enjoy the time we have together. But when I've made the booking, if it's all right with you, I suggest you cable your mother and tell her you're coming home.'

Gracie burst into tears.

Valerie rushed to her side and hugged her. 'This is no time for tears!' she chided, 'just think of the things we can do before you go.'

'I don't know how to thank you. I'll pay you back one day.'

'Indeed you won't! This is a gift. One day, Max and I'll come back for a trip and you can put us up, that's fair exchange.' She wouldn't listen to any argument and as Gracie was dressing, Valerie booked her a passage in cabin class on the very next voyage. Delighted that she'd been able to sort her friend's problem for her.

The following two weeks seemed to speed by. The women went shopping, to Radio City Music Hall, to the movies. They walked in Central Park, had lunch at Tavern on the Green and were treated to dinner by Max at the Hawaiian Room at the Hotel Lexington. Here Gracie was in her element as each diner was draped in a paper *leis* as they entered the dining room. They drank cocktails out of coconut shells, with little paper umbrellas tucked into the rim, and drank the rum-based liquor through straws, and watched the cabaret of Hawaiian dancers perform, with a running commentary as to what each move depicted. She watched the graceful movements carefully, trying to make her hands do the same, to everyone's amusement.

During the day, Valerie took her around Greenwich Village, introducing her to her shopkeepers and watching the colourful characters who made the Village such a fascinating area pass by.

'I can see why you wouldn't want to leave here,' she

remarked. 'I would think all this is pure gold to an artist and I've seen some of your paintings that prove my point!'

'I guess it is bohemian,' said Valerie, 'but I love it. Here I feel I belong!'

Max and Valerie drove Gracie to Pier 90 on sailing day. They were able to go on board with her and see her settled. Valerie had arranged for flowers and a bottle of champagne on ice to be in the cabin and a tray of canapés so they could have a little celebration of their own.

It was a time of mixed emotion for Gracie: the excitement of going home, the very fact she *was* going, thanks to the generosity of her friend; the feeling of failure in her marriage but the relief she would not have to see Jeff again, and the sadness of leaving Rick Rider behind.

She had called him and told him she was leaving. It had been a difficult conversation. She could hear the sadness in his voice as he spoke.

'That's great news, Gracie. It's what you want and although I'll miss you like hell, it's the right move for you. You take care, you hear, and I'll be in touch.'

On board, the sound of the gong brought their little celebration to an end. 'All visitors ashore!' called the steward.

Gracie walked to the gangway with Valerie and Max. There were tears shed by both women who had shared a great deal. They all exchanged kisses and Gracie went up on deck as the ship prepared to sail.

She watched the gangway being taken away, the ropes let go, the loud call of the funnels as the ship started to move with the help of the tugs and the band on the quayside started to play. She waved frantically to her friends standing on the quayside, waving back, until they were out of sight. Gracie leant over the rail, gazed at the magnificent Manhattan skyline one last time, admired the Statue of Liberty, standing tall and proud and sighed – she was going home!

Chapter Twenty-Two

As Gracie was crossing the Atlantic, Valerie's divorce case was heard in court. Ross was there with his lawyer but Valerie wasn't contesting it, so stayed away, letting her own lawyer represent her. It was pretty straightforward. Eventually, Ross was granted a decree due to his wife's adultery. Costs and damages awarded, to be met by Mrs Johnson. It took less than half an hour.

When Valerie's lawyer returned to his office, he called his client who had been pacing up and down the living room, wondering just how much it was going to cost.

'Well Mrs Johnson, this is your lucky day, Ross had asked for a large amount of money to be paid for your infidelity, but the judge happened to be a lover of art and he cut the demand by half.'

'Really?'

'Yes, really. I believe he was at your first viewing and actually bought one of your paintings. Not that he mentioned it, of course, I just happen to have that information.' He started to laugh. 'Your ex-husband was not pleased.'

'No, I bet he wasn't. Not only has he lost a wife but also one he'd hoped to help him swell his list of wealthy clients. So how much?'

With relief Valerie listened. It was less that she and Max had anticipated, knowing Ross's hunger for the dollar. She rushed into the studio to tell him the good news.

He hugged her and said, 'Thank God that's over! Well another six weeks and you'll be a free woman. How does that feel?'

'Fantastic! We can get on with our lives. It's the strangest thing. I don't feel as if Ross and I had a proper marriage, even though in the beginning we were happy. Does that sound strange?'

'Not really,' he assured her. 'Since you moved in with me, you've been able to be yourself, feed the artist in your soul and thrive on it. You couldn't have done it married to Ross.'

She put her arms around him. 'That's all due to you Max darling. Had I not been a GI bride, we would never have met.'

'Ah, but remember ages ago I told you that fate had brought us together. You were meant to come to New York!' He started laughing. 'I was just a bonus!'

* * *

Ross read the gossip column the following morning.

Valerie Johnson, the new darling of the art world, was divorced yesterday by Ross Johnson, the eminent lawyer. He cited Max Brennen as correspondent. Well that's no surprise. The two artists have been living together for the past several months. Will there be a wedding in the future?

He threw the paper across the room. He hated to lose at anything – and he'd not been awarded the amount of money he'd claimed and which he thought he richly deserved. He picked up the phone and pressed the button direct to his secretary.

'If my mother calls,' he told her, 'tell her I'm in court!' The last thing he needed right now was to listen to her outrage.

The *Queen Elizabeth*, with the help of tugs, was sailing into her dock at Southampton and Gracie Rider, beside herself with excitement, was standing at the rail with the other passengers looking for those who would be meeting them. She searched the faces of the crowd, desperate to see her mother and father. Eventually she spied them and started waving frantically, jumping up and down with glee.

The trip had been so very different from her outward voyage where she'd shared a cabin with twelve others on the SS *Argentina*, with hundreds of GI brides heading for their new lives. This time she had a cabin to herself, a steward and stewardess to care for her every need and all the facilities at her beck and call. It had been a marvellous experience and she'd loved every minute. But now, she couldn't wait to make her way down the gangway . . . then it was time.

Walking carefully so as not to slip, she reached the dockside and ran towards her parents. Clasped in the arms of her mother, the familiar scent of 4711 invaded her nostrils and she knew she'd come home. Both women started crying.

'Oh Gracie love, I'm so happy to see you,' her mother sobbed.

Her father clasped her to him then. 'Good to have you home, Gracie,' he said gruffly, trying hard to keep his emotions under control.

'Oh Mum, Dad, I've missed you both so much I can't tell you!'

They made their way down the shed and to the area marked with the letter R, where she collected her baggage, walked to the line of waiting taxies and headed for home.

As she drove through the old familiar streets, Gracie felt her heart swell with happiness. Here was where she belonged, not in America! It was not the country for her and even if she'd been happy, deep down she knew she'd have eventually pined for England – and now she was here.

Once inside the family home, Gracie couldn't help but wander around, touching the furniture, drinking in everything that she held dear and was so familiar. With tear-filled eyes she looked at her mother.

'I can't tell you how marvellous it is to be here again. I've missed you and home so much!'

Her father made them all a cup of tea, the British elixir of comfort, and they all sat down.

'You didn't say much in your cable,' her mother said, 'are you home for good?'

'Yes Mum, I am. Sad to say my marriage just didn't work out and there was no reason for me to stay in Colorado.'

'How did Jeff feel about you leaving?'

Gracie had no intention of disclosing the harrowing details of her situation – ever; it would upset her parents too much. 'We came to an agreement. Eventually I'll apply for a divorce.'

'Did he pay for you to come home then?'

'No. My friend Valerie bought my passage.' She then told them of their friendship and how successful her friend was in the art world. 'She insisted on paying for me to come back.'

'My goodness, that was more than kind. She still happily married then?'

Shaking her head, Gracie said, 'Unfortunately not. She's waiting for a divorce, but she's in love with a man called Max who is also an artist and a successful one. They'll eventually get married when she's free. He's a lovely man.'

'So what are your plans, love?' asked her father.

'I'll look for a job when I've caught my breath and if it's all right with you, I'll stay here until I've enough money to rent a flat.'

'What do you mean if it's all right? Of course it is. This is your home as long as you want!'

Gracie laughed at the indignation of her mother and she got up and hugged her.

'I think we should go out to dinner tonight to celebrate, don't you? Let's go to the Polygon Hotel and live it up!'

Which is exactly what they did.

Later as she climbed into her bed in her old room, Gracie let out a deep sigh. She was home at last and she was happy, but niggling at the back of her mind was the memory of Rick. Rick who had told her he loved her. Rick who had cared for her. Rick who said they had unfinished business . . . and she missed him.

Back in Barton, Rick slid out from beneath the car he was repairing and wiped away the sweat from his brow with a cloth. Today, Gracie's ship would have docked in Southampton and she would be with her family. He sat on an upturned box, sipped a bottle of Coke and lit a cigarette.

As every day had passed he'd missed her more and more. He was restless, unable to settle at anything but work, but tonight he was going to eat with Milly and her husband Chuck. It was his one good link with Gracie.

It was a fine evening and the barbeque was in use. Chuck wearing an apron and chef's hat was in his element, cooking the steaks, corn on the cob and pork chops. Milly had made a selection of salads and baked potatoes in their jackets. The beer was sitting in a bucket of ice.

As they sat devouring their food, the conversation turned to Gracie.

'I guess she'll be almost home about now,' Milly remarked.

'She docked today as it happens. She'll be happy to be back with her family.' Rick tried to sound cheerful.

'I'm not sure she'd have settled in this country, even if things had been different,' Milly remarked. 'America was too vast, too raw for Gracie's way of life in my opinion, and after what she'd been through with the war and all, I think she found us just too much.'

Smiling Rick said, 'She did tell me she found us all a bit loud. The Brits are so much more reserved than us and we can take some getting used to, I guess.'

'You miss her, don't you?' Milly looked sympathetically at him.

'Like hell!' he said and changed the subject.

The day after Gracie's arrival, she had breakfast and then wandered around the town, going into the shops, flicking through the clothes on different racks. She remembered moving on to the cosmetics, remembering the overwhelming smell of perfume when she first walked through the doors of Macy's in New York. She then walked down the Bargate, the remains of the ancient medieval entrance to the town, thinking that there wasn't anything this old in America. She stopped in a small café and ordered tea and a scone, thinking how very British this was as opposed to hot dogs and pretzels. She ended up in Watts Park, just sitting, watching the world go by – her world, her homeland – and was content.

Now the divorce was over and the press were no longer interested in them, Valerie and Max, decided it was the time to plan their next exhibition. They had been working hard and had several canvases each to show. They booked the same art gallery for two weeks hence. It was very well publicised and Carl Blackmore commented on it in his art column in the *New York Times*. The tickets sold out within days.

On the night of the opening, the champagne was on ice and the canapés ready. The two artists walked around the exhibition, checking that the pictures were hung properly, that the lighting was showing them at their best and hoping they would make a killing.

The doors opened and the people filtered in. Carl Blackmore walked over to them and shook Max by the hand and kissed Valerie on the cheek.

'Good luck for tonight,' he said before walking around the exhibition, taking notes for his column the following morning.

It was about an hour later that Valerie looked up and with surprise saw her ex-mother-in-law enter. She could hardly believe her eyes as Gloria Johnson slowly made her way around the exhibition, looking at the paintings, sipping champagne and eating more than a fair share of the canapés. Eventually, Valerie took a glass of champagne from a tray, drank a mouthful and walked over to Gloria.

'Good evening,' she said. 'I must say I'm surprised to see you here, Gloria.'

The woman looked at her. The hostility in her gaze was undisguised. 'My curiosity got the better of me,' she said. 'I wanted to see just what it was that you found more interesting than being married to my son . . . apart from your lover of course!'

Valerie tried to hide a smile. 'And have you found the answer?'

With a tilt of her head she said, 'I can see that you have a certain talent, but you could have still done all this with Ross by your side. He could have been a great help to you, knowing so many important people.'

'How very strange you should say that, because it was quite the opposite in fact. Ross was delighted with my success as he saw it as a great hunting ground for more clients for him. Indeed, I found him touting for business at my last exhibition. I couldn't have that happen, so I barred him from any further viewings!'

'You did what?'

'I think you heard me Gloria. Now if you'll excuse me I must circulate among my clients. Thank you for coming this evening – for whatever reason.'

She chuckled softly to herself. God she disliked that woman, but then the feeling was mutual. Almost immediately after, she saw Gloria leave the premises and when she told Max about her encounter, he couldn't believe the woman would have the nerve to visit that evening.

'Well, I do hope she noticed the red circles for the

sold sign by your pictures, that wouldn't have pleased her.'

'Frankly I don't care,' Valerie said. 'But she won't be coming to another that's for sure. So let's be grateful for small mercies!'

It was then that a reporter came up to them. Taking out his notebook, he spoke.

'Congratulations on another great exhibition,' he began, 'now tell me you two, when will the public expect to hear wedding bells?'

'You are a little previous,' Max said a little sharply. 'Mrs Johnson's divorce isn't finalised just yet.'

'Yes, I know, but it's just a matter of weeks, then I imagine you'll be off to City Hall to tie the knot?'

Valerie intervened. 'We have been far too busy to think about such things, but we'll let you know if and when.' She turned and walked away.

She and Max had been so happy just being together, they'd not discussed marriage and at the moment she didn't see the necessity to change a thing. It had now been an accepted thing, their living together. It had been newsworthy but now it wasn't, so why bother to change anything. The public knew about them and still came to the viewings and that was the most important thing. Their business wasn't in jeopardy because of their lifestyle.

The evening had been a great success and many paintings sold. To her great surprise, it appeared the 'in' thing among the higher echelon of New York society was to own a Valerie Johnson painting. She was very much the latest trend. She wasn't sure how she felt about it, as she told Max that evening.

'I would rather people bought my work because they loved it than because I was in fashion!' she exclaimed.

Max thought this was hilarious. 'Listen, at your prices be thankful. Among those who want to be fashionable are the other true lovers of the arts. There's room for both you know!'

She shrugged. 'Yes you're right and anyway there'll be something else soon that will be in vogue and my sales will fall.'

'That's true, but the true art collector will always be there, thankfully.'

The two of them were weary. Talking to clients and the public always took away their energy, but networking was part of any business and they were both very adept on such occasions. They sat down and ate sandwiches and drank coffee, too tired to cook and, having been surrounded by people all evening, with no desire to go out to eat.

'Gracie will be home among her family now,' Valerie remarked. 'I do hope she's happy at last.'

'I'm sure she is, darling. America wasn't for Gracie, she was too far out of her element. But I got the feeling that Rick, her husband's brother, was kind of important to her, am I wrong?'

'No, I think you are absolutely right, but it was the wrong time and the wrong place, at least that's what she felt.'

He put an arm around Valerie. 'We were just so lucky to

get together, despite the circumstances. I'll always love you, you know that don't you?'

She cupped his face in her hands and kissed him. 'I do and I'm a very happy woman.'

Chapter Twenty-Three

Jeff Rider was far from happy. He'd returned home to live with his parents to save money, money that he needed to fuel his gambling habit. Since Gracie had returned to England, his drinking had increased and his Friday-night poker games were keeping him poor – he'd not had a lucky run for weeks. Even Velda, who could see nothing wrong with her beloved son, was being pushed to the limit of her endurance. He'd come back drunk tonight after losing yet again, and taken out his bad temper on a wooden chair in the living room, smashing it to smithereens.

For the first time in her life, Velda was scared of him and she recalled the story Rick had told her about Jeff putting his wife into hospital. She hadn't believed it – until now.

'Stop it! Stop it!' she screamed as Jeff picked up another chair.

Her cries seemed to seep through the blind rage and he stopped, the chair held high. He saw the terrified look on his mother's face and stopped, then put the chair down.

'What on earth do you think you're doing?' she demanded. 'This is my home! How dare you?'

Even in his fuddled alcoholic brain he realised he'd gone too far.

'Sorry, sorry Ma,' he murmured, and walked unsteadily towards the stairs and his bedroom.

Velda was shaking. She sat down and clasped her two hands together to try and stop them trembling, and this was how her husband found her a short while later.

'Velda!' He knelt beside her and took hold of her hands. 'Whatever is the matter?'

She nodded towards the chair, now in pieces.

'What the . . . what's been happening here? Who did this?'

'It was Jeff,' she sobbed. 'He came home drunk and in a foul temper.'

Her husband was furious. 'Where is he?'

She grabbed his arm. 'He's gone to bed. It's no good talking to him, he won't remember in the morning and anyway, I think by now he's probably passed out.'

Sitting beside her, Ben asked. 'Has this happened before?'

She shook her head. 'No, he's been drinking a lot but tonight he went mad.' She hesitated, then she told him about Gracie being in hospital and the rest of the story as told to her by Rick. 'I never believed him, but after tonight I think it may be true.'

'Right! In the morning I'll have a chat with him, he will *not* behave like this if he wants to stay in my house. As for the other, that's despicable and I'll let him know what I think about that!'

'Now Ben . . .' Velda began.

'This is not your business Velda, this is man to man stuff and you keep out of it, do you hear?'

She knew better than to argue.

The following morning, Jeff climbed out of bed. His head was pounding as he walked to the bathroom and poured cold water over it, then he washed and shaved as best as he could with his hands shaking. He slowly dressed and walked downstairs. He looked with surprise at the remains of the chair, which Ben had made Velda leave on the floor. His father was sitting waiting for him. He rose to his feet.

'You! Outside in the yard, we need to talk.' He walked away.

Jeff followed him, puzzled by the request. As he stepped through the door he was knocked off his feet by a blow to the jaw. Sprawled on the ground, his hand to his aching chin, he looked at his father.

'What the hell was that for?'

'You don't even remember do you?'

'Remember what?'

'You came home drunk last night and started to smash up the furniture. You scared the hell out of your mother and I'm not having it! Get to your feet and take your punishment like a man!'

Jeff didn't move. He remembered only too clearly the thrashings he and his brother had taken as children when they'd been in trouble. He held out his hand to stop his father.

'Look Dad, I'm really sorry. Yes, I was drunk and yes, I don't remember, but jeez, I wouldn't do that to Ma, you know I wouldn't!'

'But you did! Your drinking's got out of hand and so has your gambling. No doubt that's what happened when you put your wife in hospital!'

Jeff paled. 'How do you know about that?'

'So you did? I may rule my house with a rod of iron but I have never ever raised my hand to my wife or any other woman. Call yourself a man? I'm ashamed to call you my son! That girl left her family and her country for you, she was a good wife and you treated her like that. No wonder she left you. Get up!'

Jeff did so very slowly, waiting for another blow, but his father said, 'Inside.' He pushed Jeff in the back, shoving him through the door into the kitchen. 'Sit down!'

Like a naughty child he did as he was told.

'If you want to stay in my house, this has got to stop – understand? No more playing poker, no more drinking. If you do, I'll throw you out and you'll have to fend for yourself. I'll disown you!'

Jeff knew his father meant every word but he also knew that Ben was right. It had to stop or his gambling and drinking would destroy him.

'Gee Dad, I'm really sorry and you're right. I have to

take control of my life. I'm real sorry about Gracie, she didn't deserve that and if I could turn back the clock . . .'

'But you can't! I'll give you one more chance, boy, and that's all. You step out of line you know what to expect. Before you go to work you owe your mother an apology.' He got up and left the house.

Velda had been watching everything through the window of the small anteroom and, when her husband left for work, she walked into the kitchen and faced her son.

He rose from his chair and made to walk towards her. To his horror, she quickly backed away from him. He saw the flash of fear in her eyes and was ashamed.

'Ma, I'm really sorry. I'm gonna change, honest. I'll buy another chair to replace this one.' He hurriedly picked up all the bits and pieces and took them outside. Then he collected the things he needed for work and left.

Velda sat down and poured herself a coffee. She'd been worried that Ben was going to really hurt Jeff. She knew her husband had a temper and was as strong as a horse. To her mind, Jeff had got off lightly, but he was on borrowed time if he didn't comply with his father's rules.

As Jeff drove to work, he could feel his jaw swelling. He'd already been teased by his workmates when Rick had given him a hiding. He'd said he'd walked into a door, but no one believed him. What would they say today?

His boss took one look at him when he walked through the door.

'Jesus, what happened to you?'

'Someone tried to grab my wallet last night as I was getting into my car,' he lied. 'You should have seen the other guy!'

His employer said nothing more, but Jeff knew he didn't believe him.

News of his brother's dilemma filtered through to Rick. Barton was a small place where everyone knew what went down. Ben had mentioned what had transpired to a work colleague and it filtered through the grapevine.

Rick was delighted to hear that his father had laid down the law to Jeff, but he also knew that as much as his brother might genuinely want to give up his addiction, he would falter eventually. It was only a matter of time.

Gracie had written to Rick, which delighted him. It was a long letter full of news about her voyage home, seeing her parents again, how great it was to be back in Britain and how she missed him. He read that bit over and over. She was now back working, saving until she could afford to rent a small flat. As she explained, it was lovely to be living with her parents in the beginning, but after being married and being her own person, she was anxious to have her very own place.

He smiled to himself as he read and re-read the letter and that night he settled down to answer it. He told her how well his business was going, about seeing Milly and Chuck, how they and all the customers missed her.

I miss you too, Gracie honey. Never a day goes by

that you are not in my thoughts at some time or another.
He didn't mention Jeff or the fracas with their father.

Jeff had managed to stay away from playing poker for three weeks and was drinking Coke instead of beer, but one night as the store closed, some of the staff disappeared up an alleyway to play craps and before he realised it he was rolling the dice.

'Come on baby, do it for daddy!'

He couldn't go wrong and at the end of the game when everybody called a halt, he left with loaded pockets. He was pumped up now, the same old thrill, which had kept him at the poker table was back.

The next evening he found out where there was a game and took his money along and played. He lost a little but he won even more. Then the madness took over. He searched out other games, not caring that he was wandering and playing in the more dangerous areas of the town. He was on a roll, nothing could stop him now. But one night something did.

In a shabby room in a seedy area, Jeff sat down to play. He had a wad of money on him, but he was smart enough to secrete it in smaller amounts in different pockets so as not to pull out a fat roll of notes, but his luck had deserted him. He looked around the table at the players with suspicion. He was sure that someone was cheating. He'd been playing the game for long enough to know when things weren't right and eventually he thought he'd found the culprit and challenged the man.

There was a furious argument, which became even more

heated until he threatened to call the police. The man he'd accused of cheating, pulled a gun on him – and a shot rang out.

Later that night Jeff Rider's body was found dumped in a side alley, his wallet and pockets empty. Only his driving licence left to identify him.

Chapter Twenty-Four

The news of Jeff Rider's murder reverberated around the town. The community wasn't without a certain amount of crime, but murder was not usual. A man walking to work early the next morning discovered his body and called the police.

Ben and Velda had been shocked when a police officer arrived at their door to give them the sad news. Velda collapsed in a heap, sobbing. Ben comforted her as best he could and called a friend in to sit with her while he went to the mortuary to identify the body.

As he looked down at his son, he was stunned. He was both desolate from the loss and at the same time angry that Jeff had thrown away his life over a pack of cards. He nodded to the assistant and left the room. Outside he lit a cigarette, drawing deeply on the nicotine for a modicum of comfort. There was none.

The police had informed him that until they had gathered all the evidence, the body would remain in the morgue. That was the hardest part. It meant that his wife would have to sit with her sorrow for even longer, waiting, in the hope that the perpetrator would be found.

When Rick heard the news from his father, he drove round to his parent's house and tried to offer some comfort to Velda. But she was still in shock. The doctor was called and he gave her a sedative and whilst she slept Ben and he discussed the tragic event.

'I warned him!' said Ben angrily. 'If only he'd listened.'

Rick placed a hand on his father's shoulder. 'It wasn't your fault, Dad. Gambling is a disease and much as Jeff might have tried to beat it, he couldn't. If a bullet hadn't stopped him, his drinking would have. He was on a downward spiral I'm afraid.'

'Will you write and tell Gracie what's happened?' Ben asked. 'She has a right to know, after all, she's still his wife.'

When he returned home, Rick took out a pad and pen, but sat staring at the blank page. How was he to go about it, he wondered? It was a hell of a thing to have to tell anyone. But in the end he decided just to give her the facts, there was no way he could soften the blow. He started to write.

Gracie heard the postman put the mail through the door and walked down to retrieve the post. When she recognised Rick's writing she was thrilled and sat at the kitchen table and eagerly opened the envelope. But as she read the contents she went cold and gasped out loud, making her mother look up from the newspaper.

On seeing how pale her daughter was, she asked, 'What's wrong love, bad news?'

Gracie looked up. 'Jeff's been murdered! He was shot and now he's dead!'

'Oh my God! How dreadful, what happened do you know?'

Gracie read the rest of the letter. 'The police think he'd been playing poker and maybe there was a fight, but they're looking into it.'

'His poor mother,' was her own mother's response.

Gracie hadn't liked Velda Rider but knowing how she felt about Jeff, Gracie did feel for the woman. 'They can't arrange a funeral yet, not until they investigate further.'

'Did he play cards often then?'

'Yes, Mum, it was something we did quarrel about, but I don't want to go into it.' She rose from her chair. 'I've got to go or I'll be late for work.'

Gracie was grateful she was employed, because for the next few hours she would be busy and wouldn't have time to dwell on her bad news.

When she got home, she sat and wrote back to Rick.

Dear Rick,

I received your letter this morning. As you can imagine the contents came as a great shock and although I was pleased to have left Jeff, I remember the man I met and married before it all went wrong and I'm sad. Especially for the manner in which he died. Please give my sincere sympathies to your parents, they must be devastated. Please let me know what happens.

Love

Gracie

She put the letter in an envelope to mail the next morning.

Over the next few weeks, the police eventually gathered the information and evidence they were seeking and the man who shot Jeff was arrested. One of the men who had been playing cards that night had shopped him, not wanting to be involved in a murder charge and so, Jeff's body was released for burial.

It was a sunny day as the hearse drove into the cemetery. Velda was dressed in black, as were the other women who had come along. Milly and Chuck were among the mourners and they stood near Rick, to give him their support.

He stood on one side of his mother, his father on the other as the coffin was lowered into the grave with the preacher standing, Bible in hand.

'Ashes to ashes, dust to dust.'

Rick felt his mother's legs give way and he held her tight to preventing her from falling.

'Deep breath, Ma,' he said quietly, which seemed to give her strength.

After the ceremony, several people returned to the house, where caterers had prepared a buffet. Rick helped his mother out of the car.

'You have to be strong now for Jeff's sake,' he told her quietly. 'Come on Ma, I know you can do it!' He squeezed her arm and led her inside.

Thankfully the wake went well. Old friends of Jeff talked about his teen years, of his leaving to join the army, his time spent fighting for his country, giving his mother better memories to hold and alleviate her grief. At last it was over and the three of them were alone and Velda went to lie down.

Ben took off his jacket and tie, then poured two glasses of beer, handing one to Rick.

'Thanks son, you were a godsend today. Without you, your mother would have gone to pieces.'

'It was harder for her than anyone,' said Rick, 'but it's over and we can get on with our lives. Ma too, in time.'

His father looked at him. 'What plans have you got for your life, Rick? Thank God I've one son with a future!'

'Oh, I'm working on a few things, Dad. I'll be fine.'

As Rick drove back to his place, he thought of his brother. He and Jeff had never been close, but he was sorry about his demise and the way he met his death. Even so, he could never find it within him to forgive Jeff for the way he had treated Gracie. But now he was free from the demons that drove him and, of course, so was Gracie, now a free woman and that made him feel good. At least she wouldn't have to go through with a divorce, which was a blessing.

Gracie had been with the family in spirit as Rick had written and told her when the funeral was to be held. She had said she wanted to arrange to send flowers, but Rick had said he'd see to that for her and had arranged for a spray to be sent along with his own. But at the time of the ceremony, Gracie found herself a quiet corner and said a prayer for the man she'd once loved. She suddenly realised she was now a widow, which felt very strange as she no longer felt a married woman. Since she'd come home, it was as if her marriage and time spent in America had all been a bad dream . . . apart from meeting Rick – that still felt very real.

She'd written to Valerie telling her the sad news. Her friend had sent a cable saying how sorry she was and would be writing.

When she'd read the letter from Gracie, Valerie Johnson had been shocked. Not that murder in the States was unusual. Guns were a way of life here, something she'd never ever got used to, but when something like that happens to someone you know, that's different.

Max was sorry to hear the news. 'It seems to me that Gracie had a narrow escape. Who knows what would have happened if she'd stayed there. Thank heavens her brother-in-law intervened.'

'Yes, he sounds a decent man and I believe there could have been something between them had things been different, but that's life.'

Valerie hadn't been feeling well and eventually Max had insisted she visit the doctor. After his examination, the doctor told her that she was about fourteen weeks pregnant.

She was shocked. 'But I've still been having my period,' she told him, but after thinking for a moment, she added, 'although the flow wasn't as heavy as normal, but I didn't think too much about that.'

'That happens sometimes, Mrs Johnson. Just take things easy for a while. Don't pick up anything heavy, but other than that, carry on. Childbirth is not an illness after all. Come back and see me in a month, unless you're worried about anything. And congratulations!'

Max looked up anxiously when she returned to the studio. 'What did the doctor have to say?'

'He told me I'm pregnant,' she said, wondering what his reaction would be. Until her divorce, they'd taken precautions before having sex and after, but once in a while, lately, passion had overtaken them.

Max looked delighted. 'Really? But how marvellous!' he took her into his arms and hugged her. 'That's the best news you could have given me.'

'Honestly?'

He was astonished. 'I can't believe you would think otherwise darling. I think it's wonderful. Are you all right?'

'Apparently so.' She did a quick calculation. The baby should be born in late March.

'Come and sit down,' he said and led her to the settee. 'We must arrange to get married. After all, we were going to do so eventually, but now I think it would be wise to do so very soon, don't you?'

'Oh Max! You don't have to marry me because I'm going to have your child,' she protested.

'I don't want to marry you just because you're pregnant. How could you think that? I want to spend the rest of my life with you, so why wouldn't I want to marry you? The baby is a bonus. Unless you don't want to be my wife?'

'You silly man, of course I do!'

'Then we'll go to City Hall and get a special licence, or did you want a big affair?'

'No I do not! After all the press coverage in the past, that's the last thing I want. Just two witnesses and a nice meal would be my idea of heaven . . . mind you, I'll need a new outfit!'

He burst out laughing. 'How typical of a woman!'

They were married three weeks later. Carl Blackmore and his wife were the witnesses and after the ceremony, they all dined at the Waldorf Astoria. It was a quiet but joyous occasion.

Valerie wore an ivory coloured dress and matching hat and shoes and an orchid. Max and Carl were in smart suits, sporting buttonholes to match. Jane Blackmore was elegantly attired in a pale green dress and hat. The party enjoyed their meal and the chef had made a small one-tier wedding cake for the occasion.

Max had been given strict orders by Valerie not to make a speech, but he picked up a glass of champagne that the waiter had just poured and remaining seated he spoke.

'I wish to propose a toast to the wonderful woman who walked into my life and today made it complete!'

They all raised their glasses and drank. 'Thank you,' she whispered and kissed her husband.

The following morning, Max and Valerie took a flight to Jamaica for a two week honeymoon. As he had said,

'You need a break now because when the baby is born, things will be different. These two weeks are just for us.'

Despite the fact that it was October, the time when storms could sweep through the islands in the West Indies, the weather was kind to them. They lay on the beach beneath palm trees, relaxed, swam to keep cool and, of course, took their paints and the opportunity to capture the tropical scene before them. They took a cab into Kingston, the capital, and shopped: buying straw hats, linen trousers and local necklaces made out of beads, sold at the roadside by West Indian women trying to earn a living from the tourists. Valerie was delighted by the custom of the shopkeepers offering small glasses of rum as soon as you entered their premises. She allowed herself just one.

Laughing she turned to Max. 'One could finish shopping and be legless here, if you accepted all that was on offer!'

'They figure if you've drunk enough, you'll buy even more is my guess,' he said.

They sat outside a café and had a cold drink as they took out their sketchbooks and drew the colourful locals, capturing the vibrancy of the Caribbean, knowing that on their return, the paintings in oils would bring onto the canvas Jamaica in all its glory.

Another day they were driven to Montego Bay, a favourite spot for tourists, but the beach was big enough to still be comfortable and when Max hired a glass-bottomed boat, Valerie was thrilled to be able to see the world deep beneath them, full of fish swimming in the sea that was an unbelievable shade of turquoise.

They dined that night at a restaurant outside, beneath palm trees with fairy lights threaded through them, moving and sparkling in a soft breeze as they danced to the captivating music of a steel band.

'Oh Max, you couldn't have picked a more romantic place to spend a honeymoon,' she whispered as he held her close.

'I'm so pleased you like it darling. This is just the beginning of our life together and the baby will make it just perfect. I'm a lucky man.'

They returned to New York and put away their summer finery. There was now a chill in the air as winter approached. But in the studio, all the vibrancy of the Caribbean was being composed on canvas as they worked. Inside it was still summer, with palm trees and a turquoise sea in the background and on another, the streets of Jamaica came alive.

It seemed no time at all before Christmas was looming. Valerie loved New York at Christmas. She thought the London shops were superb during this time, but the shop windows of New York were magnificent. At the Rockefeller Center stood a tall conifer tree, decorated with fairy lights, which reminded Valerie of the one in Trafalgar Square. There was an outside skating rink and they sat inside the restaurant watching the skaters through the window as they drank their coffee. On each corner of the streets stood a man dressed as Father Christmas with a tin, collecting for charity, and the smell of chestnuts roasting from various stands filled the air. Christmas in New York was unbeatable!

Max and Valerie had invited several friends to spend Christmas Day with them and ten of them sat down to eat turkey and all the trimmings. They pulled crackers, read the mottos and had a high old time. There was no King's speech of course, but it was only a passing thought as Valerie cared for her guests.

There had been heavy snowfalls and while the streets were cleared, Central Park was still covered and she and Max went for a short walk there on Boxing day, to try and walk off the food they had eaten the previous day. On their return he insisted she rest on the settee.

Valerie, stretched out, relieved to be quiet. During their walk in the park, she'd felt twinges of pain in her stomach and wondered what the child she was carrying was doing to her, but as she lay, the pains increased and when she went to the toilet, she was horrified to find she was passing blood. When she told Max, he immediately called an ambulance.

Max sat with her, holding her hand tightly, as they sped through the streets to the hospital. Neither said a word, both too worried about the consequences, not wanting the other to know their fears.

When they reached the hospital, Valerie was taken into a room to be examined and Max was sent to the waiting room. He walked up and down, unable to relax until the doctor came and found him.

'I'm sorry, Mr Brennen, but I think your wife is going to lose the baby, she's going into labour. I'm afraid she's having a miscarriage. It sometimes happens with a first baby, which I know is no comfort to you, but later you can both try again.'

'Oh my God! Is she in any danger?'

'No, she'll be fine, but I'm sure she would like to see you now.'

Max hurried to the room where Valerie had been taken. He rushed over to the bed and held her hand.

'Darling, are you alright?'

Tears sprang into her eyes. 'Oh Max, I'm so sorry. I'm going to lose our baby!'

'Ssh, don't fret. It can't be helped and it's not your fault. The doctor says it often happens with a first baby.'

She was suddenly convulsed in pain and Max called the nurse, who sent him off to the waiting room again, whilst she summoned the doctor.

Valerie was distraught. The nurse and doctor tried to comfort her but as the pains increased she knew that she was definitely miscarrying.

Two hours later it was all over. Max sat with his wife who was desolate and weak. Eventually she slept as the doctor came to see Max.

'We'll keep her in for a few days to make sure she's fine. Your wife lost a lot of blood so we need to build her up. When you take her home, let her rest until she feels stronger. Mentally as I'm sure you know, will take longer to heal . . . for both of you, but there is no reason she can't have another child, in time. I suggest you go home and come back this evening.' He patted Max on the shoulder. 'I'm so sorry for your loss.'

Max let himself into the apartment, sat on the settee and, burying his head in his hands, cried for his lost child.

Eventually he wiped away his tears and walked into the room that he and Valerie had turned into a nursery. The cot stood in the corner, soft toys on the mattress. He dismantled everything, packed them in boxes and stored them away. The last thing Valerie needed to see when she came home, were these things. If they were lucky one day in the future, they could be brought out again. He went into his own bedroom, set the alarm clock for two hours later, lay on the bed and slept from sheer exhaustion.

Chapter Twenty-Five

Three days later, Valerie was allowed home. Max collected her in a cab and held her close as they drove back to the apartment. He made sure it was warm inside and in the oven was a casserole he'd cooked for them to eat later.

Once inside the door, he held her close and kissed her gently. 'It's so good to have you home,' he said.

Tears welled in her eyes and she clung to him sobbing. 'I wanted that baby so much.'

'I know darling, but we can still have children later when you're ready. Now we must build up your strength. Come along, curl up on the settee and I'll make you a pot of tea. I'm told it's what the Brits do in times of stress.'

She smiled through her tears. 'Oh Max, I do love you!'

It was now early February. When Valerie was recovering and felt able, she wrote to Gracie and told her of her miscarriage, but that she was now all but recovered and back to her painting once again.

Gracie was naturally upset for her friend and wrote back at once, saying how sorry she was, then she brought her up to date with her own news. She was able to tell her that now she'd a flat of her own and was once again her own woman. As she wrote to Valerie,

It was lovely to be at home with my parents, but after being married, I wanted to have my own place again. Rick and I are still in contact. He writes often and tells me his parents are at last recovering from Jeff's death.

Who would have known in those days in Tidworth Camp when we were waiting to sail to America, what lay ahead for both of us.

As she sealed the envelope she concluded that despite everything, she wouldn't have changed a thing. She'd spent time in another country, which had been an experience and she'd met Rick. However, it was a hopeless liaison. He was living thousands of miles away. His letters were a comfort, he still told her he loved her, but what use was that when an ocean was between them? Despite that, she looked for his letters and when they came, read them eagerly over and over before putting them in a drawer.

It was Valentine's Day, the shop had been busy and Gracie was relieved when it was time to go home. Once there, she put on the kettle, kicked off her shoes and flopped onto the settee when there was a knock at the door. Muttering beneath her breath at the inconvenience, she got to her feet and opened it. All she could see was a figure whose face was hidden behind a huge bouquet of flowers.

'Yes?' she said.

The bouquet was lowered and Rick stood before her, smiling. 'Happy Valentine's!'

She felt the blood drain from her and thought she was going to faint. She grabbed hold of the door frame to steady herself. 'Oh my God!' was all she could say.

'I was hoping for a warmer welcome that that, Gracie honey!'

She flung her arms around him with a cry of joy.

'Now that's much better,' he said as he took her into his arms and kissed her until she could hardly breathe. He lifted her off her feet and walked her back into the living room. Somewhat encumbered by the flowers.

He put her and the flowers down and grinning all over his face said, 'Jeez, it's so good to see you.'

She stared at him hardly able to believe her eyes. She put out a hand and touched him. 'I think I'm dreaming,' she said.

'No Gracie, it's me, honestly and truly.'

'But what on earth are you doing here?'

'I couldn't stay away any longer. I told you we had unfinished business, didn't I?'

'You did, I remember.' She shook her head. 'You are the last person I expected to find on my doorstep.'

'I hope you're pleased to see me honey?'

'Oh Rick, how could you doubt it.' She put her arms around his neck and kissed him longingly. 'I've thought about doing that ever since I left America.'

She led him to the settee. 'Now tell me how you came to be here.'

'It's simple. There was no way we could be together in Barton, I know that was impossible, well when Jeff was alive, so I had no choice. Here I am.'

'How long are you staying?'

'As long as it takes. I've got an open return ticket.'

'What? I don't understand.'

'Well honey, the way I see it is if we want to be together we have to decide where we are going to settle. Here in jolly old England or back in the States. We have a lot of talking to do.'

'You would come here to live?' She couldn't believe what he was suggesting.

Shrugging he said, 'If that's what it takes, yes. You know we're meant to be together, where, is just a matter of choice.'

She still couldn't take in what he was suggesting but she suddenly asked, 'If you've come for a while, where's your luggage?'

He started laughing. 'Outside the door. I couldn't hold that and the flowers!'

'Oh for heaven's sake, you'd best go and get it before someone removes it.'

Gracie watched him walk to the door and retrieve his case, still hardly able to believe what had happened. Never in her wildest dreams had she envisaged Rick coming to

England to be with her, but as he walked back she was thrilled that he had.

As he sat back down beside her Gracie asked, 'What's happening to your business?'

'It's going really well. I've a guy helping me. I've left him in charge, he's perfectly capable.'

'What would happen to it if you came here to live?'

'I'd sell up of course.'

'You would do that for me?'

He gazed at her and smiled. 'If I had to, of course I would.'

'Oh Rick, I couldn't expect you to do that after you've worked so hard to build it up.'

'The only way I could keep it honey is if you came home with me. We could get married here with all your family around you first of all, of course, but I'm not sure how you'd feel about that?'

'I need time to think Rick. I mean this is so sudden, my mind is spinning.'

'Of course I understand. I was wondering, can you take some time off from your job so we can be together?'

'Absolutely! If they say no, I'll hand in my notice. I'll show you around Southampton, the New Forest, we can go to London for the day and . . .'

'Hey slow down,' he said grinning at her. 'We have the time, just take it easy.'

'I'm sorry, I'm just so excited.' She put out her hand and caressed his face. 'Oh Rick, I thought I'd never see you again.'

'There, you have no faith. I always knew I'd see you. Come here.'

Inevitably they moved to the bedroom. 'Now for that unfinished business,' Rick said as he undressed her.

Later, as they lay in each other's arms, Gracie gazed upon the face of her lover. She was overcome with joy. She knew for certain that Rick was the man for her and now he was with her she was not going to lose him again, but that meant making decisions that would affect the rest of her life.

He smiled at her. 'Oh my, Gracie honey, that was well worth the journey!'

She snuggled into him, unable to put her feelings into words.

They eventually left the bed and dressed. She went into the kitchen and cooked them a meal, grateful that she had a couple of pork chops in the fridge and as they sat at the table eating, she said she would have to go into the store the next morning to tell them she'd be taking time off.

'Great, I'll come with you and then you can show me round the town. We don't have to make any decisions right away. I know you'll need time to think and I can wait until you're ready.'

'How would your parents feel about us getting together?' she asked tentatively.

'Well, they do know that Jeff put you in hospital, which made them think differently about you leaving and believe it or not, Ma was upset about the way he treated you and Dad was furious. He took Jeff into the yard and threw a punch at him when he found out.'

'Oh my goodness, did he?'

'He did and he gave Jeff one more chance to try and pull his life together but as we know, the gambling was in his blood.'

'You know, when I met your brother here in England he was a different man, I never would have married him if I knew about his addiction.'

He squeezed her hand. 'I know.'

'You must come and meet my parents,' she suggested.

'Let's spend some time together first, honey, then when we've decided what to do about our future, we'll go see them. OK?'

She agreed.

Having taken two weeks holiday from her job, Gracie and Rick took trips to the New Forest, which he loved, especially seeing the ponies wandering wild and unfettered by the roadside. They spent three days in London taking in the sights. Rick couldn't get over the age and history of the place and when they went to see the Crown Jewels in the Tower, he was astonished by their splendour.

'Jeez, we don't have anything like this is the States,' he remarked.

They walked along Embankment in the evening, visited the Whispering Gallery in St Paul's Cathedral, which amused him greatly as he stood on one side of the gallery and spoke to her, astonished that she could hear every word. They were like a couple of tourists, yet they both knew that, eventually, they would have to sit down and decide their future together.

They returned to Southampton on Saturday and the next

day walked on the Pier, went into a café and ate fish and chips. 'The stable diet of the Brits,' he laughed, 'whereas, ours is burgers.' He looked across the table at her. 'These past days have been great, Gracie, but comes the time when we have to talk seriously.'

'I know,' she said. 'I have been thinking whilst we were away and I've come to a decision.'

He frowned and with a look of concern asked, 'What did you decide?'

'I can't expect you to give up your business. It would mean you trying to find work over here, starting from scratch, it would be unfair of me to ask it of you.'

'What are you saying, honey?'

'I'll come back to Barton with you.'

He was stunned. 'You will? But you wrote and told me how you were happy to be back in your homeland – that America wasn't for you!'

'I know and it was true, but if I was with you and happy, then I'd feel differently. After all, we'd be together, we'd have Milly and Chuck as friends, the whole scenario would be different.'

He was choked with emotion. 'Christ, Gracie! You crossed the Atlantic once already to start a new life but I promise you, you will never regret the second trip. I'll make sure we will be able to visit your folks maybe every other year. Does that help?'

'More than you'll ever know. Now I suppose is the time to go and tell my parents.'

'Oh my God! When they know you'll be going away again, they might shoot me!'

Amused at the thought she said, 'We don't have firearms so readily here, Rick, so I think you'll be pretty safe once they've met you. By the way, I didn't tell them about being in hospital, in fact they don't know why I left Jeff – only that it didn't work out.'

'Sure, I understand. Well I guess I'd better pay the bill and go and meet the folks.'

Chapter Twenty-Six

To say that Gracie's parents were surprised to meet Rick would be an understatement, but they made him more than welcome. Gracie's mother was secretly pleased for her daughter. She knew there was a lot more to her daughter's return than Gracie was ever going to explain, and she'd seen how happy she was whenever she'd received a letter from Jeff's brother. Now she'd met him, she understood why. But she and her husband were both shocked when Gracie told them her news.

'You are going back to the States?'

'Yes Mum, but first Rick and I are getting married here in Southampton.'

'That's if you'll allow me to marry your daughter?' Rick looked at Gracie's father.

'My boy, I don't think I could stop her! I've not seen Gracie look this happy for some time. Welcome to the family!' he shook him warmly by the hand. His wife came over and hugged him, then produced a bottle of sherry, poured four glasses and they all drank to celebrate.

Rick sipped his sherry then he looked at Margaret Brown. 'I've promised Gracie that we'll come visit you every other year, that way we'll still be in touch. I know just how much it means to Gracie to leave you again but I promise to make her real happy. You have my word.'

The following two weeks were a mad rush, as a civil wedding was arranged at the local Register's Office and passages booked on the *Queen Mary* for the couple to return to New York, where they planned to stay for a week with Valerie and Max before returning to Barton.

On the day of the wedding, Gracie left her parent's house and Rick left from her apartment, following the tradition that the bride and groom don't see each other the night before getting married. One of Gracie's uncles was to be best man and had stayed with Rick to make sure the groom was on time.

As the bride left with Jim, her father, in a beribboned taxi, he took Gracie's hand.

'You are sure you're doing the right thing are you love?'

'Oh, yes Dad. This time I've not made a mistake I promise you. I really love Rick and feel safe with him.'

'That's all I need to know,' he said and relaxed until the car arrived at their destination.

Gracie, wearing a navy suit and hat, with a small posy of flowers and her father, in his best suit, walked into the room where Rick and some of Gracie's relations waited.

Rick took her hand and kissed it. 'You look lovely honey,' he said quietly.

When the ceremony was over, the married couple walked outside to be met with a sea of confetti. Pictures were taken and then they all trooped off to a local hotel for the wedding breakfast. There were just twenty of Gracie's closest family and friends at the reception.

As she said to her mother, 'After all I've done this before, I don't want a big do.'

As they took their places, Rick put his arm around his bride. 'Hello Mrs Rider, but this time you're Mrs Rick Rider, I like that!'

'I like it too,' she said and kissed him back.

It was a happy day. Rick charmed the guests, most of whom were meeting him for the first time. Speeches were made, telegrams read out and Gracie, sitting listening to the messages, couldn't help but think how different this wedding was from her first one. Then it had been wartime. Today was filled with joy and it felt right.

The very next day, the two of them embarked on the *Queen Mary*, accompanied by Gracie's parents. The steward brought them drinks and sandwiches as they settled in their cabin. Her mother saying how nice it would be to make a trip on this wonderful liner.

'You would always be welcome in Barton, you know that I hope,' said Rick.

'That's nice of you, son,' said Jim Brown, 'we'll have to start saving.'

They walked around the decks of the liner, chatting, but

all too soon they heard the gong and all visitors ashore being called. The four of them walked to the gangway. There were hugs all round, a few tears from the women, then Rick and Gracie stood by the rails until the ship pulled out, waving and blowing kisses.

There was a cool breeze as the ship made its way out to the English Chanel. Rick and Gracie wrapped up in overcoats, walked around the deck, holding hands, taking in their surroundings and jumping with surprise as the ship's funnels roared above them. Then they made their way back to the cabin to unpack.

This time Gracie had someone to share the voyage. They danced each evening and swam in the pool during the day. Sat outside on the deck, wrapped up in blankets and enjoyed being waited on with trays of coffee, ate far too much – and made love. Both besotted with one another.

One lunchtime, as they sat in the dining room on a table for two which they'd asked for, wanting to be alone, Gracie looked across at her new husband thinking how very strange life was. After all, she hardly knew Rick, if she sat and analysed it. Yes, he'd found her a job, yes, he'd come to her rescue when Jeff had beaten her and had cared for her, but that had been all. He'd kissed her properly but twice, lastly when she was due to sail home. That's when he'd told her he loved her . . . yet it had been enough.

He saw her thoughtful expression and asked, 'What is it honey?'

'I was just thinking how little time we spent together before you came looking for me and now we're married. How crazy is that?'

'I guess that's one way of looking at it, but I fell for you the first day I saw you. Shortly after, I told you that you had married the wrong brother. You thought I was joking – I wasn't. But never in my wildest dreams did I ever think it would be possible for us to get together. The fact that we are is the crazy thing to me and I'm a happy man.'

'I can't wait to see Milly and Chuck,' she said, thinking of the only friends she'd made during her stay.

'They know we got married, I sent them a cable the first day we came on board. They were the only people, apart from my man at the garage, who knew I was coming over. Milly did say if ever you came back, your job would be waiting if you wanted it.'

'Really? That's wonderful. I loved working in her shop, the people were so nice.'

'Well according to Milly, you've been missed. How about that?'

Gracie laughed with delight, knowing that to be able to meet her old friends and customers would go a long way to help her settle.

Before they knew it, the journey was over and they packed their bags and left them outside the cabin door on the final evening, to be collected by the baggage master and his crew.

Gracie had insisted that she and Rick take a cab to Valerie's place after docking, remembering just how long it took to clear the ship and collect the baggage from her previous trip. As they walked down the gangway, she felt her heart beating faster. Never ever did she envisage returning to this country and, although she was deliriously happy, deep down she felt nervous. She had felt she had no choice, due to Rick having built up his business, nevertheless, there was just a small doubt in her mind as to whether she would really be able to settle here again. But she didn't voice this fear to her new husband.

At last they were settled in a cab heading for the Village and her dear friend. This Gracie was really looking forward to and when the cab pulled up in front of the apartment, both Valerie and Max rushed down the steps to greet them.

The two women embraced and then Max gave Gracie a hug and shook hands with Rick. 'Come on inside,' said Max, grabbing one of the cases.

Both of the girls couldn't stop talking they were so excited. Max and Rick looked at one another. 'Women!' they said in unison.

The two men got along so well, it was as if they already knew each other and so the first evening was a celebration – of meeting with old and new friends and a marriage to drink to. Copious amounts of champagne were drunk and a sumptuous meal had been prepared.

After, Gracie insisted that Max and Valerie take them into the studio to see their work. Rick was really impressed and said so.

'I don't understand art at all, to be honest,' he admitted, 'but even I can see how good these paintings are.' He wandered around taking in every detail of each picture. 'Gracie told me about your work,' he said, 'but I didn't expect anything like this! No wonder you're so successful.'

Max grinned across at Gracie. 'You have married a man of great taste.' Turning to Rick, he asked, 'Have you been to New York before?'

'No, I'm just a guy from the sticks,' he laughed. 'I've only been out and around Colorado. Mind you, Denver is a pretty cool city.'

'Well, we'll take you around a few of the sights before you go home,' promised Valerie.

'That would be great,' said Rick. 'I've always wanted to go to the Empire State Building and Times Square.'

And they did, as well as other favourite tourists sights. Rick was delighted.

'I feel just like a kid again,' he laughed as he bought a small flag with *I love New York* printed on it. 'I'm going to hang this in my garage to remind me of this trip, and you two must come to Barton and stay.'

Neither of them said they'd been before when Gracie was married to Jeff, it would have been inappropriate.

Valerie and Gracie had taken off together one day to shop and spend time alone to catch up with each other's news. Valerie shared with her friend the hardship of losing her baby and Gracie was able to tell her how happy she was with Rick, but was secretly concerned about settling back in Barton.

'You'll be fine,' Valerie said. 'I met Jeff and, believe me, Rick couldn't be more different. I like him and it's obvious that he adores you.'

Gracie asked Valerie how she felt about trying for another child.

'I've been to see my doctor who said there was no specific reason for the miscarriage, which was a relief, so later in the year, we'll try again.'

A week later, the four of them made their way to Grand Central Station for the trip back to Barton. Valerie and Max promising to come and visit in the fall. They stayed to wave their friends goodbye as the train pulled out.

As they walked to the exit, Max said, 'This time I think Gracie has made the right choice. I'm sure she'll be happy.'

'I think so too,' Valerie agreed, 'and I'm really happy for her.'

But as Gracie sat on the train watching the passing scenery, she wondered what sort of greeting she'd get from her mother-in-law? She couldn't bear it if Velda was still a bitch. Not after all that had happened.

Chapter Twenty-Seven

It was a long and tiring journey and when they arrived in Denver, they booked for an overnight stay in a hotel so they could shower and rest. Gracie put to the back of her mind that this was how her first visit had started, but this time, the two of them went out for a meal, then climbed into bed, curled up in each other's arms and slept, to prepare for the final trip to Barton.

The following morning they travelled by Greyhound bus to their destination and as the journey neared its end, Gracie felt a tightening in her stomach. Barton held nothing but bad memories for her and she felt tense.

Rick seemed to sense her misgivings and took her hand in his. He looked lovingly at her. 'This time it'll be different, you'll see.'

* * *

The apartment above the garage was roomy, with a large living room, a kitchen, bathroom and two bedrooms. There was a fire burning in the grate and groceries in a box on the kitchen table.

Rick looked pleased. 'Gus, my man in the garage did this when he knew we were coming home. He's a great guy, you'll like him.'

Gracie wandered around the flat, trying not to recall the reason for her last visit. The furniture was comfortable, there was a dining table and chairs against one wall and, to her surprise, cushions adorned the settee and easy chairs. She looked at Rick.

'There is definitely a woman's touch in this place, what have you been up to?'

He laughed uproariously. 'Nothing honey, honest! Milly helped me when she knew I was coming to kidnap you. She said the place needed some refinements, so I let her do her thing.'

'Well, she made a great job of it,' Gracie said and sat in an armchair. 'I really like it.'

Rick came and knelt beside her. 'You have no idea how happy it makes me to see you sitting there. I know how you feel about coming back here.' She made to argue. 'No honey, I'm not blind, I saw your expression as we neared home and it's normal to be worried after your last experience in Barton. But Jeff's gone and with him everything that made you unhappy. I love you and I will make sure you never ever regret your decision to return. Do you trust me, Gracie?'

As she looked into his face and the concern mirrored in his eyes, she put out her hand and caressed his cheek. 'Yes, totally!' How could she not? He had crossed the Atlantic to win her. He'd left his business behind to do so and had been prepared to move to England, if she'd insisted on staying there – of course she trusted him.

'Come on downstairs and meet Gus.'

Gracie liked Gus immediately. He was a big guy, with shoulders like a football player, but he had a gentle manner and greeted her warmly.

'Howdy, Gracie, I've been curious to meet the woman who has tamed this wild man,' he laughed. 'I hope you found everything upstairs to your liking?'

'Yes, thanks Gus and thank you for the groceries and for lighting the fire, that was very kind of you.'

He looked at Rick and grinned. 'Don't you just love the way she talks?'

Then Rick showed her round the garage. It was sizable, with tools and machinery neatly placed. Gus was working on a car, which was raised from the floor, and outside another waited in line.

Whilst Gracie looked around the office, the two men caught up with business news until Rick was ready to return to the apartment, looking very pleased.

Upstairs he said that Gus had managed everything just fine and more business was waiting for the two of them. 'I may have to hire another mechanic,' Rick told her. 'Business is good, so my being away hasn't been a problem.'

The next day was Sunday and they went to eat with Milly and Chuck. The two women were delighted to be reunited and in the kitchen Milly was able to talk to Gracie alone, leaving the men to chat over a beer.

'I can't tell you how happy I am that you decided to come back and marry Rick. My God that man missed you so much, he was so depressed. But look at him now, he's glowing! Are you happy Gracie?'

'Yes I am, but I was worried about coming back here. I have really mixed emotions about that if I'm honest.'

'You'll be fine, you'll see. In time you'll settle because you're with the right man and eventually all the horrors of the past will fade.' Then she said, 'The one thing I want to know is, are you coming back to work?'

'Oh, yes please! I want to meet up with all the customers again. I so loved being in the shop. The only thing I'm not looking forward to is meeting up with Velda, Rick's mother.'

'Ah well,' said Milly quietly, 'I wouldn't worry too much about that. Since Jeff's death, she's lost her spirit, sad to say. It was such a shock to her and I'm not sure she'll ever get over it.'

Gracie was able to see for herself how true this assessment was a few days later when she and Rick drove over to his parents' house.

Ben came to meet them as they pulled in and parked. Gracie got out of the car wondering what sort of greeting she would get. To her surprise, Ben kissed her on the cheek and spoke.

'Hi Gracie, it's good to see you again and congratulations. I'm sure you'll be happy this time around.'

Gracie looked over her shoulder and was shocked to see the now gaunt figure of Velda Rider standing in the doorway. The woman had aged and lost weight, her clothes seemed to hang on her. Her cheeks were sunken and there seemed to be no expression in her eyes. Gracie was filled with compassion at such suffering standing before her. She walked towards the woman, put her arms round her, held her close and said, 'Hello Velda, I'm so happy to see you.'

Suddenly Velda seemed to crumble in her arms and the sobs coming from deep within her were dreadful to hear. Gracie sensed Ben walking towards them and she held out her hand to stop him.

'Come along,' said Gracie, 'Let's go inside.' She shut the door behind them.

Ben looked at his son and said, 'That's astonishing. Your mother hasn't shed a tear since the funeral. It was as if she shut away any shred of feeling.'

'Then it will do her good to let it all out, Dad. Come on, we'll sit a bit and leave them to it.' They sat in the porch and waited.

Inside, Gracie was sitting on the settee with Velda, whose sobs had subsided, just holding her hand. Eventually Velda was able to speak.

'I treated you real bad when you were married to Jeff, but I didn't know he was being cruel to you and I'm sorry for that.'

'Oh Velda, that's all in the past. Jeff was a sick man really and neither of us realised that. It must have broken your heart when he was killed and I'm sorry you had to go through that, as his mother. I can't imagine the pain it caused you.'

'You too suffered. Rick told me and at first I didn't believe him, but later I did. Rick is a good boy, I know he'll look after you.'

'I know he will, but we have to put the past behind us Velda. You must build yourself up. Jeff wouldn't like to see you like this, I know he wouldn't and you have Ben who must be worried sick about you.'

Velda wiped her eyes and blew her nose. 'You're right! I've been wallowing in self-pity far too long.' She gave a wistful smile. 'Thank you Gracie, somehow you've managed to unlock all my emotions in one go! I'm sorry. This was no way to greet you on your return.'

'Nonsense! Let's get the men in and we can all have a coffee together.'

When they were driving home later, Rick glanced across at Gracie. 'I can't thank you enough for what you did for Ma today, honey. It's as if she's been mentally locked away for months, but after talking to you today she seems to be a bit better.'

'I think she was still in shock and somehow, for whatever reason, today as you heard for yourself, she let go and all her grief came to the fore, which is good. To keep things locked away like that is unhealthy but we all treat grief in different ways. Hopefully now, she'll be able to deal with it. We'll spend some time with them, invite them over for a meal when we're settled in.'

'You are an extraordinary woman Mrs Rider. After all I know that Ma wasn't kind to you before.'

'That was then, Rick, this is now, as you keep saying, those days are behind us. Now I feel I'll be able to get along with Velda and that's a bonus.'

It seemed no time at all, before Gracie was back in the swing of things, working with Milly, being greeted warmly by her old customers and the local storekeepers. She was deliriously happy with Rick, more than she could ever have thought possible. He brought fun and affection into her life, something that had been missing when she was married to Jeff and she thrived.

One Sunday they invited Ben and Velda over to lunch and Gracie cooked a roast beef and Yorkshire pudding, which were unknown to all of them, followed by lemon meringue pie. Velda, who was looking much better, tucked into the food with relish, complimenting Gracie on her cooking.

Another time, she and Gracie made a pilgrimage to Jeff's grave to lay flowers. Neither of them spoke as they changed the water in the metal vase, threw out the old blooms and arranged the new. They both stood staring down at the grave, lost in their own private thoughts. As they walked away, Gracie took her mother-in-law's hand and just gave it a squeeze. Words were unnecessary.

Rick's business was thriving and he'd hired another mechanic and one evening he came home with a second-hand car for Gracie.

'But I can't drive!' she exclaimed.

'I know that honey, I'm going to teach you.'

She was thrilled but also petrified, which he found amusing.

'Now don't you fret, I'll take you out on quiet roads until you feel safe enough to drive into town. There's no rush, we'll just take things easy.'

He was very patient and eventually, after a *great* deal of practising, Gracie felt brave enough to drive in the town. She proved to be very able and soon passed her test, thrilled to be able to go where she pleased. She even took Velda shopping.

When the snows came, Gracie experienced her second winter in Colorado. She'd never seen so much snow as the fall this year. Rick, Gus and Frank, the new mechanic, had to dig out the entrance to the garage and the footpaths outside. She remembered how Milly had once described a really bad winter here and now she saw it for herself. But she also learnt to enjoy it when Rick took her out with a couple of bobsleighs. They were like children, swishing down hills, tumbling over in the snow. They put chains on the tyres of the car to stop it sliding and, in time, she learnt to cope with it all. In the spring, their happiness was complete when she discovered that she was pregnant. Gracie sat down and wrote to Valerie, telling her the good news.

Valerie Johnson opened the letter from her friend and was overjoyed when she read of Gracie's pregnancy. She and Max had also been trying for a baby. They felt the time was right, but so far they hadn't met with success. The doctors assured them that nothing was wrong so they kept trying and after another exhibition they decided to take a visit to see Gracie and Rick, thinking a change of scenery and a break from city life was what they needed.

As Max said, 'We need to get away from the hustle and bustle of New York. We've both been working far too hard, it's time to take a holiday.'

Spring in the Rockies was a beautiful time of the year. The mountaintops were still covered with snow and the pine trees were verdant, however, storms had been forecast and these could be traumatic. Gracie had been warned but she wasn't prepared for the downpour that followed. The air was filled with the sounds of thunder, lightning flashed, making her jump, and then hailstones bounced off the sidewalks. She had never experienced anything like it. Some of the roads were flooded, making her journey to work somewhat hazardous and Rick insisted on driving her to and fro. He was concerned about her driving herself now she was carrying a child.

Business in the shop came to a standstill as no one was coming out unless it was absolutely necessary. Eventually, at the end of another quiet day in the store, Milly told her not to come in until the storms had subsided.

Valerie and Max had flown into Denver just before the storm struck so they stayed in the city. For Valerie it wasn't such a surprise after living in Singapore, where such weather was part of the tropics. She and Max stayed in the hotel and relaxed. They swam in the pool, ate in the restaurant and rested until several days later the weather begun to clear.

Max hired a car and they drove to Barton, where Gracie was waiting for them in the apartment. The three of them sat chatting, drinking coffee and eating sandwiches, catching up with each other's news until Rick came home to join them.

That evening, they were all sitting round the dinner table when the phone rang and Rick excused himself to answer it. He came hurrying back carrying his jacket.

'Ma's been rushed to hospital', he said. 'She's had a heart attack!'

Gracie looked at Valerie. 'I'll have to go and leave you, I'm sorry.'

'Of course you must go,' her friend replied. 'Don't you worry about us and I hope you come back with good news.'

When they arrived at the hospital they found Ben sitting waiting as the doctors examined his wife. He looked pale and drawn as he greeted them.

'Thanks for coming,' he said. 'We were having a meal when suddenly Velda felt unwell and went to lie down. I called the doctor and he called an ambulance. He said she'd had a mild heart attack.'

Rick sat on one side of him, Gracie on the other. Until the doctor came to find them.

'We have to operate,' he told Ben, 'but before we prepare her perhaps you'd all like to go and see her. Just keep her quiet and I'm afraid I must ask you to keep your visit short.'

They all walked into the room where Velda lay, looking very pale. She gave a wan smile.

'I'm sorry to be such a nuisance,' she said in barely above a whisper.

Ben took her hand. 'Don't be silly,' he said in a choked voice. 'You are going to be fine.'

She looked at Gracie and held out her other hand, which Gracie took in her own.

'You take care of my grandchild, you hear?'

Gracie leant over and kissed her forehead. 'You get better soon and you can help me look after her – or him.' But her heart was heavy as she spoke.

The nurse ushered them out of the room. But as they left, there was a sound of a bell being rung from inside and suddenly there was a rush of nurses and the doctor.

It was pandemonium for a moment and the family stood by, hearts in their mouths wondering what on earth had happened.

Twenty minutes later the doctor emerged and walked towards them.

Gracie felt a shiver run down her spine, waiting for him to speak. He looked at Ben.

'I'm sorry Mr Rider, but your wife suffered another heart attack and I'm afraid we couldn't save her.' He placed a hand on Ben's shoulder. 'I'm very sorry for your loss.'

Ben looked stricken and was unable to speak. Gracie led him to a nearby chair and sat with him while Rick spoke quietly to the doctor. Then Rick came over to his father.

'We can go and see her if you like, Pa.' He looked at Gracie. 'I think you had better sit and wait honey. We must think of the baby, I don't want you getting upset.' He leant forward and kissed her cheek, then took his father by the arm and led him into the room to see his wife.

Later, Rick and Gracie insisted that Ben come back with them, they didn't want him to go home to an empty house. Rick said he would stay with his father that night but first of all, they had to let their visitors know what had happened.

Both Max and Valerie were solicitous towards Ben Rider. They all sat down and had a strong drink together, trying to understand what had happened.

As Ben sipped from his glass he said, 'She never got over Jeff's death and I figure she died of a broken heart.'

They let him talk. It was the outpourings of a man trying to grasp the fact that he was now alone, but unable to fully understand what had happened because it had been so sudden. Then Rick took him home.

When they were alone, Valerie turned to Gracie. 'Are you all right?' she asked with a worried frown.

Placing her hand on her bump, Gracie assured her that she was.

'Well, I think you should go to bed,' Valerie insisted. 'I'll come and sit with you for a while.' Having lost a baby, she was concerned for her friend, worried that the sudden trauma may have an adverse effect on her.

She came back downstairs a little later. 'She's fast asleep,' she told Max, with great relief.

'She'll be fine,' he said, trying to comfort her. 'But what a sad time for the family. What with Jeff and now his mother, they've been through it one way and another.'

'We'll stay and help Gracie,' Valerie said. 'There will be a funeral and all that that entails, I don't want her to have too much to do, if that's all right with you?'

'Of course, that's what friends are for. If there's anything we can do to help, we will.'

Gracie was so pleased to have Valerie and Max during the days that followed. Valerie insisted on doing the cooking, leaving Gracie free to support her husband who was arranging the funeral and trying to keep his father together mentally and physically. It was as if they were all in limbo, all coping in their different ways.

Eventually it was over. The funeral was a quiet affair. Friends of Ben and Velda came to pay their respects and gathered after at the Rider's house to a buffet, which Valerie and Gracie had prepared. When it was all over, Ben thanked them both, profusely.

'I don't know what I'd have done without you all,' he said, tears brimming his eyes. 'But now, we can get back to the real world. After all, life has to go on.' He put an arm around Gracie. 'Soon there will be a new life in the family and that will be wonderful. We must now concentrate on that and not the past.'

He had insisted that Rick return to his own home. 'I'm fine, son. You have been a hero in my eyes, but now you must care for your wife and unborn child.'

As they curled up in bed together that night, Gracie looked up at her husband. 'Your father called you a hero, well you certainly are mine, the way you looked after him when your mother died.'

He pulled her close. 'It was the right thing to do. Now I can spend my time looking after you, so don't you dare give me any trouble.'

The next two days were spent with Valerie and Max. Their visit hadn't been as they had planned but they made up for it during the short time that was left and as they got ready to say goodbye, they promised to keep in touch and meet up again after the baby was born.

As she gave Valerie a hug as she was leaving, Gracie said, 'I hope that you'll soon be able to send me some good news too.'

Her friend chuckled. 'I have to say I'm enjoying trying any way!'

'You are so bad!' laughed Gracie as she held the car door open for her. 'And thanks for all your help, you have been an angel of mercy.'

As she watched them drive away, Gracie thought back to the time the two of them first met. Little did either of them know then just what good friends they would become and how thankful she was that they had met.

Chapter Twenty-Eight

It was now early December and the snow lay deep outside. Gracie was near her due date and was heavy with child. Rick wouldn't let her walk outside on the icy streets without him, in case she fell. It was so cold that she didn't relish being outside too often. They had decorated the second bedroom as a nursery and Gracie would go in there, sorting through the baby clothes and diapers, they'd bought in readiness.

She was naturally excited about the forthcoming birth but in her heart she longed for her mother to be with her and at such times she was overcome with homesickness. Not that she shared these thoughts with Rick, who was looking after her so well. He had a woman come in once a week to clean the apartment and in the evenings he sometimes cooked the meal to give Gracie a break.

One morning he told her that he had to drive into Denver and if she needed anything she was to call Gus, who would be on hand in the garage. He assured her the roads had been cleared when she showed her concern about his journey.

'Listen honey, in the States we're well equipped to cope with winter snows. If we weren't, the country would come to a standstill. The roads are clear so it's perfectly safe. Now you take a rest after lunch and I'll be back early this afternoon.'

Feeling weary and heavy, Gracie went to the bedroom to rest, placing a pillow under her swollen stomach for comfort, and fell into a sound sleep. She woke to hear Rick's voice.

'Gracie honey, wake up!' She stirred and saw his smiling face. 'You all right darling?'

She stretched languidly. 'Mm, what time is it?'

'Half-past three. You need to get up, we have a visitor.'

'Oh, right.' She climbed off the bed thinking that it was probably Milly who had popped in, as was her habit if business was slack, when she would leave the shop in the hands of her assistant. She quickly brushed her hair and followed Rick into the living room.

'Hello Gracie love,' said the woman standing by the window.

For a moment, Gracie looked at her completely stunned, then rushed into her arms.

'Oh Mum! Is it really you?'

'Yes, it's really me.' She hugged Gracie as tightly as she could with her bump getting in the way. 'Heavens! Are you sure you're not carrying twins?' laughed her mother.

Gracie looked over to her husband who was grinning

from ear to ear. 'You kept this quiet,' she said.

'Rick paid for me to come over,' Margaret Brown told her.

'I knew you'd want your mother around when the baby came,' he said, 'so we made arrangements between us. We wanted to surprise you.'

'Oh Rick, what can I say?' She walked over to him and kissed him. 'You have no idea how much this means to me.'

'Oh I think I do. I know you so well, honey. Although you never ever said anything, I see sometimes that expression that means you're feeling homesick. It doesn't happen often but just lately it's been there. Every woman needs her mother at such a time, so here she is!'

'I'm sorry it has to be winter when you come, Mum, with all the snow and everything.'

'My God Gracie, I've never been in such a cold place. The coldest English winters seem like autumn when you feel the cold bite into you here. It's well below zero Rick said.'

'I know, I hope you brought some warm clothes.'

'Rick did warn me, fortunately, and I wore my winter boots, thank the lord!'

'How's Dad? I hope he didn't mind you coming on your own.'

'No, of course not. He sends his love. Rick is going to send him a cable to say I've arrived in one piece.'

Gracie looked admiringly at her mother. It must have been an extraordinary experience for her to make this journey and she said so.

Margaret smiled coyly. 'Well I was a bit overwhelmed

when Rick suggested it, but he arranged for me to be looked after all along the way and here I am. I feel quite adventurous if truth be known. Wait until I get home! What tales I'll have for my friends. They'll all be jealous!' She laughed gleefully at the thought.

Rick had bought a single divan to be put into the nursery for Margaret to sleep on, under the pretext that should they have a visitor, they could accommodate them. The room was big enough to take it and, if they did have a guest, the cot could be moved into their room. Margaret settled in.

One day she was taken to meet Milly and Chuck, walked round the shop and bought some things to take home as gifts and for a short time tasted the American way of life. She loved her trips to the diner and listening to the special language the girls used when ordering. She said when she went home she'd ask her husband, Ken, if he wanted his eggs sunny side up and giggled at the very idea.

'He won't know what I'm talking about so I'll ask him if he wants them served on a raft!' She thought this hysterically funny.

Two weeks passed and then Gracie woke in the night with pains, which came and went and increased in time. Margaret and Rick sat with her until her pains were coming every five minutes, and then they all got into the car and headed for the hospital.

When she was settled in her room, they both stayed with her, holding her hand when the pains were violent, mopping her forehead and trying to comfort her. Rick, who had insisted on staying, was beside himself.

'Oh God Gracie honey! I'm so sorry to put you through all this. We won't have any more I promise!'

As another pain gripped her Gracie yelled out and, looking at her husband, said, 'You make me pregnant again, I'll sue for divorce!'

Margaret just smiled to herself, knowing that once the baby was born, they'd think differently, but she did wonder if Rick was going to be able to stand the strain. With every pain his wife suffered he grew paler. The sweat stood out on his forehead as he watched her. He looked at his mother-in-law for help.

'It's fine,' she assured him. 'This is quite natural in childbirth.'

'Oh dear, Margaret,' he said as he wiped his wife's brow with a damp cloth. 'So much pain doesn't seem natural to me!'

Several hours later, Gracie gave birth to an eight-pound boy. As the doctor wrapped the baby in a towel and put the child on her chest, Margaret let out a sigh of relief. Rick had tears streaming down his face as he gazed at his son.

'He's so beautiful Gracie, thank you so much.'

'Well I didn't manage this on my own you know. You did have a part in it!'

'But I didn't have the pain,' he said and leant over the bed and kissed her.

Margaret went and sat down on a chair away from the bed to allow the new parents to enjoy their moment. She was so happy to have been there and silently thanked

God for giving her such a thoughtful son-in-law. What a fine family they looked, she thought. She'd be able to go home knowing that Gracie had made a good marriage and, once she was back in Southampton, she and her husband would now have no worries that she was so far away.

Three weeks later, Margaret said goodbye as she prepared to leave, she kissed her grandson and hugged her daughter.

'It was lovely to be with you, Gracie and I've really enjoyed my stay, now I can go home knowing all is well. Rick's a good man, you look after him.'

Both of them were fighting tears as they walked to the door. Then with one final hug, Margaret left and climbed into Rick's car to be driven to Denver.

'Thanks for coming ma-in-law,' he said smiling at her. 'It helped Gracie so much having you there.'

'I'm so lucky to have had the chance and I've you to thank for that.'

'In a couple of years, we'll come over to England and see you and your old man. I'm sure he'll want to meet his grandson. Meantime, I'll take lots of pictures and send them to you.'

They drove on in companionable silence. A bond had been born between them during her stay and a shared affection so when Rick took Margaret to the train and settled her in her seat, he hugged her. 'Thanks for everything.'

She, too choked for words, just hugged him back and kissed his cheek.

* * *

Robert Kenneth Benjamin Rider thrived and true to his word, proud father Rick took many photos of his son and sent them to his in-laws, making sure they shared in the baby's growth. Rick was a hands-on father, changing diapers and feeding Robbie, as they called him. Much to Gus's amusement. As he said to Gracie one day, 'Who'd have thought it? Rick Rider, wild boy, feeding his baby!'

Intrigued, Gracie asked, 'What do you mean by wild boy?'

'Well, Gracie, once upon a time, he was the worry of his parents' life. Off on his motorbike for weeks on end. He liked dancing, was quite a hit with the girls, although he never stayed with one for long. I have to tell you he broke a few hearts around Barton. Look at him now!'

'Ah well, it took an English girl to make him settle!' she laughed.

Chapter Twenty-Nine

It was now April and in New York, Valerie was out with her paints and easel in her beloved Greenwich Village. She had decided to do a series of canvases of the Village. One of a quiet residential tree-lined area with its rows of houses in bright red brick, stairs up to the front door, with its matching wrought-iron railings. Overhead the fire escape ladders, the balconies outside the windows, where the residents would sit on warm evenings, window boxes brightening the place. Others of the different busy thoroughfares with their stores, water hydrants, delivery vans and yellow cabs driving through, which made the pictures throb with activity. Washington Square with its impressive arch and park, the folk sitting on the grass enjoying themselves.

She needed a goal to work towards to fill her time to stop her longing for a child. Every time she looked in a pram and saw a baby she felt the loss of hers so much more. Max, who was well aware of the ache within her, tried his best to comfort her.

'If it's meant to be, then we will have a child. If not, then we have each other and our work which, is so much more than some people have.'

She knew he was right, but the longing stayed with her.

To help her think of other things, Max had arranged for them to sail to England in September where they were to hold an exhibition in London. Carl Blackmore, the art critic had suggested it.

'I want the two of you to be known internationally!' he exclaimed, 'and I can help you to achieve this.'

Valerie had written to Gracie and Rick telling them of their intended visit and what a thrill it would be to be going home for a whole month. She and Max would be able to stay with family and, of course, her parents would be able to go to London to see the results of her work and appreciate her new career, apart from meeting their new son-in-law. It was his first visit too, so there was much to plan.

Gracie knew her friend wouldn't feel the need to return permanently as she was so settled in New York with Max. Although she was deliriously happy with Rick and baby Robbie, Gracie still felt the pull of home and wondered if this homesickness would ever leave her. However, Rick had promised that they would all go back to England the following year, which gave her so much to look forward to.

* * *

The months seemed to fly by and before Valerie and Max knew it, September had arrived and the trip to London was only days away. They were booked on the liner, *United States*. Their canvases carefully packed and crated ready to be delivered to the docks and put in the hold of the ship.

It was a large exhibition. As Carl had said, 'Put in everything! This is your one chance to make an impression. Don't waste it.'

It had been hard work for the past months and when the two of them walked up the gangway and found their cabins, they were weary. Max lay on the bed and sighed.

'Thank God we've got five days to rest. I am so tired. Please don't ask me to go dancing tonight.'

'You're not the only one that's tired Max Brennen! After dinner and a walk round the deck, bed is on my agenda – I don't know about you.'

'Sounds wonderful.' He got up. 'Come on, let's find a bar and have a drink, I think we've earned it.'

Five days later, rested and ready to go, Max and Valerie arrived in Southampton. They were met by James Grant, an agent Carl had recommended, who was overseeing the exhibition. He assured them that he would see to the safe delivery of all their canvases and then saw them onto the train with details of their hotel, the address of the gallery in Knightsbridge and his telephone number.

'I'll see you there the day after tomorrow in the morning

about ten o'clock,' he told them. 'By then everything should be unpacked and ready, then we can decide where to hang the paintings.'

They settled in a first-class carriage for their journey to the city.

Max was intrigued by the passing countryside, the verdant greenery, slowly turning to autumn shades, the fields full of animals. The sheep, the cows and horses grazing.

'How very peaceful it all seems,' he said to Valerie. 'The pace is so much slower here. I'm really going to enjoy my visit.'

When they had settled in their hotel room, Valerie rang her parents to tell them they'd arrived. She sat in an armchair listening to the familiar voices of the people she loved and could hardly wait to see them. They of course, were coming to the opening night of the exhibition and had booked into a hotel for three days.

'I can't wait to see you,' said Eve, her mother, 'your father is delighted that you and Max are here. Are you happy darling?'

'More than I ever thought possible,' Valerie said, 'and when you meet Max, you'll understand why.'

Two days later, Valerie and Max took a taxi to the gallery to oversee the hanging of their paintings. It was a long and arduous task, setting out the canvases of various sizes, but after a break for lunch and with the help of many hands, by early evening, it was done. They stood back and surveyed the walls. The gallery was big and on one side, Max had his paintings, on the other were those by Valerie. With the lights above each picture, the interior became one of colour, with landscapes, portraits, Valerie's series of Greenwich Village, a section of vibrant scenes of Jamaica from their holiday there, watercolours and oils. It was like a gigantic feast and they were delighted with the result.

Carl, using his connections, saw that the publicity for the event was vast. There were enormous posters, announcements in various newspapers and ticket sales were good for all seven days of the exhibition. The outlay financially was considerable, so they both prayed that it would be a success. The next day the exhibition would open to the press and invited guests, critics of the art world, then the grand opening was to be the following evening, after which it would be open from ten o'clock in the morning, with tickets on the door for those who hadn't bought them already.

Valerie and Max retired to the hotel and ordered food to be sent up to their room, as they were too weary to seek food elsewhere. As they sat at the table, which had been set up by the window, they discussed the day's work.

'Well darling,' Max said, 'This is going to be really important for us and I feel good about it, don't you?'

She was more reticent. 'You know me, Max, I'm always surprised by our success, but we have to try and if it goes well, we can come back and do it again in a couple of years. Anyway it'll be an experience.'

He smiled fondly at her. 'You never cease to amaze me

that you still don't realise how good an artist you are!'

'Well, we'll find that out by the end of the exhibition, won't we?'

They were surprised and delighted that so many members of the press attended and several art critics, along with several members of the London A-list, who appeared at all such openings, with their pictures appearing later in *Tatler*, who were represented by their reporter and cameraman. James their agent was most efficient, making sure that Max and Valerie spoke to the most influential people there and more importantly, didn't miss talking to every member of the press.

Champagne and canapés were handed around at regular intervals, which helped the ambience of room. To their surprise, some of their paintings sold that evening, which was a bonus and at closing time, James assured them it had been a great success.

'There'll be a review in several papers tomorrow morning,' he told them. 'I'll get copies and bring them to your hotel at breakfast time, if you like?'

They agreed, as they were more than anxious to see if their journey was worthwhile.

'Join us for breakfast, James. We'll be in the dining room just before nine o'clock.'

James duly arrived the next morning, carrying a selection of newspapers, all turned to the relevant pages. He was thrilled with the results.

'You two have caused quite a storm in the art world,' he told them. 'Here, read the reviews.'

And indeed they were more than complimentary, urging the public not to miss the exhibition of the two artists. Making a point that Valerie had been a GI bride. They were delighted.

'There! Didn't I tell you?' Max exclaimed. 'Now perhaps you'll believe me.'

Valerie was still reading one paper, thrilled with the review. 'Yes, I know,' she retorted, 'but you never can tell. What works in the States doesn't always work here. But this time, thank the lord, it seems to have done so.'

'I'm really looking forward to this evening,' said James. 'After this publicity, it should be very well attended.'

Which indeed it was. But the two people that Valerie wanted to see more than most, were her parents, who arrived just after the exhibition opened. There were hugs all round and Max was introduced to his in-laws, Eve and Giles Brampton.

After a few words, he said, 'Come and see your daughter's work, she's so talented and I'm so proud of her.'

As they walked over to the other side of the hall, Eve whispered to her daughter, 'I like Max, he seems a lovely man.'

As they stood before the paintings and walked slowly round them, both were amazed at what Valerie had produced.

'I remember your sketches,' said Giles, 'but these paintings are really terrific. I had no idea you could paint.'

'Max is a good teacher,' she said.

'But the talent was already there,' Max interrupted.

At that moment, James called them away to talk to some reporters who had come along after reading the reviews and wanted to meet the artists, leaving Valerie's parents to themselves.

When at last the exhibition closed, the four of them went to a nearby restaurant for a meal and to catch up with each other's news. It was a time for reminiscing, of laughter and discussions about the future. It was here that Valerie told Eve and Giles that she was happy living in New York and that she wouldn't be coming back to England to live permanently.

'Why would you?' her father said. 'Obviously you and Max like living there, it's where your work is known, it would be foolish to be anywhere else!' he looked at Max. 'We as a family are like nomads really, as I've had to travel the globe in my job, so we understand better than most.'

'Perhaps you'll be able to come and visit sometime?' Max suggested.

'I'm going to take early retirement in a few years, so we will, if not before.'

After the meal, they went their separate ways until the morning, as James said they were not needed at the gallery and to take a break.

As they lay in each other's arms in bed, Valerie nestled into her husband. 'My mother thinks you're nice,' she said.

'Ah, your mother is a woman of taste . . . like her daughter who realised I was a good catch!'

'Well, you're not bad, I'll grant you that.'

'So tomorrow you can show me around London as a reward, now let's get some rest because it's going to be a long day and I'm beat.'

For the following three days, the four of them toured the sights for Max's benefit. They took him to the Tower of London, Westminster Abbey, Buckingham Palace and for a boat trip along the Thames to Windsor where they walked around the castle. Max was intrigued with the history of the country, the portraits by famous painters adorning the walls. The splendour of the rooms.

As he said, 'I can imagine kings and queens wandering around here. It's incredible!'

When their time was up, the Bramptons returned to their home, knowing that Valerie and Max would be visiting them for a few days before they returned to New York.

Left to their own devices they went to the V&A Museum, the Tate Gallery and the National Gallery in Trafalgar Square. Here they spent a few hours studying the Old Masters, discussing their use of colour and techniques. For Valerie it was like getting another lesson in her art as Max discussed various details of the pictures and the use of oils in their various ways.

They spent other days around the city with sketchbooks and paints, collecting scenes of history and historic buildings. As Max said, 'We Yanks are fascinated by the

"Old Country" and these pictures will market well.'

When they left London to stay with Valerie's parents in Lymington, they again used their time to draw, this time the quiet countryside with the New Forest ponies, the marina with its many yachts around Lymington itself and, for good measure, thatched-roofed cottages.

Max was introduced to friends and other family members during his stay and with his usual charm, endeared himself to them all . . . and then it was time to leave.

As they were being driven to Southampton to join their ship, Max opened a letter from James Grant, which had been sent to them in Lymington, with the final figures from their exhibition. He was delighted with the result.

Waving the letter he turned to Valerie. 'Well darling, it was certainly worth the visit!' He showed her the figure at the bottom detailing the takings. 'We can come back in a couple of years, that's for certain.'

She was more than surprised that they had sold so many paintings. Valerie wasn't really interested in the money side of her career, for her it was all about putting brush to canvas and now she wanted to get home and start on the scenes of her homeland. She realised of course, to continue to live comfortably as well, that success was important and she was delighted for her husband.

'I'm so pleased it went well, Max and that I was able to show you my country, but now I can't wait to go home.'

He leant forward and kissed her. 'To hear you call New York home, is music to my ears,' he said. 'I did wonder how you'd feel after returning to the States after being in England with your family.'

She squeezed his hand. 'Don't be silly, you are my family now, where else would I want to be?'

Chapter Thirty

It was now October and in Barton, winter was approaching. Now that young Robbie was five months old, Gracie placed him in day care four days a week to allow her to return to work at Milly's shop. The two women had become firm friends and for Gracie it was a joy to spend time with her, both at work and socially.

Rick had moved into bigger premises and taken on a third mechanic to help with the ever-increasing business. He had bought a three-bedroomed house with a garden and Gracie had spent time furnishing it and making it habitable, but this time, Rick had paid a man to decorate the interior before they moved in.

'You have enough to do, looking after the baby,' he'd said. But he had left her to choose the colours. When it was all finished, she was delighted with the result, but wished that her parents could come and stay to see for themselves how well her husband was doing and, of course, their grandchild.

She had made new friends with some of the mothers she'd met and sometimes invited them over for morning coffee where she served homemade scones and fruit cake for her friends. They now made the 'English scones' as they called them, from her recipe, so she felt she was helping with international relations. Sometimes she held tea parties with cucumber sandwiches and sponge cake, too. The American women thought the idea of tea in the afternoon was 'real cute', as they put it. But as she did this, she knew that deep down she was still feeling somewhat homesick and this went some way to alleviate the longing. But when she received a letter from her mother to say her father wasn't well, she was beside herself with worry.

'What does your mother say is wrong with him?' Rick asked when she told him the news.

'They're not sure. He's having blood tests and X-rays. Mum said she'd let me know the result.'

He tried to comfort her. 'It may be nothing, Gracie honey. You know as people age, they begin to have various complaints; it's the way it goes. Try not to worry until you hear the results.'

But two days later, Gracie received a cable saying that her father had been rushed into hospital after suffering a heart attack.

Gracie was in tears. 'What if he dies?' she cried. 'He won't ever have seen his grandson and I won't be with him and Mum!'

Rick didn't hesitate. He booked his wife and son on the *Queen Mary*, which was due to sail from New York four days later.

Those days passed in a haze for Gracie. Things were packed hurriedly. Valerie met her and Robbie in New York from the train, and they stayed overnight with her and Max. They both took her and Robbie to the docks and saw them safely on board.

'If's there's anything we can do . . .' Valerie gazed at her friend and saw the fear in her eyes. 'It may be better than you expect,' she said. 'Call me and let me know. Reverse the charges.'

The five-day crossing seemed an eternity to Gracie. Having to take care of Robbie was the one thing that saved her sanity, but when she left him in the nursery in the afternoons to have a nap, in the care of the nursery nurse to give herself a break, then her inner fears would surface. She would walk the decks in tears until one day a deck steward stopped her and asked what was the matter? When she told him, he led her to a deckchair and brought her a pot of tea and some cakes.

'Now you sit there love and relax. You'll be no good to your mam in this state. You come here every afternoon when your baby's asleep. A cup of tea will do wonders, you mark my words!'

She could have kissed him.

At last the liner docked in Southampton and her mother was there to meet her. Never had Gracie been so pleased to see her.

'How's Dad?' were her first words.

'A bit frail,' said Margaret Brown, 'but he knows you're coming to see him. That's cheered him no end.'

After they'd collected the baggage, they found a taxi and drove straight to the hospital.

As she walked down the ward carrying Robbie, Gracie thought her heart would leap out of her chest it was beating so hard, but she took a deep breath as they approached her father's bed. She was shocked when she saw the pale drawn face staring back at her, as her father gave a wan smile as he recognised her.

'Hello love,' he said. She thought her heart would break. She smiled back and kissed him.

'Hello, Dad. I've brought your grandson to meet you.' She sat the baby on the bed.

Jim Brown took hold of the baby's hand. 'Hello son and how are you?' He looked up at Gracie. 'My, but he's bonny!'

'How are you feeling?' Gracie asked.

'Bit battered love, but I'll be fine given time.'

But as she gazed at him, Gracie wondered just how long that would be. In her heart she felt it wouldn't be that long and shortly after, she was able to have a word in private with the doctor who was caring for her father.

'Mr Brown had a severe heart attack,' he explained.

'And the prognosis? Please be totally honest with me.'

'Not good I'm afraid. We'll keep him as comfortable as we can, but I'm afraid that's all we can do.'

'How long has he got?'

'Difficult to say, but not long, a matter of weeks is all I can give you.'

She rose from her seat. 'Thank you, Doctor, for your honesty. Does my mother know?'

'Oh yes, she asked me the same questions as you did. I'm really sorry.'

Gracie stood in the corridor and wept quiet tears before returning to the ward.

Her mother took the baby outside to give Gracie and her father some private time together. Her father took her hand.

'Don't be sad love. I've had a good life and now you must go and live yours. Your mother tells me that Rick is a good man. So you look after him.'

'He is good, Dad. He's doing really well in his business. He bought us a nice house with a garden for Robbie to play in as he grows. He loves us both and I love him.'

'That's how it should be. I have a life insurance so your mother will be looked after financially.'

'Oh Dad, don't talk like that.' Tears welled in her eyes.

'Listen love, you have to look life in the face and take what it sends you. It's no good pretending, what's the point? I've made a will so there should be no difficulty when I've gone to meet my maker. I just want to tell you how much I love you and how proud I am of you. It wasn't easy to leave here and you did it twice. That took guts Gracie!'

'I still get homesick Dad.'

'That's natural, but your life is in America with your husband. Mum says Rick told her he'd bring you home every other year, so think how fortunate you are.'

'But if you're not here . . .'

'No one can live for ever Gracie, we all have to go sometime.'

At that moment Margaret returned with Robbie.

'The baby's tired, Gracie. I think we should take him home, feed him, give him a bath and put him to bed.'

'Go on love, your mother's right. I'll see you tomorrow.'

Gracie kissed him goodbye and left the ward.

Jim Brown passed away in his sleep that night. They got the call just after midnight.

Gracie rang Rick to tell him what had happened.

'I'm so sorry honey, but at least you were in time to see him and for him to see Robbie.'

'Yes, that was a blessing. I have to stay and help Mum with the funeral. I don't know how long I'll be staying after. It all depends on how Mum is.'

'That's fine. Do what you have to do, just make sure you come back to me eventually, that's all.'

That made her smile for the first time in days. 'I won't let you loose on your own Mr Rider! I'll be back!'

She then rang Valerie as promised.

'Oh Gracie, I am so sorry. When you do decide to come back let me know and we'll meet the ship. You can stay overnight and we'll put you on the train for home. We'll be thinking of you.'

Two weeks later Gracie and her mother sat down to discuss the future. The funeral had been a quiet affair, with just family and close friends attending. They had been through Jim's clothes and given them away to the Salvation Army.

The will was waiting for probate and at last the two women could relax.

'How are you going to manage, Mum?' asked Gracie.

'I'll do what a million women did who lost their husbands in the war. I'll get on with my life. I now have a widow's pension and the insurance from your father, so I'll manage. I might find a part-time job to fill my time and in the spring I'll come and visit you. I can afford to do so now!'

'That'll be marvellous. The last time you came it was winter. Spring will be so much better.'

Margaret gazed across at her daughter. 'I think you should go to the Cunard office tomorrow and book your return passage.' Seeing the consternation of Gracie's face, she said firmly. 'You have a husband to care for. It's time for you to go home.'

'Are you sure?'

'Yes, Gracie. I will get used to being alone because I have to. You have to go home for the same reason. Anyway it isn't long until the spring.' Seeing the look of uncertainty on her daughter's face she added, 'Gracie love, we are both strong women and we rise from the ashes like the phoenix when we have to. You did it twice. I will now do the same. Life has to go on. I'll be fine!'

'You are an extraordinary woman,' Gracie said.

'And I brought my daughter up the same way. Now you do the same for my grandson.'

As Gracie lay in bed that night, she knew that her mother was right. Life had to go on and fortunately now her mother would be able to be a part of their lives with her visits to America, and soon she would be home with Rick. She smiled as she realised, at last, that she thought of America as home. It had taken some time, but it was all due to the man who loved her and she would be forever grateful for that.